HONEY, HONEY

REBEL CARTER

Copyright © 2021 by Rebel Carter

All rights reserved.

No part of this book may be reproduced in any form or by any electronic or mechanical means, including information storage and retrieval systems, without written permission from the author, except for the use of brief quotations in a book review.

Edited by Bria James.

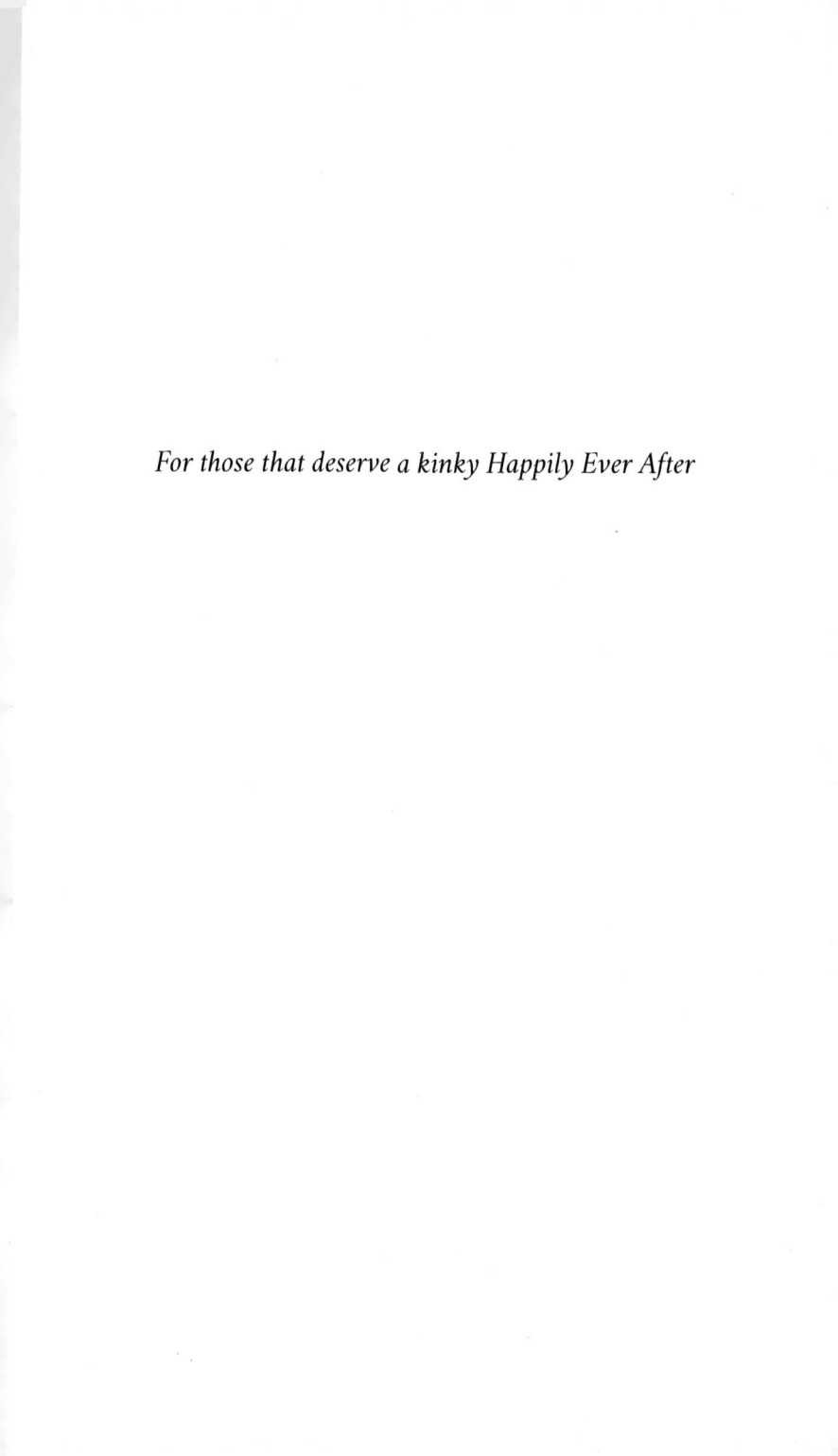

For those that deserve a kinky Happily Ever After

READER WARNING

Honey, Honey is a darkly sweet and steamy Daddy Dom BDSM romance novel with age play, DDlg, spanking, ex mafia ties, estranged family, dirty talk, restraints, impact play, and a creepy lurking ex. All sex is explicitly consensual and deliciously enjoyed by all involved.

If this isn't your jam, please stop reading and find yourself a different thrill.
   Love y'all either way.

CHAPTER ONE

LAW

I turned, adjusting the cuff of my jacket and frowned up at the sky. It was bleak, the sun hiding behind a low blanket of clouds that gave the early morning the feel of twilight rather than a new day.

It was cold. I hated the cold.

Summer couldn't get here fast enough, but this was bearable for the simple fact that I knew it wouldn't last. I turned up the collar of my jacket and kept walking, hands in my pockets and a frown on my face. I was practically stomping down the sidewalk to get my coffee and when I saw a look that could only be described as scared shitless on the face of a passing woman who did her best to give me a wide berth.

My steps slowed and I turned to glance at myself in the shiny glass of the building to my left.

"Shit," I whispered, seeing the angry look on my face.

I was narrow eyed and glaring, my lips pulled into a thin line that was bordering on a sneer. With my hands stuffed into my pockets and my shoulders up by my ears, I was...formidable. I was a big man, and even if I was minding my own damn business while being pissed at the weather, it was good to keep a handle on what other people saw when they looked at me. The hours I was keeping, near round the clock for the past few weeks, didn't help. I was eating like shit, not sleeping, and way too caffeinated for my own good. I looked haggard as fuck, with shadows under my eyes. My cheekbones were too sharp from lack of rest and food, and I knew I had the look of a man that was one hop, skip and jump away from punching someone. Twenty two days of constant work and high profile dealings that had far too much sway over the future of my company did that to a man. That woman had probably thought I was going to mug her or some shit.

I sighed, breathing in deep, and pinched the bridge of my nose as I forced myself to suck in another deep breath. "This is not good. Get a grip. Relax."

I'd already been relegated to decaf by my

assistant for being, "a total and complete dickhead." I couldn't even tell Addie she was wrong, because I *had* turned into an ass this month. The shittiest part of it was that I'd done it to myself when I had hijacked her scheduling program and over booked myself like a stupid fuck.

And since I'd done it on my own, that meant Addie got to tell me things like I was "a total and complete asshole," and ban me from having anything with caffeine in it in the office. I was going to have to get her a nice gift, or reservations at a nice restaurant she would never think to go to, when all of this was over.

"One more week," I muttered. "One more week and this is over, and then I am never being this stupid again." I was lying, of course. I would do it again, and again, *and again* for as long as I was able to. Work was the only thing I had. Work I understood. Work I knew. Work was the constant in my life that made sense to me.

Law Acquisitions was at the top of its game because I was relentless. I had always been that way, but now I was on the up-and-up. I didn't have to watch my back when I went anywhere and I didn't shower in water so hot that my skin was left raw in an attempt to burn away the memory of what I'd been paid to do by my employer. I didn't answer to the highest bidder in the market for violence anymore.

I called the shots now, and that was a kind of power that I would never give up. I answered to no one and I liked it that way. But at the same time it meant I didn't have anyone. Not anyone close to me that would be waiting on me, or wondering where I was after another late night at the office. It might be sad if I gave a shit about any of that. I took companionship when I needed it. There never was a shortage of partners looking to spend time with me when I came up for air.

That was a lot less frequent these days, though. The last time had been at the start of this, nearly a month ago and my palms itched remembering just how fucking sweet that weekend had been.

I grimaced and set off again towards my destination. If Addie had banned me from getting caffeine at the office I was going to have to do it on my own. Hudson Yards was a pot of things, up and coming playground to the rich, a little slice of New York that toed the line–eco and green living with a hint of Bohemian. Albeit carefully curated bohemian, while catering to the rich tastes of the upper crust. Everything was luxe or created to be one of a kind. The kind of place that never let you forget it was "artisan", if artisan consisted of fuckwads of cash, mostly gleaming building fronts and immaculate windows I wasn't sure had ever seen a speck of dirt since being installed.

Hudson Yards was not accustomed to a man looking as irritated as me storming down the street. You don't look irritated, you look murderous, I reminded myself. I clenched my jaw, pushing the thought away, because I did look like I might snap. I could almost hear Addie sighing at me from behind her desk, where she no doubt would be regarding me with an annoyed look while she tapped her ballpoint on the fat appointment book she kept my schedule in.

"Suck it up. Smile," I ordered myself. If I was going to be moving in this world, one of money and squeaky clean windows, then I needed to at least try and not attract unnecessary attention walking down the damn street for coffee.

Otherwise what had been the point of all the shit I'd done to get here?

I wasn't a thug. I was a businessman. Corporate head of a multi-billion dollar operation, and I only stood out when I chose to. Now was not one of those times.

I shrugged and rolled my shoulders, trying to release some of the tension there. I needed to relax. After another few minutes of walking, I was feeling a little clearer and by the time I was pushing open the door of A Different Brew, I felt more settled.

That was until I clocked the curvy brunette behind the counter.

"Fuck," I huffed out, freezing in the doorway when she flashed a bright smile my way.

"Good morning, sir. How are you?" Her voice was like summer and sunshine, and whatever else made you go hot on a good day. It was sweet, but real. She wasn't faking the smile, or the chipper tone I heard.

I didn't answer her, just continued to stand there staring at her like a dumb fuck with one hand on the door and the other in my pocket to stop me from putting it up on the doorframe to steady myself. A move like that would clue the smiling woman in that she'd had an effect on me.

I didn't like anyone to know that type of shit.

I was cool in boardrooms, I was cool waiting for a big mouthed guy who'd said one too many things while I loaded my forty-five. I didn't get flustered like a school boy from a smile and a 'good morning'— no matter how beautiful the woman was.

"Sir?" She tipped her head to the side, looking at me with a raised eyebrow. My dick twitched at that one word. *Sir.* God, I needed a day off if a good morning and one word was getting me hard.

"I, ah." My voice came out in a splutter and my brow furrowed at my stumble. I did not stutter. Not for any woman. The small coffee shop was warm and inviting, just like the woman's smile, but I didn't move forward and didn't step into the shop until someone behind me let out a delicate 'ahem' and I was forced to move.

"Morning there."

I glanced to the left to see a bright eyed blonde smiling up at me. I gave a grunt of acknowledgement and then turned my attention back to the counter in front of me. It was all shiny white quartz that sparkled in a ray of sunshine that managed to get through the morning gloom. I turned my neck seeing the sun had broken through the low hanging clouds. It would be beautiful today given a little time.

I looked at the barista who was still smiling my way, and she reached up tucking a loose strand of her hair behind her ear. She was beautiful too.

"I couldn't help but notice you work in the area." The woman at my side said, and I jumped in surprise. She'd vanished from my thoughts the second my eyes had hit the barista, but there she was, still looking up at me expectantly. "Do you come here often?"

It was just a question, but I prickled. I knew what she was playing at with her too interested look. I didn't have time for this. Even if I did, this blonde couldn't handle what I was into.

"Ah—"

"Can I take your order, sir?" Beautiful Barista asked in her warm sunshine voice that made me want to bolt. My eyes darted back to her and I saw she was leaning forward, an innocent smile on her face, her hands on the counter. Her arms framing her tits and pushing them together for just enough cleavage that I had to fight to keep my eyes on her face.

Sir.

Every time she said it my brain shorted out. And her teasing with her tits. Fuck. I scrubbed a hand over my face and gave myself a mental kick. How the hell was a woman knocking me on my ass with a simple 'sir'? She made me want to reach out and grab her, bend over the counter and paddle her ass and tell her that her innocent smile wasn't fooling anyone.

She bit her lip and I stepped forward. Beautiful Barista was playing with me.

I opened my mouth to order, but the blonde I was trying to forget stepped with me and scoffed.

"Laying it on thick, aren't you?" She asked, narrowing her eyes at Beautiful Barista. Both the barista and I looked at her in surprise. I knew then she hadn't seen the blonde, she'd only seen me, which suited me fine. I liked that she hadn't noticed anyone else.

"Sorry?" She inclined her head, blinking in

surprise at the blonde, who tossed her hair over shoulder and flicked a finger at her.

"If you pushed them up any more they would be on the counter," she said.

Beautiful Barista's eyes widened and she blushed. Not the kind that I would want to see on her pretty face. She was embarrassed. She looked away, a deep red flush spreading up from her throat and across her cheeks. It made her even prettier, made me think of what that color would look like if I had her laying across my lap, her ass in the air while she sobbed, my hand turning her flesh red. If she was mine, I'd have her like that, ass tinged pink and raw, a reminder that she wouldn't forget, making sure she knew she belonged to me. She would want it like that. The security my hand brought, wrapping itself around her until nothing bothered her. Because she knew her Daddy would be there. She would be untouchable even if she was at work serving coffee to assholes who thought they could talk to her anyway they wanted.

Daddy. What the fuck was I thinking?

"I'm sorry. I don't kn—" Beautiful Barista began, but her voice wasn't like sunshine anymore. There was a waver and the warmth that had drawn me in was gone. I gritted my teeth and turned to look at the blonde who was drawing herself up to her full height, which was laughable. She barely cleared my shoulder and that was in heels. But the way she was glowering at the goddess in front of me made her out to be 6 feet tall.

"Don't tell me you don't know what you're doing. It's pretty obvious by the way you're practically flashing him, that you do. Is this the kind of trash this shop hires?" She asked, though she was speaking to no one. I knew this was meant to be one of those rhetorical fucking moments by the way she turned and looked around the coffee shop and looked towards the other patrons.

She turned then and gazed up at me with a sympathetic simper. "You don't deserve this. A man like you."

My brows shot up at her words. A man like me? What the fuck did that have to do with anything? What did she even begin to think she knew about a man like me?

Whatever it was, I didn't like it.

"Listen, lady," I began but she was waving her hand at someone behind me.

"Gus! Please come here. There's a matter you need to attend to."

If I wasn't so damn annoyed I would have laughed at her imperious tone. A matter he needed to attend to? We were in the middle of a coffee shop, not some ballroom scene from one of those tv specials they aired nonstop around the holidays.

"Be right there!"

I heard a man's voice behind me and Beautiful Barista's eyes widened. She bit her bottom lip and took a step back, her arms coming up across her chest and I felt my chest go tight. This wasn't simple embarrassment, even if the entire shop, small as it may be, was watching her. She was worried. I turned my head to look at the man she had been watching.

I had to do something.

"What seems to be the matter?" The man was in his fifties and was dressed casually enough. Salt and pepper hair and a mustache that made him look like a goofy uncle, but he was standing ramrod straight while the blonde rattled off her grievances.

"That barista is practically flashing this man," the blonde said, swinging a hand from Beautiful Barista to me. "He doesn't deserve that. This man works at Law Acquisitions," she told him as if she were anyone to me.

I raised an eyebrow at her words. How did she know that?

"Honey, what's going on?" He asked looking her way, and I almost groaned at the sound of her fucking name. It would be something sweet. *Honey.* For crying out loud.

The blonde scoffed. "Honey? What the hell kind of name is that? A stage name?" She sneered.

Honey flushed again and I got angry. "I'm

sorry," she began, but I was done with this morning scene. I hadn't even had a cup of coffee and not one, but two women were making my morning a nightmare.

The blonde for being an asshole. Honey for making me want things I shouldn't want. And the blonde bitch was attracting attention. The something I had thought about doing needed to be done— and I had to do it now.

"It's the name of my fiancée," I ground out. The lie came too naturally, but I wasn't going to think about that. Right now, I was making things right.

Gus blinked in surprise. "Ah, what?"

The blonde spluttered. "Your what?"

"My fiancée. My girl," I said, taking a step away from them until I was standing in front of Honey, shielding her from the pair of them. My hands went to my hips and I leveled a hard stare their way. "I came here to kiss her good morning and grab a cup of joe since she didn't make it for me this morning, and you," I jerked my chin at the blonde who was now staring at me with an open mouth, "started yelling at my girl for smiling at me. Isn't that right, Honey?" I asked, still watching the couple in front of me.

She swallowed hard, dark eyes darting from me to the idiot blonde and her boss. "Uh, I—"

"Honey," I said, a note of warning in my voice

indicating that she needed to get on the same page as me, and fast. "Isn't that right?"

Another woman with flaming red hair leaned out from behind the espresso machine and I barely had time to register the gleeful look on her face, or the barely restrained squeal she let out, before Honey was answering me.

"Yes! Yes, I mean, I was just–yes, sir," she blurted out and I had to clench my hands into fists, while she added a feeble, "Baby, yes."

I didn't like that as much as sir, but what were you gonna do in a situation like this? Beggars couldn't be choosers, after all.

"I don't appreciate my girl being yelled at," I told Gus. "She's working hard for you, it's not right. She needs to be protected from this kind of shit while she's working."

He shook his head. "No, I'm sorry." He leaned to the side to speak to Honey, and I had to fight to not lean with him to keep her hidden from view. "I'm sorry, Honey."

"That's okay, Gus."

I looked at the blonde now who was fast realizing she had no power here. Not anymore. "And I don't just work at Law Acquisitions. I own the damn thing."

She gasped. "I didn't—"

"Get some manners. Don't treat service workers

like they owe you something just because you're on this side of the counter," I growled.

We all looked at each other for a beat before Gus cleared his throat and gestured towards the door. "I think you should leave now," he said to the blonde who looked like she was about to pass out.

"Leave? Why would you ask me to leave?" She wanted to know, but the murmur of answers from patrons around her answered her question before the owner could say a word.

"You're causing a scene."

"Who yells at people like that?"

"She's his fiancée! Can't even say hello to him without a Karen telling on her."

This was going to handle itself just fine. I sighed and rubbed my temples before I turned back to Honey and stepped up to the counter.

I jerked a thumb over my shoulder. "I'm really sorry about that."

"You have nothing to be sorry for. You saved my ass." She shook her head at me and held up her hands. She had nice hands. Long fingered, nails painted with a sweet pale blush that went with her tan. I looked away. I shouldn't be noticing her hands.

"What can I get you?"

"Quad americano, black, please."

"Of course. It's on me," she rushed to tell me, but I stopped her with a shake of my head.

"What kind of fiancé would I be if I let you do that?"

She grinned, the light I had seen earlier returning to them. "What kind of fiancée would I be if I didn't pay for it, after you just rescued me?" Her eyes focused behind me and she turned her head, hiding a giggle in her hand. I could hear the blonde being hustled out of the coffee shop by Gus and the outright disapproval of the other customers.

"You don't even know what you just did," she said, reaching out and putting her hand on mine. It was just a brush of her fingers but it made my blood sing. Seeing her fingers resting on the back of my hand, the pink of her nails contrasting with the ink on my skin made my head swim. It looked fucking perfect. I jerked my hand away from hers and looked away when I saw the hurt in her beautiful eyes. I couldn't have her touching me. Couldn't have that side of me waking up and wanting her more than I already did.

The redhead joined us then and she beamed in my direction. "You didn't say you had a fiancé. What the hell, Honey bun?"

A near shriek sounded behind me, but I didn't bother looking. I knew it was the blonde trying to save face. "He owns it? A man like that with her doesn't make any sense!" She was insisting to someone, probably that Gus guy, maybe just anyone in earshot. Either way I ignored her.

"Don't listen to her," I advised Honey when I saw her flinch at the bullshit the blonde was spewing on her way out. "She's just trying to look less shitty."

"You mean classist," the redhead said with a nod towards the blonde. "She comes in here every day acting like she's Marie Antoinette, and I for one always wanted to take her bleached head off, so thank you for that," she said, nodding at me.

I grunted a reply that had the redhead giggling and skipping off to the espresso machine but not before she flicked a finger at Honey. "You have a lot to tell me about after this rush, Honey bun."

"Sure," Honey answered, voice weak. She looked back at me and took the card I was holding out to her. It was heavy and black, and she turned the metal over in her hands for a second before she looked at me. "She's right, but thank you for what you did," she said, swiping the card.

I frowned. "What the fuck do you mean she's right?"

She looked startled at my question but answered me all the same. "A man like you wouldn't be with someone like me."

My throat tightened. I could see she believed that. Thought I wouldn't want a woman like her. I shook my head at her. "Listen to me, a woman like you doesn't want a man like me. Men like me are dirty."

"Wha—"

"Men like me don't deserve sweet."

Her eyes dropped to my mouth for a beat before they met my stare. "I'm not sweet." Her voice was husky, a touch too low to be proper. Christ. I loved the sound of her voice. I scoffed, reaching out to take the black card she still held. Our fingers brushed and I sucked in a breath at the slight slide of her skin against mine. She was soft. I knew if I kept touching her she'd be soft all over. I couldn't touch her all over, not without losing control, but that didn't stop me from brushing a calloused finger over her knuckles.

"You couldn't be any more sweet if you tried, Honey," I said, her name rolling off my tongue like I'd said it a million times.

Her eyes went soft and she bit her bottom lip. "Sir," she began, and I groaned at the word. Her eyes went wide but it was too late. I closed my hand around her wrist and pulled her towards me. By now the entire morning crowd at A Different Brew were pretending they didn't see us. Our coupledom having been established via a bitch fit, and none of them seemed ready to take me on in the pursuit of caffeine.

God how had she known to call me that?

"You shouldn't go around calling just anybody Sir, little girl. You might have to answer for it," I warned her, the words slipping out of me before I could stop.

She let out a soft exhale and then smiled at me, her eyes still soft on me. "I think I'd like answering to you."

Fuck.

My fingers flexed on her wrist and I could feel the pull between us ratcheting up. I needed this woman. It didn't matter what was going on around us, the blonde could be screaming her head off beside us and I wouldn't have given a shit so long as Honey kept looking at me like she was.

I needed this woman to be sweet for me. Sweet and needy. Dark eyes soft on me while she screamed for me. I could see it plain as day, her dark curls spilling over her shoulder with her head thrown back, legs wrapped around me while I bounced her on my cock. She would feel good–no, better than that. She'd be perfect.

It would be perfect.

"Quad Americano, black, for Honey bun's man!"

Honey jerked back and took her hand with her. My fingers tingled from where our skin had touched and I blinked and shook my head, coming back to myself.

"Do you think—"

"That's me. I gotta go," I said, cutting off whatever it was she was about to say. A feat fueled by pure strength of will. I wanted to hear whatever it was she was about to say. I would listen to this woman all fucking day if I could.

She opened her mouth again and then nodded at me. "Have a good day, sir."

I gave a jerky nod but was already moving before that blessed word fell from her perfect mouth. How could a soft 'sir' put me on my ass like this? I didn't even know her, but I knew without a doubt that I needed her.

"Thanks," I murmured, taking the cup from the redhead.

She winked at me. "You got it, boss man."

I gave another grunt and kept moving. I shouldered through the crowd that was now falling back into motion, the earlier scene and my nearly pulling a barista over the counter and into my arms already old news, and finally fucking made it onto the sidewalk.

It was only then that I let my weak ass look back at Honey. She was already waiting on another customer, a smile curving her lips. I took a sip of my coffee and winced at the unforgiving temperature of the drink. I swallowed it down and kept watching her for another minute before she looked up at me.

Our eyes met and I felt the pull between us again.

It didn't matter that there was a counter, a crowd of people and a whole damn door between us. The pull was there, and I knew she felt it too. Which is why I turned on my heel and started walking.

Nothing good would come out of me tasting Honey.

CHAPTER TWO

HONEY

"Hey, when the fuck did you get engaged?"

I blinked and looked up from the cappuccino foam I was making. "What?" I asked, shutting the milk wand off and turning to look at Tiffany, who was glaring at me with her arms crossed over her chest.

"Don't you 'what' me," she said, jerking a thumb over her shoulder in the direction of the door. "Where's the rock that big man gave you?"

"What rock?" I looked over her shoulder where she was still jerking her thumb and had to swallow down the disappointment I felt when I didn't see the man she was talking about.

My fiancé.

We'd locked eyes after he'd stepped out of the

coffee shop. After he'd saved my ass from whatever today's Karen was ready to unleash on me. I knew he'd seen me watching him, and that he had looked right back at me before he'd stormed off. When he'd paid for his coffee and taken it from Tiffany I hadn't so much as seen him slow in his steps on the way out the door. But that look on the sidewalk? I knew I had seen it, and that it had as much interest in it as mine had, even if he didn't much seem like he wanted to be in the shop.

He had looked tired. Haggard even. Like he hadn't had a good night sleep in a week or more. His clothes were impeccable, even if I could see the fatigue on him. None of that really took away from how handsome he was. He was a big man, dark hair peppered with silver that was thick and lush but cropped close. The silver that threaded through his hair might have made some men reach for a box of hair dye, but on him? No. On him it worked, on him it looked well earned, hinting at the life experience he possessed. That dark and silver paired perfectly with his eyes, eyes the color of blue that looked like the expensive bottled water sold in all the shops I worked in, the kind that I couldn't afford so I drank tap. And fuck, his cheekbones and jawline? The man was all sharp angles and chiseled bone structure, even if his nose was slightly crooked, the look of a body part that had been broken once or twice. I could see tattoos on his hands, thick inky lines that covered the backs of his hands and disappeared beneath the sleeve of his expensive coat. There were the telltale lines poking up and over the crisp collar of his dress shirt which told me he was probably covered in tattoos.

A man like that might scare some. His bulk, height and demeanor pushing them away, but me? I found him beautiful. I'd give my right eye to see the art on his chest. It had to be gorgeous. Just like him.

My chest tightened and I swallowed hard knowing I was blushing just thinking about the man's bare chest. Remembering how his cerulean eyes had dropped to mine when I had...well, I don't really know what the hell I had been doing when I greeted him. I didn't flirt at work. Not ever. It wasn't smart to shit where you ate–even if where I ate changed daily. I didn't like taking chances like that but the second I had laid eyes on him I knew he was different.

This man woke something up in me. Something I kept a very tight hold on in normal circumstances but that had come tumbling right out of me the damn second our eyes met. I'd wanted him to come close and grab me. His hands firm and warm on my body, to drag me close and shove me over the counter before he slipped his hand down the front of my jeans, strong fingers sliding down to cup my pussy. My nipples ached thinking about the day dream that had suddenly forced itself back in my brain.

All of that had led to me greeting him with a little more enthusiasm than I normally did. I might have pushed my tits up too. I frowned. That damn blonde had gotten in the way because she'd seen the same thing I had in him. She'd seen it and didn't like that he'd noticed me, so she'd done her best to get in the way.

I got it.

I mean it sucked, because it was real shitty how she did it. But I understood what happened when a man like that was suddenly in front of you. You'd do crazy things for a man like that. So the blonde has shown her hand. Too bad for her it'd been the wrong play, but even still–I understood her motivation to act.

There was a certain elegance to a man that looked like he could take you apart and have you begging for him to keep going with each and every piece that you lost to him. He'd scoop up the broken parts of you that had fallen to the floor and take them with him, filling his pockets with you on his way out and leaving you alone and wanting more.

The fucked up thing was he probably didn't even notice the effect he had on women. A man like that was in his own world.

But even still....

If this were a romance book he would come back and smile at me. He'd had a terrific smile. One that warmed his whole face up and made him look years younger. He would stroll up to the counter while I tried to pretend I hadn't been staring after him and he'd slip his number, printed on fancy card stock and he would ask me to dinner. All of this would make our meet cute. A story we would laugh over at dinner, regrettable but ultimately so perfect because it had brought us together. He'd kiss me goodnight after a lovely evening and we would date. Everyone that saw us would just know we belonged together. An unlikely pair that *just fit.*

But because this wasn't a romance book he didn't come back. Shit like that didn't happen to women like me. This was real life.

The sidewalk was empty save for a nanny and toddler scurrying past holding hands, their heads bowed and collars upturned from the morning chill. I sighed, turning back to the cappuccino foam in front of me and hoped that Tiffany wouldn't see my face.

"Uh, don't "what rock me", you little secret keeper. I'm talking about the rock you're not wearing on your hand. Letting all of us know you're gonna marry that hunk-o-burning love." She jerked a finger towards my hand as I poured foam into a cup and only when I had placed it on the counter and called out, "Dry cappuccino for Aaron!" Did she snatch my left hand and give it a shake.

"Where is the rock?!"

"You keep saying that, but I honestly don't—"

She shook my hand at my face. "He said you were his fiancée. Don't play with me. He told all of us you were his fiancée," she said, gesturing out towards the cafe that was full of customers looking our way curiously, if discreetly. "I bet they tell page six about this."

"About what?" I squeaked, and pulled my hand back with a jerk.

"That the owner of Law Acquisitions is a friend of the working class," Tiffany said gleefully. "And that he's in love with you."

"No, Tiff—" I shook my head, ready to set her straight on the kindness he had done me when she continued on.

"Lawson Sokolov, is like one of the city's most eligible bachelors and they are going to lose their shit when they find out he's off the market. It's going to be *awesome*." The way she said awesome made my stomach drop while simultaneously fluttering with excitement. I shook my head. No, I could not like awesome, not when it came to Lawson Sokolov's fictional dating status.

"He's what?" I asked, pushing away the dread and excitement that was brewing in my stomach.

She raised an eyebrow at me. "How do you not know that?"

I bit my lip and glanced towards the front of the shop. The big windows were bright and glittering with sunshine, making Lawson's earlier entry into my world seem like it had happened in another universe, not that morning.

"Don't know what?" I hedged, and Tiff scoffed.

"Don't play coy, you little minx."

I would have given anything to have met him before today. Anything for the words that I didn't know that man to be a lie. Lawson Sokolov was a stranger to me. I should have told her she knew more about him than I did, that until this morning I had never laid eyes on him or heard the man's name but for some reason the words wouldn't come. Instead I kept hearing him say *"my fiancé. My girl,"* and even if it was fake it felt too good, felt perfect, to be his. Even if it was all a lie.

I'd been raised to lie with a smile on my lips, bending the truth to fit whatever fucked up reality my mother spun around us. But this wasn't like that. This was warm and it was Lawson. The way people had looked at me in the shop when he'd claimed me had changed. Even the screaming Karen had been knocked on her ass thinking I was his.

Being Lawson's girl would be far better than anything I'd known. Even if he'd hightailed it out of the shop without so much as a pause in his step. He'd looked back.

Being Lawson's was worth a lie.

So I didn't tell her the truth.

I aimed a smile in Tiffany's direction and shrugged. "He doesn't talk about that with me," I demurred.

Tiffany blew out a sigh and bumped my shoulder with hers. "It makes sense that you're in and out of shops so much with the app if you're with a man like that."

"What do you mean?" I asked, wiping down the counter in front of me and surveying my work station. Everything was orderly and neat, just the way I liked it.

"I didn't get it really, but now I do. Keeps you free for a man like that."

I paused and glanced at Tiffany, she was looking out the windows in the direction Lawson had gone earlier, no doubt thinking of the man just the same as I had been.

"Free...yeah, that's it," I finally said, clearing my throat and forcing the smile on my face to stay in place.

"Super smart of you. If the paps had found out where you worked, it would be a circus. If you keep moving around then they'll never catch on to it."

I nodded. "Exactly. Makes things simpler that way." I put away the towel in my hand and straightened, glancing at the clock at the far end of the shop. My shift was over in a few minutes which would be the perfect excuse not to talk about the colossal lie I had just told my very brand new friend.

"Just got a few minutes left on the clock. I'm going to do a quick restock, okay?" I said, jerking a thumb over my shoulder towards the small back room where we kept the dry goods.

Tiffany's eyes went to the clock and she blinked in surprise. "Holy shit, you're done in ten. How did that happen?"

"Time flies when you're having fun."

"Definitely," she agreed and beamed at me. "A shift with you is more fun than I deserve at work."

"Flattery will get you everywhere, Tiff," I laughed, but I flushed at her praise. It was nice to hear that you were wanted. Even if Tiffany's words were casual, they were needed and warming all the same. It was another reminder why I liked being around the other woman.

"Awesome, then do you want to get dinner later this week?" she asked, and I stopped my search for the clipboard with the inventory supply list.

"That sounds great. I'm in," I told her. I could use

a little more of Tiffany's warm demeanor in my day-to-day.

"I know a great little Korean barbeque spot in Queens. We can check it out and stuff ourselves on the all you can eat meat dinner special." Tiffany bounced on her toes, practically radiating energy and excitement. She looked so happy and eager at that moment and I knew dinner would be a fun night.

"You had me at all you can eat dinner special. I'm free any night since," I gestured around the coffee shop with a circle of my finger, "coffee is an early bird game."

"Perfect! Are you free Thursday night?" she asked.

"I am."

Tiffany pumped her fist in the air with a grin. "It's a date! I'm so excited. We are going to have so much fun."

"What's going on over here?" Gus asked, leaning against the counter to watch while Tiffany broke out into a mini dance.

"Honey and I are going out on a date. It's going to be awesome."

Gus nodded his head and smiled, watching Tiffany hop around. "I'm glad you two are getting along. Friends are important," he said and then he looked my way, "which brings me to this morning. Can we talk a minute, Honey?"

I bit my lip and gave him a quick nod. A wave of uneasiness swept through me but after a reassuring smile from Gus, I forced my shoulders down and took a step towards him. "Sure thing, Gus."

"I just wanted to say how sorry I am about this morning."

The breath I hadn't been aware I was holding left my lungs with a little *whoosh* and I came forward until I was at the counter. I set the clipboard on the shiny quartz and shook my head. "It was a lot, please don't worry about it."

He held up a hand and shook his head sadly. "I do worry, and it wasn't okay, not at all. That woman was out of line, Honey. I'm so sorry you had to put up with that and in front of your fiancé of all people."

The little tightening in my stomach that accompanied a lie came to life but I batted it to the side and gave Gus a practiced rueful smile. I'd perfected this one the summer I had turned eleven and my mama had refused to pay 'one more dollar for useless activities' when I'd been set on playing softball in the summer city league. All of her cash was to be spent on getting herself ready for a tour she was certain would be her big break. My slightly embarrassed, definitely sympathy-inducing smile had worked to stave off my coach's inquiries over league fees for the entire summer. I'd proven to be a pinch hitter that couldn't be beat, which had been the perfect motivation my coach had needed to ignore my ever increasing balance of dues owed.

I turned that look on Gus now and watched as he softened. "It isn't your fault. It's just one of those things," I told him.

"It is, but even still. That woman should not have been comfortable coming in here and acting that way. She's banned. I just wanted you to know that."

"Banned?" I asked, eyes wide in surprise. I hadn't expected that.

"Yes, banned. I want you to feel happy and safe coming in to work here when you can. You're Tiffany's favorite and you're amazing with the customers. I love having you in the shop."

"Thank you, Gus. That means a lot."

"Anytime," he said, giving the counter a tap. "You are always welcome here. I want you to know that."

I made a mental note to scoop up any shifts at A Different Brew, each and every one that I could get my hands on. "I do, thank you, Gus. I like working here."

"Maybe one day I can convince you to take on a permanent spot."

Unease settled in my chest at his words. I knew he meant them, but settling down wasn't something

I knew how to do. I'd never learned. I held up a hand and waved him off. "Oh, I don't know, Gus. I like my freedom."

"My offer stands if you ever get tired of all that freedom."

"She can't take on a spot here," Tiffany butted in. "She's gotta keep the paps on their toes, Gus. If she locks in here she's going to blow her cover."

Gus blinked. "Her what?"

"Her cover, duh," Tiffany said, waving a hand at him and then pointing out towards the street. "She's Lawson Sokolov's fiancée, remember? Can you imagine what Page Six will look like if they know where she works?"

I rolled my eyes at her. "I don't know about that, Tiff."

"It's true and you know it. And you're going to tell me all about it, over all you can eat meat."

Gus nodded at her, even though I could tell he had zero idea what she was talking about. "I'll take over that, Honey. You're out of here now, go enjoy the day and all that sunshine."

"Sure thing." I handed the clipboard over to him and made for my purse and hoodie. As much as I liked A Different Brew, I was eager to start my 'day off'. He was right, it was a beautiful day outside, one that would be perfect for a stroll and window shopping. I might even treat myself to something and splurge in one of the little shops I loved so much. Things were tight with my budget but not that tight, not anymore. I could treat myself. I shouldered on my bag and turned, waving goodbye to Gus and Tiffany who returned it with goodbyes and waves of their own, while Tiffany shouted out about how we were going to eat our weight in Korean barbeque. I paused in the doorway and looked over my shoulder at the pair. Tiffany was chatting while Gus restocked.

He obviously had no clue what she was going on about. Still. But that didn't stop them. This was a daily occurrence, maybe hourly even from what I had seen while on shift, and I smiled at the familiar little dance the two of them did together.

It was a sweet picture. One that I was glad to recognize as familiar, one that I was a part of if only occasionally. And it was with a smile that I set off to enjoy the day's sunshine.

CHAPTER THREE

LAW

"Why are you brooding?" Adelaide asked.

"I'm not brooding," I replied, not looking away from the spreadsheet on my computer I was reviewing. I heard Adelaide scoff, blowing out a sigh before she tsk'd at me. I kept my eyes on the figures in front of me, even if I had been reviewing the same line for the fifth time. None of the shit I was supposed to be doing was coming easy or making sense to me that morning and I hated every last second of it.

Nothing was making sense since that morning.

Since the barista.

No, not the barista. *Honey*. Since fucking Honey.

"You are too brooding," Adelaide said. She marched up to my desk, her high heels clicking on the marble of the floor and stopped in front of me.

"Addie..." I growled, hand going tight on the pen in my hand.

She sucked on her teeth and laughed. "Oh, it's Addie now? Trying to distract me, I see."

I looked at her and frowned. She was smug, arms crossed with her planner tucked close and she tipped her head to the side, brown eyes considering me. I had picked the woman to be my assistant for a reason. She was damn good at her job and part of that job was reading me. Normally, her uncanny ability to see past whatever walls I had up was a blessing, but right now...

"Who is she?" She asked.

Right now I fucking hated it.

"Addie," I gritted out. "I have to finish this," I gestured down at the spreadsheet and then flicked a finger at her planner, "if we are going to make all the appointments you have in there."

"There's plenty of time for me to dissect exactly why you have your panties in a twist."

"I don't wear panties," I replied.

She rolled her eyes, tossed her planner onto my desk and took a seat in one of the leather backed chairs in front of my desk. "Whatever, boss. You know what I mean. Someone---no, not someone, some *woman*, has you twisted up in knots and I want to know who she is and where you met her."

I opened my mouth to tell her she was wrong,

but Addie shook her head. "No lying boss, secrets don't make friends."

I sighed, pinching the bridge of my nose. How the hell had this happened? I'd left the coffee shop and returned to my office, a cup in my hand and my mind squarely on the woman that had made the coffee. That had been hours ago, the coffee long gone cold, sitting untouched on the corner of my desk. If I drank it...well, I didn't fucking know what it would mean, but I was reluctant. If I did then I would have to throw away the cup—all reminders of that morning would be done and gone.

Honey would be gone.

A sharp pain shot through my chest. I held in a growl. *What the fuck.* My eyes landed on the damn cup and my lips pressed into a thin line. *What the actual fuck was I doing? Feeling?* Not drinking coffee? Holding onto paper cups as a goddamned memento from some chance meeting with a woman I didn't fucking know?

"Eyes off the cup and on me, boss man," Addie ordered.

My eyes snapped up to meet hers and I sighed heavily. "I'm not looking at a cup. I'm looking at the spreadsheet."

Addie hummed. "So it happened while getting coffee. Interesting."

Shit.

"Nothing happened," I snapped, and when she crossed her arms with a smirk, I cleared my throat before I went on in a calmer voice, "Nothing happened, Addie. Drop it."

"Drop it?" She inclined her head and held up a finger. "That means something definitely happened. Who is she?"

I sighed and leaned back in my chair. "Is the conference still happening at the end of the week?" The best way to change the topic was to throw work at Addie. She loved it, thrived in bringing order to the chaos of the constantly changing day-to-day of Law Acquisitions. I'd built the company from the ground up and kept it moving forward through a grueling work schedule and sheer determination. We were growing by the day, a feat for the largest acquisitions company in the city, and Addie at my side was one of the major reasons we were continuing to grow at our current pace. Driving her attention back to work was the key to getting her away from her line of questioning.

"I know what you're doing." She said with a scowl.

I arched an eyebrow at her. "Work is what I'm doing. What we're both supposed to be doing."

She sighed heavily. "You're no fun when you're in a grump funk."

I wasn't even going to touch on that. "Work, Addie. I need an update on the conference."

"Oh, all right," she sighed, snapping open her agenda book. "It's still on. You have meetings starting first thing tomorrow morning."

I relaxed at her words. Good. "First thing is good," I said. If I was busy with work, then I wasn't going to be thinking about a barista, or the way her name rolled off my fucking tongue like it was a name I had said a million times before--like it belonged there. I didn't like the taste of that shit.

Not one fucking bit.

I rose from my desk and grabbed the tablet to the side of my desk. "We need to go over the numbers for the Kinishewa merger." I was off and walking, already having crossed half of the room when I heard Addie stand from her seat with a heavy sigh.

"I'll get those right to you, boss."

I gave her a jerky nod and continued forward. "Good. I need to speak to Williams about an invoice. I'll meet you in five." Addie made a noncommittal sound and I knew she didn't like my decision to skip her topic of choice, but that she was at least on board with work. I opened the door, holding it for Addie to pass by me and then I set off towards Williams' desk. It wasn't completely true. I'd already seen the invoices and triple checked the figures for the Kinishewa merger, but that didn't matter. What mattered was a convenient get away which, for better or worse, was for a man like me.

I almost grimaced at the thought. A man like me….what the fuck did that even mean anymore. All I did was work, eyes focused on tomorrow. I was driven to never see the bottom again, but the more I grabbed the more I wondered why.

Why any of it really?

I didn't have to work. Not another day in my life if I didn't want. But if I did that I'd be going soft. My lip curled at the thought. Soft. Turning into some paunch-bellied out of touch idiot that spent more time on a golf course or throwing their weight around at an overpriced bistro while they fell into an existence that was equal parts irrelevant and self-loathing.

Soft.

That was never going to happen, not if I had a damn thing to do with it. I'd rather fight every damn day of my life than be that kind of man. Money was nothing if there was no power behind it, and power came from respect. If I had to work every last day of my life it would be worth it to stay at the top. And that was why I worked the hours I did, why I turned away from any comfort or attachment that might weaken me.

Why I had to stay away from a woman like Honey.

She was gentle and soft. I could see it, even if she tried to hide it. Knowing that she made an effort to keep it close and secret had me wanting to protect her, let her be as soft and gentle as she wanted. Because there was nothing to fear with a man like me at her back. If she was my woman, my little girl… there would be nothing in the world that wouldn't be hers. The bitchy blonde's face swam back into my vision and I gritted my teeth.

She'd treated Honey like trash. Like she was beneath her. If I hadn't been there things would have gone south for Honey. I knew down to my bones the big mouth blonde would have caused a scene until Honey was forced to bend and break.

But would it have happened at all if you hadn't been there?

I huffed out a breath, walking faster. Honey had gotten shit from the blonde for flirting with me. If I hadn't been there, she would have been safe from a Karen's power trip.

Would she have been?

"She would have been fine," I muttered out loud, but the words sounded hollow. That'd only be true if Honey didn't have the mind to flirt with anyone that morning. There was nothing to stop her from turning her smile on someone else and still catching shit.

I felt my eyes narrow. A spark of anger coming to

life in me at the thought Honey might give anyone else even half the attention she had sent my way that morning.

She shouldn't be flirting with anyone else but me. The anger roared to life like a wildfire and swept over me in a rush. If another man got close to her... They wouldn't lay a single finger on her beautiful tanned skin, her smile, her body...her fucking body was for me and me alone. If she even fucking looked at someone else I would put them through the wall.

"She's mine."

Those two damn words came out of my fucking mouth before I could stop them and I let out a silent prayer of thanks I was alone. It was bad enough I'd said the fucking thing. I didn't need anyone knowing I was losing my mind over a woman I had met that morning and spent less than 15 minutes with like a lovesick pre-teen.

I scrubbed a hand over my face. "Get it together. Stop talking to yourself," I growled. "Forget her." I straightened my shoulders and set off down the hallway. I went to Williams' office even though I already knew what the numbers would be.

Anything was better than thinking about her, or the fact that I hadn't bothered to throw away the coffee cup that still sat on my desk.

CHAPTER FOUR

HONEY

I climbed the stairs to my apartment with a groan and a roll of my shoulders. I was soaking wet from the early spring downpour I'd gotten caught in and I shook out my drenched hoodie. I hadn't planned on staying out as long as I had, but there'd been no way around it with the way my jobs had been spaced out that day. Uptown, midtown, hell I had even been clear out in Brooklyn before finally coming home.

Rain had only made it all worse. Rain in the city always made things inconvenient, toss in a couple of shitty shifts I'd picked up on BaristApp and it was downright exhausting. These gigs hadn't been the highest paying, but I'd been desperate. Usually my week was filled out with a nice selection of shops and shifts to pick from, but for whatever reason today had been a straight up bust.

It hadn't been the weather. Rain always meant people calling out of work while potential customers looking for a cozy place to wait out the rain went up. I usually made bank on rainy days, but today hadn't gone to plan. I grimaced looking down at my shoes. Black sneakers with a heavy sole. Perfectly sensible attire for being on my feet all day, but terrible in the rain. They squished with every step, my socks soaked through enough that I wondered if I'd have blisters from my long walk back from my subway stop.

The tips hadn't even been worth it. Between four shops I had barely managed to pull in sixty dollars, which was unheard of. Sixty dollars was my usual take from one shop on a slow day. Today hadn't just been slow though. Today had sucked. I shoved my key into my door and turned it with a jerk of my hand.

"I just want to lay down," I murmured, shouldering open the door and slipping inside with a sigh of relief. I kicked the door shut and slid the lock home before I started yanking off my shoes. I kicked them aside and stripped off my soaking hoodie, tossing it onto the coat rack by the door.

"I need tea." I made a beeline for the kitchen, hopping out of my jeans as I went and before long I was standing in my kitchen in my underwear and putting on a kettle to boil. "I need to get dry," I whispered a second later when I had gotten the kettle nice and piping hot. In my hurry to get dry, I hadn't exactly thought about staying warm. I turned, dashing towards the thermostat and flipped it on, the ancient furnace kicking to life with a rumble that told me I'd soon enough have a semi-warm apartment.

I was luckier than most with an apartment as old as I had, the damn thing had been built in the early thirties as tenement apartments but had been thoroughly renovated, not enough to give me creature comforts like central air, shiny appliances or floorboards that didn't creak and groan with every step, or you know windows that weren't prone to drafts— but I did have a pretty reliable and powerful heating system that went beyond wall radiators. So what if the crown molding was missing in some spots or if the paint was a little chipped here and there? Scuffed floorboards and doors that didn't quite shut when closed were small potatoes when it came to living in this city. What my apartment did offer me was a warm and dry place---a *safe* warm and dry place where I could rest easy knowing my neighbors weren't going to break in and take what little valuables I did have.

There was a sweet older Mexican woman, Juana

Mendoza, that had lived in these apartments since she was a young newlywed. She always kept a watchful eye on me when I was late coming home and I could always count on her coming round to invite me over for coffee or fresh tortillas when she was cooking on a Sunday. Juana helped alleviate the touch of homesickness I hadn't really realized I carried with me. My mother might have never given me a home, but I did miss South Texas from time to time. Then there was the nice family at the end of the hall that always had a friendly smile and chit chatted while we used the common laundry room. I loved their pre-teens Molly and Evan, and Elaina, their mother, always ate up whatever gossip I could offer her. She worked long hours at the nearby hospital as a RN and would take any sense of a little normality she could vicariously live through.

"You're young. You should be out partying and dating every good looking man within 15 city blocks," she had insisted one day.

It was a nice place to live, even if it was older, and I was glad to have it. Hell, it was even a decent sized space for the rent. I made a decent amount on my current work schedule but rent in New York was not for the faint of heart and for what I was paying I should be living in something more around the size of a postage stamp. Instead, I got a sprawling-*ish* loft with drafty windows and semi-decent heating. I even had neighbors I liked. For New York City, I was practically living in the lap of luxury. The size of the apartment wasn't even a huge deal to me, It wasn't like I had a ton of possessions to store anyways.

I glanced around my apartment while I waited for it to warm up. It was sparsely furnished, something I insisted was because I was a minimalist and definitely, not at all, because I was afraid as hell to set down any kind of roots that would require me to actually have to plan and coordinate a move. I liked knowing I could grab a bag, stuff it with essentials and be gone before anyone even thought to wonder where I'd gone.

You are your mother's daughter.

The ugly whisper came before I could stop it and I squeezed my eyes shut, sucking in a deep breath through my nose. We'd moved around a lot when I was a kid, even more when I was a teenager, and it had become second nature for me to keep a bag close by my bed. My thoughts were always leaving my present situation, always skipping ahead to the next thing or place. How I might start over in whatever new place my mother dragged us to—how it might, if I was lucky, be the last place we moved.

Except that it was all hopeful wishing. It was never the last place. We never stopped moving. And somewhere along the way I picked up the habit of always having an escape plan. Ready to go, even when I had exactly zero plans to leave the life I had built behind. I wasn't going to be moving. Not today, not tomorrow, not at all.

This was home.

"No, I am not. I am not like her," I whispered, eyes still closed. I had to shut that little voice down and I had to do it now. If it took hold...if it took hold, there was no telling where I would go, and I was not about to tempt fate.

The room was big and open, the windows that normally flooded the space with light showing me the dark and gloomy silhouette of the city. A television was at one end of the room, against the wall and a nice modern couch that I had picked out one day while wandering around the swap meets in Brooklyn, sat opposite of it. There was a bookcase that was filled to the brim---I had always thought about getting another one, but instead had just started stacking books on the floor beside the bookcase instead. I had a few stacks at about hip height leaning precariously against the wall. A small two person dining table and a pair of matching teal chairs were behind the couch in a makeshift dining room that spilled over into the kitchen. My tea kettle was rattling merrily along on the stove and I swallowed hard looking at the small kitchen that was cute, homey, but still didn't possess the same lived in quality that Elaina and Juana's kitchens did. Those spaces were alive and warm, while mine was just occupied.

A gust of wind threw another wave of rainwater at the windows and I shivered, wrapping my arms around myself. The rain had been nearly knocking me sideways before I'd managed to get inside. I hurried into my bedroom to grab a hoodie and socks. Standing around in my wet underwear was doing absolutely shit for keeping me dry. I dressed quickly and went to the bathroom, splashing warm water on my face and drying my hair out in a towel.

I stopped and looked at myself in the mirror. "You are not your mother's daughter. This is home." I insisted once more, staring at my reflection as if I could will it to come to life and agree with me, agree with me or I didn't know, fight me. Argue and tell me I was lying. Anything to fill the quiet of the apartment and the words that sounded too thin on my lips.

If this was home then why did I refuse to put art up on the walls? I had lived in this place for two years and so far had only managed to buy one small print that I had hastily taped to my fridge, because no place in the apartment seemed right. My bedroom was just a bedroom, not a place to rest, it was where I slept, nothing more.

It wasn't right. None of this was right. When was I going-

EEEEE!!!

The shriek of the tea kettle made me jump and I turned on my heel, striding into the kitchen to turn it off. I was grateful for the distraction and set about making myself a cup of tea--cherry blossom plum--to settle my nerves. I turned off the stove and reached for the cupboard to the left of it. The second I pulled open the heavy wooden cupboard doors the scent of flowers and herbs hit my nose and I smiled, taking in a deep breath. I might not have a lot in the way of furniture or art, but tea?

Oh, I had that.

Green, black, herbal. Bitter, sweet and savory. Caffeinated and not, It didn't matter, I wanted to try it, and had even begun blending my own teas. I'd found an apothecary in town that offered classes and made sure to take as many as I could, usually one a month to keep learning about the herbs and teas available to brew. I liked learning the different temperature requirements, how to store and care for the prettiest rolled flower teas and what might happen when I added a dash of citrus to some--the answer was that sometimes it turned blue like a potion out of a fairytale, and sometimes it was just a mistake I couldn't drink.

It was an art, a ritual that worked to calm my mind, chase away that voice I hated. That infuriating voice that I carried around. The one that surreptitiously reminded me that it didn't matter how many places I moved, or didn't move, how many days and years I spent trying to be someone else. That I would, inevitably, slip up. I frowned, grabbed down the jar I wanted to use and flipped open the top, taking a deep breath of the familiar floral and tart smell the cherry blossom and plum mixture offered me. I had worked on this one just last weekend and it was my current obsession when I was feeling a little tense, which apparently right now I was.

I sucked in another deep breath and held it for a beat before I released it and opened my eyes. "That's better, now unlock your damn jaw," I ordered myself while I forced my shoulders down from around my ears. I never failed to get twitchy whenever my thoughts got away from me. But that didn't matter. Because I was here, and I was happy. Or at least, I was okay. I was definitely okay. I looked back up at the tea on the shelves in front of me and ran a finger along the glass jars that held the blends and herbs I had stocked my home with.

"No one can be unhappy with this kind of tea hoard," I said, nodding at my words. It was true. You just couldn't be unhappy with this kind of stash, and this wasn't even counting my coffee collection. I had a whole other cupboard dedicated to that. Beans of different origins and roasts, my fancy little drip cold brew maker, my Aeropress, the beautiful espresso machine I had sprung for was all neatly tucked away on the corner of the counter and I ran a hand over it lovingly. No, I might not have a ton of possessions but if I ever had to leave I'd mourn the loss of my tea and coffee hoard.

This kind of beverage power just left a woman blissed out and happy.

"And I *am* happy," I told myself, pouring the water over the tea leaves with a nod. The gentle floral smell of cherry blossoms wafted up to me, and I smiled. Yeah, this was better, much fucking better all right. I leaned a hip against the counter and rolled my shoulders and stretched my arms over my head with another deep breath.

Breathe in. Breathe out.

My shoulders dropped and I nodded in approval. I was relaxed, dry, had a cup of tea brewing and my apartment was semi-warm. It didn't really get better than this after a lackluster day. I picked my cup up and made my way to my couch where I settled, balancing the cup on the arm of the couch while I picked up my phone and began scrolling mindlessly through sites and social media I didn't keep up with in the slightest.

It was here that I was hit with a little shock that popped the bubble of relaxation I was weaving around myself.

"She's my girl."

Lawson Sokolov makes records with newest acquisition. Will he continue to defy the odds?

I swallowed hard, staring at the screen I held. Right there on my phone was a picture of the man in question. It was a good photo, capturing him in profile with his gaze to the side. My eyes moved along the strong line of his nose and over his full lips, and down to his jaw. The man had a great jawline, sharp and strong, just the kind that made me weak in my knees. Again, I swallowed, fingers moving away from the screen of my phone to grip the tea mug beside me. I could see Lawson's jaw, plain as day, clenching in anger in the coffee shop before he turned to face down the blonde woman that had gone after me. I sipped from my tea, the hot liquid burning down my throat because I hadn't bothered to wait to let it cool.

I closed my eyes, focusing on the tea induced ache in my throat. Anything other than think about him, jaw clenched, eyes narrowed in anger, the morning sunlight glinting off his hair that was a mix of brown and gold, the sides shorn short with a peppering of gray adding silver to his profile. He'd been on the warpath when he'd told off the woman, but then...but then he'd been there defending me, making up a lie about me being his fiancée to save me. God, he was absolutely beautiful, even when he was angry. Then there had been the way he'd looked at me when he'd turned to me.

"I'm really sorry about that."

He'd spoken to me in a gentle tone, his voice a sharp departure from the way he'd talked to the blonde. This was intimate as a whisper between lovers and he'd come close, one big hand resting on the counter between us. His eyes had been soft on me. Dark hazel with ocher flecks in them that I kept seeing everywhere I went. Under normal circumstances that would be pretty stupid, but under these? A made up fiancé? A swooping in and saving my ass like a knight in shining armor? It was absolutely ridiculous and cringe worthy, but god, if there wasn't a woman alive that wouldn't understand me and what my imagination was forcing on me.

I kept seeing his beautiful face everywhere I went. Anytime I saw a man in a dark suit with a slightly rumpled air, I wondered if it was him and I felt my heart rise up in my chest, forcing its way up and up until it was lodged in my throat. I knew that if it was him, I wouldn't fucking know what to say. I'd just smile and blush, the words getting all confused and twisted in my mouth while my brain spun furiously, trying to put my feelings in the right order. Things like that never came easily to me. I'd been shaking when Lawson had left the coffee shop, the words I had managed to get out to him a blessing. But then the man would turn my way and it wasn't him. Never Lawson. It was just some man. Not Lawson, larger than life and calling me *his girl*.

His girl.

Why the fuck did I like that so much? I didn't even know the man.

"Because I'm borderline pathetic and don't own any furniture," I muttered, taking another sip of scalding hot tea and wincing. I had even taken another shift at A Different Brew just yesterday, a whole two days since I'd first seen Lawson, which was honestly huge for me. I didn't take repeat jobs in the same neighborhoods in the same week, let alone the same shop, but there I was working the espresso bar with Tiff while I hoped I would run into Lawson again. I sighed, letting my head fall back against my couch because I'd watched the front door the entire day like a hawk, but each and every time someone entered the shop it hadn't been Lawson. It was so bad that Tiffany had taken to teasing me about "having it bad for my man," but I couldn't really say much in my defense, because it was obvious that I was looking for him. And besides, she thought he was my fiancé, so why would I even try to rebuff something like that?

The short answer was that I couldn't, so I did what any self-respecting modern woman did when faced with such a situation: I continued to lie.

I didn't like lying, especially to someone that had the potential to be a friend. A real and honest one at that, but there was really no way to tell Tiff that I'd lied the first time when she asked. I could have come clean then, but I hadn't. My bed was made and now it was time for me to lay the hell down in it and figure the rest out.

I huffed out a laugh. "What the hell was I thinking?" I asked the empty room, but there was no answer. Only the tapping of the rain against my windows and the rumble of thunder. I took another quick drink of my tea, eyes going back to the phone in my lap, back to Lawson's photo.

The man really was gorgeous. There was no way anyone was really reading this article to learn how he was making deals, not when they could look at his face. I sighed, ready to settle in for a night of staring longingly at Lawson's photo when my phone buzzed in my hand with a message.

See you at eight tonight. Bring your stretchy pants.

I laughed seeing the message from Tiffany and swiped up, opening it so that I could answer her. Messaging Tiffany was good. If I was doing that then I wasn't staring at the article on Lawson like it was the latest Teen Beat. I'd agreed to dinner at Korean barbecue earlier that week and today was the day. Even if it was pouring outside I was up for braving the storm for a chance to see Tiff. The woman made me smile, genuinely made me happy, I knew that a night stuffing my face with her was the thing to get me out of lingering over Lawson for too long.

Consider it done. See ya then! :)

I sent the text, closed the browser with Lawson's stupidly handsome face and saw that I had exactly enough time to get dressed, finish my tea and get my ass in gear to meet Tiffany. The place she had picked was just down the block from me and it wouldn't take me very long to get there, which was a blessing considering the storm that was still raging.

I hopped off the couch tossing my phone behind me and made for my bedroom with my cup of tea in hand. I sipped at my tea, my mind already skipping ahead to dinner while I dressed. When I was done getting ready and yanked on my rain boots, Lawson Sokolov was the furthest thing from my mind. I made sure to double check my phone, keys, wallet, the routine of it working to further center me in the now. Once I was sure I was good, I left my apartment already feeling lighter. I waved at Juana, who was on her way home for the evening.

She raised an eyebrow at me when we passed but waved back all the same. "Where are you going in this rain? And at night too," she asked, and I grinned at her question. Some people might find it nosey, but I didn't. It felt nice to have someone looking out for me while I was coming and going in the city. I didn't have family to do it, which made a nosey neighbor more than welcome.

"To dinner with a friend. Just over at Sik Gaek," I told her, stopping at the top of the stairs.

Juana hummed, a hand going to her hip. "Is it a date?" she asked, not even trying to hide her curiosity. She was always wanting me to find a "good man to settle down with," so her question was one I wasn't surprised to hear in the slightest.

I grinned and shook my head at her. "No, it's a friend, I swear. A girl I work with."

"Girls can be more than friends too," Juana insisted, apparently not willing to give up on her hopes of me finding myself someone.

I laughed. "Not this one. She's just a friend. Pinky swear, Juana."

She sighed at me and then waved a hand at me. "Come here."

I walked forward without hesitation but still asked, "Why? What's up?"

"You need an umbrella," Juana pointed out, already moving into her apartment.

"Oh I'm okay. It's not that far and-"

"Honey." I could tell by the way she held on to my name Juana was not going to be arguing on this one. It was going to be easier to take the umbrella in the long run.

"Okay, okay," I sighed, coming forward to follow

her into her apartment. The space was cozy with pale yellow walls that warmed the big loft in a way mine lacked. Juana had plants filling every available space, rugs covering the floors and the familiar smell of spices—cloves and cinnamon—filled my nose the second I crossed the threshold. It was a happy place, somewhere I knew I was welcome anytime and I grinned watching her rifle through her closet until she emerged with a pink umbrella triumphantly.

"Here's an extra that I don't need anymore," she said, holding it out to me with a smile.

"I'll bring it back," I hedged, taking the pale pink umbrella that looked as long as my arm. A flouncy bow could be seen peeking out from the bottom of it and I turned it over, seeing there were more bows circling the bottom of it. This thing couldn't have been meant for anyone over the age of twelve, but even so my soul sang at the sight of all that pink. The bows made me want to run my fingers over them, twisting the material around my forefinger and thumb until it cut into my skin. It would be soft, I knew that. It was a perfect umbrella really, but that didn't change the fact that it was meant for a child.

Not a grown woman. Which I was.

I looked at Juana nervously, wondering why she had given me this umbrella. The old woman saw more than she let on and a finger of fear crept up my spine and made me wonder exactly what it was that she saw in me that made her give me a pink bowed cupcake of an umbrella.

Juana rolled her eyes at me. "That's your umbrella now, Honey. I've had it for years, it's not like anyone will use it, so don't tell me that you can't take it when it's just taking up space in my closet." The fear that had touched my skin vanished and I let out the breath I had been holding. She didn't know. It was all a coincidence. "Now come here, give me a hug and go eat, and make sure to eat seconds. You don't eat enough."

I opened my mouth to protest but right on cue my stomach growled. Traitor. It was true I did skip meals but it was just because I was so...scattered. I didn't know where the time went, or where I was when the time went, but my mind was somewhere else. Lost on a thought or busy thinking about what I needed to do *later*, that I just forgot about what I needed to do right *now*.

"Oh, all right," I sighed, obediently hugging her. Juana was a small woman, short and slight, her body felt light against mine and I closed my eyes when she squeezed with more strength than her small body indicated she had. She patted my back and leaned back, smiling broadly at me.

"I'll keep an ear out for you when you get back. Be careful crossing Queens Boulevard, you know how they drive. Todo loco," she said with a shake of her gray head.

I smiled and leaned in close to her, pressing my lips to her cheek. "I know, I'll be careful."

"Have fun."

"I will." I raised the umbrella and gave her another smile. "Thank you for this, Juana. I mean it."

"De nada, mija," she said, and then shooed me towards the door, "now get a move on, or you'll be late for dinner."

I left Juana's apartment, my footsteps sounding loud on the wooden stairs as I descended to the street level. When I shouldered open the heavy metal door I was hit with a wave of chilly wet air that had me frowning and opening my umbrella with a jerk of my hand. It unfurled, the great big whoosh of it's canopy extending above me making me jump. The pink material of it was...well, it was fucking great, and I smiled watching the pink bows bounce merrily along as I walked.

It was a sweet umbrella. I wouldn't tell Juana but I loved it far more than she would ever know. I reached out, touching the soft pink end of a ribbon briefly before I adjusted my grip on the surprisingly large and heavy handle. The umbrella was a lot bigger than I had anticipated and I shifted, making sure to hold the curved pink handle with both hands when a man's shoulder grazed, it but he was effectively bounced back and away by the sturdy umbrella canopy. The pink bows danced merrily and I was only vaguely aware of the man's frown as I lifted the umbrella to get a look at what had made contact with me. I was going to have to concentrate on navigating the busy street if I wanted to get there without knocking anyone down. But because of its size and height, plus the sheer overwhelming power of it's bubblegum pinkness, the umbrella did wonders for helping me slice through the crowd. It was a little oversized, the canopy of it forming a pastel bubble around me that kept other walkers a foot away from me. Then I knew why Juana had given me the umbrella. Not for the pink material or the big bouncing bows I loved, but for the distance that it put between me and the other people in the city.

Juana was a smart woman. But not even she had figured out my secret. And that secret was that I was, at the core of me, a *Middle*.

A Middle with a taste for BDSM and submission.

I shifted, gripping the umbrella tighter. Would Juana like me if she knew? I didn't know. Probably not. Not that she would ever be let into that part of my life. Not that anyone I ever held in my day-to-day existence would discover the secret about who I was.

Not that it matters on account of how far away you

keep everyone, the voice in my head insisted, and I flinched. There were times I hated my thoughts and now was one of them. I hated it when my thoughts told me the truth. I did hold everyone at arm's length, but that didn't have a thing to do with the person I chose to be when I put myself in the hands of a Daddy Dom. My skin tingled, the blood rushing to the surface in a mix of adrenaline and lust that warmed me through better than any shot of alcohol could ever hope to. I barely felt the cold rainwater sloshing off my umbrella and onto my arm when I turned the corner sharply to avoid careening into a pack of school children gleefully screaming and running down the street.

Daddy.

That one word was enough to make me weak. I bit my lip, fingers gripping the hard plastic handle tighter, checking before I joined the group of pedestrians crossing the street. It had been awhile since I'd played, which probably explained why I was so in my head lately. I needed it. Craved the release of letting someone else have my control, even if only for a few hours. The time spent being a Middle reset me. Let me breathe a little easier when I could let Daddy make the decisions. Although...it wasn't like I would be docile about it. I made up my mind to play that weekend. There were only so many days a woman could go on like I was, with zero play and all work. I would go to Cairn and put out my feelers for just the right Daddy. Because not just anyone would do. I needed a Dom with a strong hand, but also with a soft spot for brats.

I liked giving it as good as I got. The sassier side of me, the sharper edges I kept carefully hidden away from the world, had no qualms at revealing themselves to those who also participated in the lifestyle. It was easier to reveal all those jagged and raw bits of myself to others who chose to lay themselves just as bare. There was a vulnerability in kink that went unnoticed by much of the public who either didn't have an interest in, or hadn't experienced the delicate dance of release through kink. I loved it when I was able to sink into my role as a Middle. I was absent more than not lately with my work schedule and it had only added to my anxiety and general scatteredness.

Tonight with Tiff would help reset me some though. Good people, good food, the closeness of dinner and gossip with a new friend would come close to taking the edge off the ball of anxiety I felt growing in my chest. Tonight would be good. Just what I needed. I knew it. My lips turned up in a smile, steps quickening as I all but set off in a jog to stay with the flood of foot traffic.

Overhead thunder rolled, the crack of it reverberating along the tall buildings and I swore I could feel it shaking up through the concrete as I ran, trying to get out of the rain that didn't seem to be letting up any time soon. Water splashed my legs but I kept going and before long I saw the familiar lights of Sik Gaek come into view. The warm glow of it made me smile as I walked toward the door, and I began to wonder how long Tiffany wanted to stay out—as in how many bottles of Soju I might be able to persuade her to order with me tonight.

With the way I was feeling whoever I played with would have their work cut out for them.

I could not wait.

CHAPTER FIVE

LAW

"You're brooding."

I glanced up from my cellphone to look at Addie. "This is just my face. We've been over this."

She snorted but tilted her head to the side and placed a folder on my desk. "Liar." It was an early evening on Thursday and the end of another work day. We should be gone by now, but I'd lingered as usual, and Addie hadn't strayed from my side, also as usual. A crack of lightning flashed across the sky, lighting up the city better than any sunny day. It was blinding and I squinted with a frown.

"I'm having the car brought round to take you home."

Addie waved a hand. "I'm fine on the subway."

I shook my head. "You know I don't like that you

insult me by taking that damn thing to begin with," I jerked my chin towards the window where another brighter than daylight lightning strike was making itself known, "I'm not having you do it now when you stayed to work late."

Addie blinked hard. "I'm fi-," she began, and I pinched the bridge of my nose."

"I'm calling the car. That's final. Or you are banned from staying to work late for a week," I threatened.

"But boss-"

"A month," I threatened.

She stamped her foot and crossed her arms. "Fine, *fine*. I'll just go get my coat then." I knew she would cave when I brought work into it. There was nothing Addie loved more than working—she would stop at nothing to keep herself in all the late nights she could handle. Some people had hobbies they did to relax, but from what I could see Addie worked to relax. The woman was a machine. I was sending her to a damn beach somewhere once the next fiscal term was over.

"See that you do."

Addie glowered in my direction but I ignored her in favor of my phone. She was getting home, dry as a bone, and that was that. I didn't need my assistant turning up sick. I hit the button for my driver, Taylor, and a ring later they were answering.

"Sir?"

"You're taking Addie home tonight. She'll be down in five. Don't let her out until she's home."

I heard Taylor huff out a laugh. "Understood."

"Good man." I ended the call and turned, looking out at the rainstorm. It was practically a fucking hurricane and Addie would have been blown sideways if I'd let her make her own way home. I rolled my shoulders, letting some of the tenseness out. If Taylor had the order it would be carried out. He was a man who had a similar understanding of this world, someone who had worked his way off the street to lead a quieter life. Someone looking for, and willing to protect, one very important thing.

Normal.

Honey's dark eyes came to mind and I almost groaned. As plain as day I could see her eyes, those ocher flecked brown eyes that I'd seen four days ago. I glanced towards the empty cup of coffee sitting on my desk. It was from A Different Brew, courtesy of Addie, of course. The damn meddling woman had caught on that something had happened in the shop and had made her play to force a reaction from me. I kept myself calm and in check the first time she gave me the cup, though I might have held onto it for a minute too long, the memory of Honey coming to me and waking me out of my early morning routine.

"Something the matter, boss?" Addie had inquired, watching my face carefully.

I didn't answer, favoring a noncommittal grunt before I took a swig of the coffee before stalking back into my office. Addie had let it slide, but she had made a point to bring in a cup every day since I'd seen Honey.

Not just seen, but claimed her as my own.

My palms itched and I rubbed them against my thighs in frustration. Thinking about Honey, just what her eyes looked like when staring back at me, made me like this. Too restless, like my body was overheating, blood rising and making me want.

I shouldn't want.

I had everything I had ever wanted. A man like me didn't want, because when I wanted something, I fucking took it. But that was when it came to things, people, anything that wasn't Honey. She deserved better than that.

You didn't just take a woman like that. She'd come willingly enough if I asked. I could see it in her. Even in the brief interaction we'd had in the coffee shop, I knew if I so much as held my hand out, Honey would take it. She'd been intrigued by me and not just because I'd taken up for her, but genuinely. I hadn't missed the stunned look in her eyes or slightly flushed color that had dusted her cheeks when I'd done it. *When I'd called her mine.* Honey wasn't taken, she offered herself, and if she did that to me...My palm prickled again. I clenched my fingers, chasing away the feeling, and scrubbed my hand across my thigh. It would be like offering a starving man a feast on a silver platter.

There would be nothing left of her. I would do what I always did. The only thing I knew how to do. I would have her, have all of her and consume every last bit of her until she couldn't tell where she ended and I began. I would fill her so full of me that she would be ruined for anyone else.

"Don't even know her," I reminded myself.

I didn't know her and I was going to keep it that way—no matter how many coffees Addie brought me from A Different Brew, five counting today, or how often I daydreamed about Honey like some shitty high schooler crushing on a pretty girl they didn't know how to handle. I knew exactly how to handle Honey—and that was the problem. A woman like that would bend and form in my grasp, every bit of her mimicking her namesake as easily as if I were pouring her from a heated spoon into my morning coffee. She'd be sweet. I knew that, god she wouldn't just be sweet—she would be perfect.

I snatched up the empty paper cup from A Different Brew and stared down at the stamped logo, a mug inked in black, little curlicues of steam wrapping itself around the shop name, and I glared at it. It was what Addie would declare to be 'cute,' but I didn't have time for cute, not in my real life.

I tossed the paper cup into the wastebasket beside my desk and tagged the leather folio full of that week's numbers before sinking down into my chair. I would be here for a while longer, plenty of time for Taylor to finish dropping Addie off and return for me. This was what I needed to focus on. A night at the office. Work. Numbers. Nothing that asked too much of me. Certainly not a pretty woman that would be far too fragile to handle my taste for control and sex. If I wanted cute, if I wanted sweet, I knew where to find it.

The Cairn.

Not in a woman I met in my everyday life. Not even a woman that I declared to be mine in a shop full of strangers. I would take my pleasure not in a woman, but a submissive who understood my wants and needs.

A submissive that understood why I wanted them to call me Daddy.

One that would relish being broken and put back together by my hands, and they would thank me for it. My fingers flexed on the leather of the folio and I paused before opening it. My mind was already being a fucker and not concentrating, thoughts of submissives and pretty pink lips whispering, 'Daddy,' were settling in too damn easily for my liking, which meant only one thing.

"All work and no play makes me a fucking asshole," I muttered, reaching out and picking up my cellphone in favor of the folio. I hit the number that I had saved and waited. It rang once, twice, and then it was answered with the cool, even voice that I knew well.

"Hello." That was it, no fake ass customer service voice cheerily greeting me, no explanation of where the fuck I was actually calling, because only the city's most affluent with a taste for more had this number. Calling it by mistake was not done. If you called, you knew.

"Connie, how are you?"

I could practically hear her smile through the phone when she said, "Sir, what a pleasure to hear from you and so soon after your last visit. I can say that you left quite an impression on your *little* guest."

I grinned and leaned back in my seat. That weekend she referred to had been just over a month ago. Time that I had taken out at Addie's demand before I'd launched myself into a month long marathon of work and well, more fucking work, that I'd managed after high-jacking Addie's planner.

My assistant hadn't been pleased and the price had been a weekend of mandatory fun I'd enjoyed at The Cairn. I'd returned from it balanced and ready to take on my work. If my brain and dick seemed insistent on thinking of Honey, of conjuring up images of pretty submissives splayed out for my attention, then why not give it what it wanted?

Scratch the itch so to speak. If I fucked a submissive into next week, then I was sure Honey's hold on me would be put to rest. It had to fucking work. Anything to stop my idiot brain from putting Honey in the place of the submissives it was already craving.

That would be a stupid as shit thing to think.

"I'm glad to hear it. She needed to be taken care of."

"Indeed." She paused and then asked, "Will you be joining us for another weekend?"

"Not sure if I'm in for the weekend, but a night would do me right."

"Mmm, let me check the books, but I'm certain we have your suite available."

"Thank you, Connie."

"Anything for you. Now let's see here…" Her voice trailed off as she checked the appointment book for the weekend. I drummed my fingers on the desk while I waited, the nervous energy in my body taking hold until I was bouncing my knee. I gritted my teeth, forcing myself to sit still. How the fuck had Honey gotten me this wound up from a meeting that meant nothing?

I turned my head and almost kicked the wastebasket when my eyes landed on the paper cup displaying A Different Brew's logo. I glared at it. Cute. It was too damn cute. No wonder she worked there. I was still glaring when Connie began speaking again.

"We do have Saturday evening open for you, if that fits your schedule."

"It does."

"Perfect. I'll pencil you in, and as always I'm happy to know we'll have you with us, if even for a night."

I smiled hearing the genuineness in Connie's voice. I didn't hear sincerity often, not in my line of work, and I appreciated it where it was offered. "Thank you, Connie. I'll see you then," I told her, and I was glad to hear my voice already sounded less stressed.

"Have a good evening, sir."

"Same to you."

The line went dead after that and I put my phone down with a sigh, shoulders dropping down from where they had hunched up. I rolled them, relaxing into my chair with a nod. I picked up the folio then and with nothing else to do, I did what I did best.

I worked.

CHAPTER SIX

HONEY

"So we are getting the pork belly, right? If we aren't, then I'm going fucking home and I don't care if I have to swim home in the storm outside. I'm doing it." Tiffany crossed her arms and stared at me with a look that told me she meant it. Storm or no storm, she was out if I didn't say yes we were getting the delicious fatty pork.

"You're in luck," I told her, picking up my spoon and digging into the egg Gyeranjjim, "because I insist on the pork belly. And if we don't get at least two bottles of Makgeolli, then *I'll* swim home in this monsoon."

Tiffany's eyebrows quirked, and she grinned. "Oh, I like it! Upping the ante and in only the best way."

"You know it," I told her, eating a spoonful of steaming egg with a moan of pleasure. "God, I'm starving. I could probably eat three of these," I said, gesturing at the steaming metal pot the egg dish was served in.

"That's because you don't eat anything, ever."

"I eat," I told her, shaking my head.

"Yeah, okay, cool story."

I rolled my eyes at her and picked up the menu in front of me. The server was walking our way and I didn't intend to waste a damn minute getting my fill of delicious Korean food and wine. We ordered and in no time had an assortment of banchan, a bottle of chilled rice wine sitting in front of us with pork belly sizzling on the grill at our table.

Life was good. This was exactly what I'd needed after the day I'd had. Today had felt...draining. The week had been lonelier than usual, which put me on edge. I was able to mostly keep myself occupied, my mind flitting from this project or that, the app on my phone pinging away with available shifts in the city. It was enough to distract me, but it had felt empty. Not even the book I had been reading did much to curb where my mind seemed determined to go, which was in the direction of one person.

Well, one man to be fucking exact.

Lawson Sokolov.

I licked my lips and raised the ceramic cup my

makgeolli was in and took a hasty sip. I didn't need to be thinking of that man. Not now, not when I had decided that I was going to be paying the Cairn a visit. What I needed to do was focus on tonight and on enjoying Tiffany's company.

"I love all these side dishes," Tiffany sighed, stuffing her mouth with tofu and grinning at me. "Hey, I'm really happy you came to dinner with me. I've been wanting to hang out. You know how hard it is to make friends as an adult."

I laughed. "It's fucking terrible. So awkward."

"Beyond awkward! How do you make it not weird that you like another adult and want to spend time with them? It was so much easier back in school, you know?"

"I get it." I nodded along as if I understood, even if I didn't. Making friends had never come naturally to me. I was always a beat out of step with everyone else. On the outskirts of everything even when I was in the thick of it. I'd never been able to make the transition to putting down roots and making genuine connections when I was sure I was going to be moving on whenever a new wind blew my mother a different direction. The awkwardness of school hadn't lessened when I'd left home, it had only seemed to amplify, with me questioning each and every one of my decisions.

Making friends hadn't ever been easy. It was

painful for me, even when I wanted it to happen. I smiled at Tiffany pouring her a drink. Needless to say, I really fucking wanted it to happen with Tiffany. She was good people. I needed more good in my life.

"Okay, so what do we have to do to make you sign on to be full time at the shop?"

I blinked in surprise at her. "A Different Brew?" I asked.

"No, the donut shop. Of course, A Different Brew. I want you working with me regularly, woman. How do I make that happen?"

"Are you offering me a job?"

Tiffany raised her cup and took a deep drink, rolling her eyes at me as she did. "Duh," she said when she slammed the cup down and gestured at the makgeolli bottle. "Another, please."

I nodded at her and poured more in her cup. "Listen, I don't know…you might only like me in small doses, you ever thought of that?" I asked, while I flipped the meat on the grill.

"Oh, please, I know I love you already. I want to see your amazing face all the time, and besides you know how to man a Korean barbeque grill, which makes you a top quality woman in my book."

I laughed and set the tongs down. "Doesn't take a lot then."

"Honey, stop that." There was a tone in her voice

that made me look at her. When I met her eyes I saw that Tiffany was staring intently at me. Her cup raised halfway to her lips, she gestured with it towards me. "You always do that."

"Do what?"

"You make it sound like being your friend is a chore, and it's not. You're the best."

"You hardly know me," I pointed out.

"I know enough. Also, Gus is on board because we are so tired of being understaffed and you know you want to get off that stinking app." She waved a hand at me and I leaned back in my seat, sipping my drink.

"I like BaristApp."

She scoffed and took another sip of her drink. "What? No one likes that app."

I tapped a finger against my chest. "That's not true, Tiff. *I* like the app, and I'm sitting right here to prove it."

She put down her cup and picked up her bowl of rice, spooning kimchi and fish cake onto it. "Okay, but maybe you just like it because you have a billionaire boyfriend," she said, and then held up a chopstick, "oh, wait, not boyfriend but fiancé, my bad."

My cheeks heated at the mention of my make believe fiancé. "I don't know what Lawson has to do with it."

"He has everything to do with it. You don't need

to work with a man like that calling you his girl." She winked at me when I tried to protest. "No shame in the game, Honey. I'm glad you got someone like that pulling for you. New York isn't a kind place. You need someone with a little power in your corner, you know?"

I closed my mouth, eyes dropping back to the sizzling grill in front of me. "Yeah, I know," I said, because what she was saying was 100% gospel. The city would chew you up and spit you out if you didn't have some steel to you, but New York was also a 24/7 grind that wore a girl down. It helped to have support, especially if that support was Lawson Sokolov. I could see why Tiffany thought I was set, and sitting here looking at her with her big smile and earnest eyes, I wished not for the first time that what she was saying was the truth.

God how I wished Lawson Sokolov was well and truly mine. Of course, he wasn't and never would be, but that didn't mean I could tell Tiffany that. Not when she thought it was the truth, and not when we were on our way to becoming friends. How quick would that end tonight? I could just see her look of surprise and then bewilderment. She'd leave. I knew it. If I could take back every lie about the man…I shook my head and quickly speared a pickled radish. I couldn't even finish the thought, because it wouldn't be true.

When a man like Lawson Sokolov claimed you, if even for the moment, you grabbed hold of it with both hands. There was no morning, day or night that I would not do what I had done. There was no world where I didn't lie about being Lawson's.

"So like I was saying, when you want to kick the app to the side and settle down...you know our shop is right down the road from your man's work. You two could come into work together and be cute before he scoots off to his big building." She grinned at me triumphantly while I pretended to consider her words. If we were a real couple and not just a lie, she would have a great selling point.

I pulled our meat off the grill and began dishing it out to her, cutting it quickly with scissors before sliding some onto her plate. "I'll think about it, okay? Can't spring it on a girl on our first friend date and think I'm going to agree. I'm hard to get, Tiff." My words were light and I knew they would come across as a joke. It would be enough for me to change the topic of conversation and enjoy the rest of the night with Tiffany.

"Okay, all right," she said, throwing up her hands and pouring sesame oil into a dish beside her meat. "But don't think this will be the last time I bring this up. I want you working with me, Honey."

I hummed and took a bite of my food. It was good food and I savored it while I poured myself and

Tiffany another drink. I downed my wine quickly and refilled my glass, which earned me an excited clap from Tiffany.

"Wait for me! Wait for me," she laughed, quickly throwing back her wine and pouring us another round. "If we are getting a little drunk, I'm game."

"Then we are getting a little drunk."

"Oh, what a perfect night." Tiffany was smiling at me. The wine had begun to go to my head which was my signal to not only drink some water from the carafe beside us, but to also down more of my food. It was going to be a long night, even if it was going to be a good one.

CHAPTER SEVEN

LAW

Korean food on a rainy night was heaven. On its own the cuisine was perfect, the right mix of spicy and savory. There was sweet and pickled, the crunch and snap of vegetables both fresh and preserved, the meat flavorful and tender, fatty in the right ways.

It was one of my simple pleasures and it was one that I indulged in when I burned the candle at both ends. The long day, the damn deal that went sideways and had cost me a cool 40 million, and the fucking weather had me in a shit mood. I needed a damn hot meal, a dry place to relax, and a beer.

Korean food it was, which meant I was crossing the bridge and going into Queens for it. I nodded my thanks at the hostess who handed me a menu and took my coat with a smile. I was in a private room, one that was meant for parties. The unused places at the long table could be seen as wasteful by some, but I didn't think there was anyone that would be excited to dine with me after the day I'd had.

The empty room suited my mood for space. For quiet.

A server came and quickly took my order of soju, a beer, and galbi. I added on an order of stew as well, my rumbling stomach reminding me that I hadn't had much that day by way of food. I couldn't remember consuming anything beyond the coffee I'd drank that morning. I frowned, closing my eyes, and leaned back in my chair, head falling back in annoyance.

Coffee.

Coffee.

Honey.

"Fuck," I grunted, eyes opening as I sat up. It wasn't just the money or the long as fuck day. The weather had little to do with why I was in a piss poor mood. It was Honey. I'd spent nearly all day trying to keep the woman from taking over my thoughts, and by how I felt, ticked off and sulking in a Korean restaurant, I knew I'd done a shit job at it. The more I tried to push her to the back of my mind the more she rose to the forefront. Her eyes, those pouty lips, fucking gorgeous tits that I knew were waiting for me beneath her shirt. She'd be soft, her skin would be like silk under my hands, and I could practically hear the gasp from her when I touched her. Fingertips lightly tracing the underside of her breasts before I caught her dusky nipples between my fingers, rolling the plump flesh between them until-

The door to the room slid open and I forced myself not to jerk in surprise. The server gave me a quick smile and placed my drinks, side dishes, meat and a pot of bubbling stew in front of me. "Thank you." I meant to be succinct but even I could hear the gruffness to my words. They were barely more than a grunt.

"No worries." She flashed me another smile, but this one was tentative and she cleared her throat, looking like she might keep speaking, which was the last thing I wanted or needed. I nodded at her and reached for the beer she'd placed in front of me. I needed at least half a beer in me before I was going to entertain small talk. I popped the top off while the server flipped on the grill in front of me. The flames sprang to life and the familiar sound of it relaxed me. I took half a swig of my beer and was already reaching for the tongs beside the platter of meat when the server spoke again.

"Will there be anything else?" The server, a pretty dark haired woman, asked me with another quick smile. But this one didn't have the same veneer associated with friendly customer service. She was searching for something. Her eyes scanned my face and she came forward, the tray against her thighs, fingers clutching it so tightly I could see her knuckles were turning white. She was nervous, but forced herself to come closer.

I paused and reassessed her. She wanted something from me. Even if I wasn't going to give it to her I wanted to know what it was. From the look of her it wasn't the small talk that I'd dreaded. She was blushing, the blood rising to her cheeks and painting a pretty pink flush across her pale cheeks. She had plump lips she'd painted blood red and she bit her bottom lip, A flash of teeth and a nervous giggle aimed my way were meant to entice, even if I could tell she was too scared to voice what she wanted from me. A woman like this would wait for me to make the first move. She'd fall in line the second I showed her the smallest bit of interest, which suited me fine. I wasn't going to so much as breathe in the server's direction, and I wasn't putting off the most sociable aura, which would take care of any lingering doubt. On another night I might indulge her, might encourage the little display of cleavage she was currently treating me to with her artfully crossed arms that boosted her tits into a generous display of skin. She was beautiful but she wasn't the woman my body wanted, not the one that made my dick twitch and my palms itch.

No, that belonged to someone else. That belonged to the beautiful woman running through my damn brain. A woman that I'd spent all of five minutes around, a woman that I'd claimed as mine and then walked away from.

My gut twisted and I frowned. "No, nothing," I told her, looking away. I poured myself a glass of beer and reached for the bottle of soju. "Thank you."

"If you change your mind…" she said, voice going soft in a way that I knew. I'd heard it a hundred times before. It was the voice subs used when they wanted to pull my eye, when they were letting me know that they saw something they liked in me, and that if I was game so were they.

I raised my eyes to hers, and gave her a slight shake of my head, but even then I said, "I'll find you."

She beamed at me, my dismissal too subtle. "See that you do, handsome. I'm Melissa." She winked at me and I almost chuckled at her little display of flirtation, but she was gone and dashing out the door with a giggle.

I downed half of the beer before I poured the other half of it into my glass. I added an equal amount of soju to my glass and then took a healthy drink of that before I turned my attention to the grill. If my hands were busy then I could go on autopilot. The calm that I was looking for used to come easier before I went legitimate. Mostly because when I was working on a mark, when I was hunting someone down or enforcing the boundaries, it was natural. I never thought so much as reacted, it was one of the reasons I was so good at what I did.

It came naturally. I didn't have to think to be a killer.

I just was.

That calm and Zen gifted by giving over my body to the task at hand was good for the stress. But now it was all meetings, conference calls, endless email chains. And deals gone wrong, fucked over by rats like Martin D'Amato. I grit my teeth and added meat to the grill, the sizzle of it a good chaser to remembering what D'Amato's smarmy smile looked like at the end of the video conference.

He'd swooped on a deal I'd had locked down, raised the price by 25% even though it wasn't worth that. He was going to be losing money by going through with it but I knew full well, it wasn't about profit with that fucker. It was about screwing me over and letting me know he'd done it on purpose. D'Amato was sending a message with the shitty deal, and unlucky for him he now had my full attention.

"Gonna get that little shit," I said to no one, flipping the meat and taking another swig of my drink. I was going to need at least two more of these before the night was over. I glanced over at the button at the side of the table that would bring my server, Melissa, running back and sucked on my teeth. I'd wait some before I resorted to that. I wanted to enjoy a little peace and quiet before I called her back in. After today, I'd earned that much.

CHAPTER EIGHT

HONEY

"This is so fun!" Tiffany was red faced and giggling. "Everything here is so yummy. You know that right?" She asked our server who laughed and nodded at her. "Isn't it amazing?" She asked me.

"It is, especially when we're drunk," I replied, throwing back the last bit of soju in my glass.

Tiffany scoffed. "We are not drunk. We both agreed to get a little tipsy, and that's what we've done."

"Sure, sure," I laughed. "But we're calling a rideshare after this." While Tiffany might be in denial about our current state I knew better, the warmth in my belly had spread to my limbs, the rain outside was forgotten in favor of the easy laughter and the slight sway I felt when I stood up. I was drunk, all right. We both were and even if she didn't believe me, I'd make sure she got home safe and sound.

Tiffany rolled her eyes but then a second later she brightened up. "Okay, fine, then I'm going for it," she said, snapping the seal on the bottle of soju with a turn of her hands. "But that means we need more beer, because I can't just do shots of this stuff."

I pushed away from the table and stood up with a wave of my hand. "I'll go ask for more."

"Awesome! You're the best, Honey!" She called after me and then added, "Oooh! Can you get more kimchi too?"

I laughed as I started to wend my way backwards through the crowd and held up a hand with a thumbs up. "I'm on it!" I walked out of the back dining area we were sitting in and turned down the hallway towards the front of the restaurant. The kitchen was between the two seating areas and I was pretty sure I'd have a better chance of snagging our server's attention that way to get the beer and kimchi Tiffany wanted. Besides, the bathrooms were this way which my body suddenly let me know I needed badly.

I was making a beeline for the bathroom with a little more sway in my step than normal, when I ran into our server, a bubbly woman with dark hair. I think she'd said her name was Melissa, so I went with that when I called out to her.

"Hi, Melissa?" I tried.

She turned immediately to face me. Bingo. "Can I get you anything?"

"Yes, I was worried I got your name wrong but I'm glad I was right! And sorry for coming to find you but it seemed a little easier that way since stuff was really busy tonight, you know?" She nodded, still waiting for me to go on. I gave her an apologetic smile. I was rambling, the alcohol obviously loosening me up. I licked my lips and cleared my throat. "We were hoping for two more beers and more kimchi, when you had a chance."

"Got it." She reached into her apron and pulled out her notepad, scribbling the order. "I'll get that to ya in just a bit, okay?"

"Thanks, a lot. Appreciate it." I nodded, swaying slightly and made to move towards the restrooms but Melissa stepped in close, a conspiratorial smile on her face that made me stop.

"It's just that there's this super hot man in one of the private rooms. He requested me specifically."

My eyebrows shot up. "Oh, wow!" I exclaimed, because that seemed like the thing she wanted to hear from me. I was half a bottle of wine and a beer, plus a couple of shots in, so I couldn't be sure. I put a hand out on the wall because I was right earlier—I wasn't tipsy. I was drunk. And, I was doing what drunk girls the world over did best, I was being supportive as hell when a woman was dishing on some hopeful man news. Why she was choosing to tell me this information I had no idea, but I was going to cheerlead as best I could, because that's what you did.

"I'm pretty sure he's going to get my number soon, or you know, like ask me to stay and have dinner with him."

"Really?"

She nodded, biting the end of her pen and grinning at me. "Oh, yeah, he's been eye fucking me all night. I've seen him before. I've waited on him all the other times he's been in and I don't think it's a coincidence that he requested a private room in my section. I think he's finally making his move tonight."

My brows furrowed and my drunk girl support faltered. "You don't think that's a little weird? What if he's stalking you?"

Melissa laughed at me, and even drunk I knew the look she was giving me was a little pitying. "It's not stalking, it's romantic," she said with a shake of her head.

I nodded along as if she made sense, because I knew she didn't. Showing up at someone's work was the opposite of romantic. It was one of the things I liked about moving around so much with BaristApp. If someone made me uncomfortable, I didn't have to worry about them being able to find me again. There was safety in anonymity. But putting down roots? Choosing one place to work and exist was risky. Always had been, always would be.

I couldn't take Tiffany up on her offer, even if the tips at A Different Brew were amazing.

"Anyways, I'll get those drinks to your table, okay hon?" She stopped and gave me an assessing look as if she were really seeing me for the first time. "You good though?" She asked.

"Yup," I said with a bigger nod than was needed, "just on my way to the little girl's room. It's that way, right?" I pointed behind her.

"First door on the right."

"Thanks, Melissa."

"Sure thing." She gave me another smile, this one didn't seem so bubbly and then she was off, her dark ponytail bouncing as she hurried away. Probably back to her private room with her sexy stalker man.

I screwed up my face and shook my head. "Why would anyone think that's romantic?" I asked, walking down the hallway and towards the restroom. I stopped when I got to the end of the hallway and saw there was no door in front of me. Shit. I'd gone too far. What had she said? The door was on the right...or was it the left? I turned back and looked around the hallway.

"Did she mean her right or my right?" I threw out my hands in frustration and then settled on the door in front of me. It was to the right of where we'd been standing and it was the first door, so this *one was probably it.* I was about 95% sure this was it, so I reached out and slid the paper door open, striding into it with all the confidence in the world. It was only when I had slid the door closed that I realized I was definitely not in a bathroom.

"Oh, I am so sorry," I blurted out. There was a table with sizzling meat and a man sitting at the end of it. He had his head bent over his phone, tongs in his hand while he scrolled. "Shit, I am so sorry," I continued, reaching behind me for the handle of the door and missing. I accidentally pitched to the side and bumped against the wall. I winced, but was grateful he was still looking at his phone, but then he was lifting his head and looking directly at me.

Blue eyes the color of tropical waters hit mine and I felt like the air had been punched out of me. Those eyes. I knew those eyes. I'd been thinking about those fucking eyes all week and now here they were when I was drunk and lost on the way to the bathroom.

"Fuck," I blurted out, because my stupid brain

refused to keep my inside voice on the inside of my fucking head.

"Honey?"

That sucker punch felt more like a body slam because–he remembered my name? He didn't just remember it. Lawson Sokolov didn't even hesitate to say my name.

"You remember me?" I asked, because my brain was still hosting a revolt and bent on embarrassing the fuck out of my drunk ass.

Lawson gave me a slight nod, his eyes scanning over me before he stood from the table and set down the tongs. "What are you doing here? Have you been drinking?"

"I came here because I was hungry and I had a bad day," I said, mouth continuing on before I could stop it. I shook my head, "Wait, do you mean here like *this room*, or the restaurant? I thought this was the bathroom and-"

"Why did you have a bad day?" He was striding towards me now and I backed up again, hitting the wall and bouncing off it slightly, my arm going out to the side to steady myself. Lawson caught me then, a hand at my waist with the other curling around my outstretched arm. "You have been drinking." He was frowning at me and I blushed hot under his attention. I didn't like that he was frowning.

"Honey, who are you here with?"

I licked my lips and dropped my eyes to my feet. "A friend."

Lawson's fingers flexed on my waist and he stepped closer to me until there was no space between us. I went tense where we touched. We were flush together, my waist against his front. I could feel the hard muscle of his chest against my breasts. My breath caught, nipples hardening at the pressure because he was so close. Too close, really, for people that didn't know each other. Okay, we were too damn close even for people who did know each other in a non-sexual way.

This was not platonic standing. But I didn't care because since Monday, I'd had Lawson Sokolov on the brain. I arched my back, pressing myself to his front and when I felt his thumb on my chin, tilting my face up, I let him.

"Is it a friend, or is it a date?" His voice was lower and I felt the octave change down in my belly. Fuck, he was hot.

"I've been thinking about you," I said instead of answering him. I watched him clench his jaw, the line of it hardening just like I remembered, and I smiled. "You're hot when you do that," I said, nodding up at him. "But you probably know that."

"Answer me, Honey." His thumb brushed against my bottom lip and I hummed, as my eyes drifted closed.

"Why did you tell everyone I was your fiancée?" I asked.

"You know why I did it. What are you doing here drunk?" The hand at my waist flattened and slid up my side until it was at my back, cupping my shoulder and pressing me towards him.

I lifted the shoulder beneath his fingers and shrugged. "I needed to blow off some steam."

He looked away and towards the closed door, brow creased. I frowned and reached up, touching his forehead. The gesture was slight, but his eyes snapped to me so suddenly my hand fell back.

"I'm sorry," I began, but I didn't get any further because whatever I was going to say got stuck in my throat when Lawson caught my hand before I could pull away completely. "Lawson."

His blue eyes met mine and he stared at me for a beat before he shook his head. "We shouldn't be doing this."

"Doing what?"

"This," he said, giving my hand a light shake. But even as he did he was sliding his hand against mine and threading our fingers together. The lines inked into the back of his hands stood out against my tan skin and I swallowed hard. It looked good. We looked right.

We looked perfect.

"But I like this," I told him.

He sighed heavily and pressed our bound hands back against the wall behind me. Outside the door, I could hear laughter and talking. Footsteps from a passing diner clicked by, and my mind dimly registered that Tiffany was probably going to come looking for me if I didn't get back to her soon.

Lawson lowered his head, lips close to my ear and I bit my lip when the soft warm air of his breath hit my skin. If I turned my head towards him I could meet his lips with my own, but even as drunk as I was I wasn't that drunk...or brave. "If you were mine..." he growled, lips grazing the top of my ear and I shivered.

"If I was yours I wouldn't be here," I replied, barely able to stop the pout I felt pulling at my lips. It was my default setting. Bratty. I didn't know what to think about it coming out to play in front of Lawson.

His fingers tightened on mine and he pressed me back into the wall. "No, you're right. You wouldn't be. If you were and you chose to get *this drunk*, you wouldn't be able to sit down for a week."

My eyes shot open. "What?" I whispered, turning my head to look at him. If I wasn't mistaken Lawson Sokolov just threatened to spank me. The familiar warmth of desire and lust began to wake up in my body and it worked to sober me, because I couldn't have heard him correctly. There was no way this man was saying he would spank me, I must have heard wrong. With my thoughts on the Cairn and my earlier need to find release and structure within the familiar bounds of BDSM, I had to have misheard. Lawson Sokolov was not into what I was into, he-

"If you were mine I'd turn you right over this damn table and spank the fuck out of you, little girl." He leaned back and stared me down, he wasn't happy, but there was more there now than just annoyance. He was interested, a spark in his blue eyes that was hungry. "Someone needs a firm hand, don't they?"

Holy fucking shit. He was into what I was into.

My mouth fell open and closed, then it opened and closed again. I knew I looked like a fish out of water, but I'd had a lot to drink and the man I'd been obsessing over for the better part of a week had suddenly materialized on my way to the bathroom and was now saying he wanted to spank me.

Little girl.

Yeah, and he'd called me that. He was pushing all my buttons, lighting them up as easily as if he had taken his hand and slammed them down the side of a skyscraper elevator bank's worth of buttons. We were going from the ground floor to the 85th floor at warp speed with each and every button lit up like a Christmas Tree. Was this really happening or was I just that drunk?

"Are you for real?" I rasped out, finding it hard to talk now that my tongue felt like it was about two sizes too big for my damn mouth. I almost groaned at myself, but didn't dare move a muscle because Lawson was shifting.

His lips pressed into a thin line and he dropped his head so that he was eye level with me. "Deadly."

I audibly swallowed. "Oh no," I whispered. I might have said more if the door to the private room wasn't sliding open. The sound of the restaurant in full swing of a late evening dinner rush spilled into the room along with the server from earlier.

"Hey, handsome, I just wanted to-" She broke off when she saw us pressed together against the wall. "What's going on? What are you doing here?" She asked, and there was no missing the pointed tone in her question. She glared at me and I sucked on my teeth. She was pissed, but what for? She didn't even know Lawson, so why was she looking at me like she wanted to throw me out in the street? If anything I should be mad that she had just interrupted me getting to the bottom of what Lawson was, wanted, or maybe still would do to me.

"It's just that there's this super hot man in one of the private rooms. He requested me specifically."

Oh. *Ohhhhhh.* Shit. This was that man. The hot one that she was sure was going to ask for her number. The one in the private room. The private room we were currently all standing in like a weird sitcom gone wrong where the love interests have an intruder in their midst. I cleared my throat nervously and hoped I wasn't the intruder in this scenario.

"I'm pretty sure he's going to get my number soon, or you know, like ask me to stay and have dinner with him."

God. I was the intruder, wasn't I? Shit fuck. How the hell had this happened? Oh, right, when I had drunkenly stumbled into this room instead of the bathroom. That's how.

"Hey, um, I'll just get out of here. I got lost," I told Melissa with an apologetic smile. "I didn't mean to-"

She crossed her arms over her chest and jerked a thumb over her shoulder. "I had your beers sent to your table. You can leave now."

"Yeah, sure." I made to move from Lawson, but he didn't let me go.

"She's good. She's not going anywhere."

Both of our heads snapped in his direction and I saw that he was looking at her with that slightly pinched expression that I knew meant he was genuinely unhappy. It wasn't like when he was telling me he wanted to bend me over the dinner table and spank the shit out of me. That made me feel good. I knew I shouldn't take as much pleasure as I was in Lawson shutting her down, but I did.

Melissa was silent, her eyes darting between the

two of us, and I could see what she was thinking. She was thinking I'd stolen her man. Made a move on her territory, which was just insane given that Lawson and I had been alone for all of five minutes in this room. It had to be apparent that we knew each other previously in some capacity.

"I won't be needing anything else but the bill. I'll get that at the door when we're ready to leave," Lawson went on. Melissa's eyes narrowed at his words, her hands going to her hips and she sucked in a deep breath when he was done speaking. "Thank you," he added, as if it were an afterthought. The man was gruff, but he was trying for manners in front of me. Which was sweet for a man who had threatened to spank me. I liked that he was trying, even if it felt unpracticed by him. Trying was *something*.

"She's shit faced drunk, you know that right?" She blurted out. *Ah, there it was.* That was what she'd been deciding on. "I told her about you in the hallway and she decided to come see for herself. You're being played."

Lawson straightened up, let me go and stepped in front of me. "It's time for you to go now. I'll get my bill at the door when we're ready to leave," he said, but this time I could tell the man wasn't going to bother playing at civility.

Melissa gasped. I leaned to the side to see, and

found that I *was* actually still drunk, because I didn't just lean around Lawson, I stumbled into the wall beside me. Melissa's eyes landed on me and scoffed with a shake of her head.

"Whatever, have a good night, *sir.*" She tossed the last word out like an insult and I couldn't help the giggle that bubbled up in me. Melissa left the room with a bang of the sliding door and Lawson looked over his shoulder when I kept giggling.

"Why do I get the distinct feeling that you're trouble?" He asked. I clapped a hand over my mouth when he said that and shook my head at him.

"I'm not trouble," I insisted.

He didn't look convinced and pointed a finger at me. "You are."

"Really? Because from here *you* seem like trouble. You're the one threatening to spank me," I reminded him.

He gave me a dip of his chin. "Because you're trouble.'

I opened my mouth to argue but didn't, because one very important thing came rushing back to me. "I have to pee," I blurted out. *"Now."*

CHAPTER NINE

LAW

"What the fuck are you doing?" The question was to no one in particular, seeing as my ass was alone and standing in a hallway outside of a women's bathroom. I glanced towards the shut door and repeated the question. "What the fuck *am I doing?*" There, that was right, the clarification of that question made all the difference in the world.

What was I doing? I glared at my phone and shoved it back in my pocket. I'd texted Taylor letting him know I was going to need him to bring the car around and that we'd be making a detour before home. There was no if's and's or but's, I was going to be taking Honey home the second she got out of the damn bathroom. I leaned back against the wall and looked at the door. The door to the bathroom Honey was currently in. How had this happened? One minute I'd been eating dinner and responding to emails in a private room. The server had been a little intrusive, but she was easily brushed off. I wasn't interested and hadn't given her an in, so when the door had slid open I'd thought it was her checking on me again and interrupting the peace I was enjoying. I hadn't looked up from my email, choosing to focus on work. I'd let the silence speak for itself when she tried to strike up a conversation with me for what felt like the hundredth fucking time that night.

I'd already made a mental note to let the owner know on my way out that when I said private, I meant *private*. She knew me from the days when I'd been a familiar face on the streets of New York. She'd make sure I had my quiet while I dined.

But then I'd heard that first breathy 'sorry,' and I'd known exactly who it was. It wasn't my nosey server, it was Honey. Just like that, it was like a switch being flipped in my brain—I'd just known it was her. Something in me had changed the day I'd met her, the second I'd laid eyes on her, heard her voice, had her smile at me. Something in me had shifted, the compass of me reoriented to zero in on Honey. I'd recognize her in a crowd, pick her low and sweet voice out no problem even in a crowded room.

Sonofabitch. How had that happened?

And then I'd been crossing the room and putting my hands on her before I could stop myself. She was drunk, which I hated. Having a good time was fine by me, but pushing boundaries until the lines of safety and recklessness were blurred and twisted together was beyond what I tolerated. I did not allow for my subs to get out of control, to abuse themselves like that, and I'd threatened to spank the shit out of her if I had the chance. Which brought up a whole different issue altogether.

Honey was not my submissive. She was not my little girl, not even if I used the title once I had my hands on her. I'd lost my head the second I had her hand in mine, because I'd found out I was right. She was soft as silk beneath me, her skin warm and smooth under my hands, and her body had been perfect against mine. She fit in all the ways that mattered, soft and pliant to the planes of my body. I could have done exactly what I threatened if that damn server hadn't barged in and tried to piss all over what I had going with Honey.

The moment had been ruined, but that was fine. I wouldn't have taken it any farther anyways, not with her looking up at me with drink-hazed eyes. She liked what she was hearing, but a sub made bold by alcohol was not what I wanted. I rubbed a hand over my eyes and sighed. Was she even a sub? I didn't know, we hadn't talked about it. Honey made me want to lose control, to let the Dom out to play. All the dark in me felt like she'd stirred it right up and begged for me to pour it out into her waiting hands. But did the woman know what she was waking up in me? Or was she simply drunk and letting her mouth get ahead of her. I turned when the door handle began to jiggle and watched as she exited the bathroom with a slightly chagrined look on her face.

"Hey, sorry. I mean, thanks for waiting," she said, pointing a finger at the door. "I should go, my friend that I came with is probably worried about me."

I felt my hackles go up at the mention of the friend. "You never answered my question."

"What question?"

"Is it a friend or is this date?" I didn't know why the fuck it mattered to me when I didn't know this woman, but it did. It mattered because I wanted her for myself and it mattered because now I knew what her tits felt like pushed up against me.

"Friend," she said with a quick shake of her head, and then she looked past me, down the hallway, towards the back dining area. "Her name is Tiffany. We work together. I really like her and want her to be my friend, but she's going to be so annoyed at me for being gone so long. I have to go back now. Do you know how hard it is to make friends when you're an adult? I hope she isn't mad at me." She pushed past me unsteadily and I stopped her by hooking an arm around her waist and drawing her back into my side.

"Come on, we'll go find your friend." I put her arm around my waist, pinning her wrist to my side while I continued to practically hold her up with my other arm. How had I ended up babysitting her, wanting to do the damn thing and feeling an uncomfortable pull in my chest when she leaned her head against my shoulder and smiled up at me? It was a drunk smile, but it was a smile all the same.

"She's back here. I see her!" Honey exclaimed, raising an arm over her head and waving wildly at a woman sitting at a table. It was the redhead from the coffee shop and she was waving back just as excitedly.

Honey didn't charge across the room like I expected her to, instead she looked at me. "You don't think-" she began but I stopped her, knowing exactly what she was anxious about.

"I don't think she's mad at you," I told Honey. She was worried about what her friend thought, which was understandable, but the way she had looked to me for reassurance... Her quick, breathy little *"Do you think-?"* was still ringing in my ears with all the reverberation of a gunshot at point blank range. She had my head fucking spinning, my ears ringing with the sound of that half asked question. She'd wanted me to set it right, and I had without even thinking about it. Because it's what I needed to do for this woman.

"Really?" She asked, a tentative smile forming on her lips.

"Yes, she's practically falling out of her chair waving at you. Come on, let's get you over there and get the bill settled. I have to get you home."

"But I'm in charge of getting Tiffany home," she informed me with a shake of her head, digging her heels in when I started towards the table.

"You were," I told her with a shake of my head. "Now I'm getting you both home."

"But why?"

Because that's what you did when you couldn't shake a woman from your brain after a solid week. Because that's what you did when you threatened to spank her. Because that's what you did when you wanted to bend her over and fuck her into next week.

I cleared my throat and shrugged. "Seems like you need a little help right now."

She bit her lip and looked away. "I got a little carried away. Sorry," she whispered, barely audible over the din of the restaurant. If I hadn't been this close, or this fucking attuned to Honey, I would have missed it. "I didn't mean to."

I dropped the hand that I'd been holding to my

side and reached out, tipping her head back with a finger, so that her eyes were back on my face and not on the floor. "It happens," I told her in a reassuring tone meant to soothe. That didn't mean I was fine with her drinking choices tonight, "you need to be careful in the future, Honey. I won't always be the man you run into when you're drunk."

"I'm safe with you," she said, giving me a lopsided smile. "I can tell."

"You're not," I told her. Her eyes widened slightly, pretty mouth opening with a barely audible *'Oh,'* and I nodded at her, leading her in the direction of her friend. 'Oh' was right, but I wasn't going to get into it with her, not in this damn restaurant when I still had to get her and her friend home. Not when I had to get her inside of her house while keeping her safe. Not when the biggest risk to keeping her safe was keeping her fucking away from me.

"Hey! I was worried about where you disappeared off to, but now that I see you with Mister Perfect, I get it." The redhead shot us a finger gun and a wink. "I'm Tiffany by the way and I'm fast becoming your lady love's best friend," she told me, extending a hand when we were beside the table.

"Lady love?" I asked, looking at Honey who was shaking her head at Tiffany and giving me a look that could only be described as panic. Someone had been telling lies.

"When did you get here?" Tiffany asked, when I shook her hand. "Honey didn't say you'd be joining us."

I pulled out a chair and nudged Honey into it, before I took the one beside her and sat. "Honey gave me a ring. Told me you might need a little help getting home."

Tiffany clasped her hands in front of her and smiled wide at me. "You're amazing for rescuing us. A real gentleman!"

I waved off her thanks. "It was no trouble. I was having dinner nearby."

"Oh, so you've eaten. That's great news! Then you can have a drink with us before we go, because we finally got those beers. Even if our server has been totally giving you the stink eye since you two showed up." Tiffany leaned over the table and stage whispered to us. "What do you think her deal is?"

Honey giggled and I turned my head, unable to hide the smile on my face at the sound. It was light and carefree. Sweet like her namesake, sweet like I knew her mouth would be when I kissed it. I frowned, the smile vanishing from my face at the thought. I should not be wondering if I would kiss her or not. I should not be going there. Not tonight.

"Let's have that drink," I said, reaching out and snagging the bottle of beer from the table. I poured us all a round and followed it with a soju chaser for each of us. Taylor would be coming any minute to get us—all three of us, with Tiffany's addition.

"Cheers!" Tiffany exclaimed, lifting her glass in the air.

"Cheers," Honey and I said joining her, but I noticed Honey's cheers were softer now. She was watching me with a worried look on her face. She knew her little lie about our relationship was out in the open now and she was trying to gauge my reaction. Her big brown eyes were trained on my face, even as she spoke to Tiffany, her fingers twisting in the sweater she wore. I reached out, sliding an arm behind her chair and carried on the conversation with Tiffany. She was a nice woman, open and caring, and I could see I was right. Honey had nothing to worry about in terms of making a new friend.

My phone buzzed and I reached for it knowing it was Taylor. "Ladies, I need a minute." I stood and nodded at them as I pulled the phone from my pocket. Taylor was out front. It was time to close out the bills and get Tiffany and Honey out of here. I passed the server from before on my way to the front, and I didn't miss the rigid look to her when our eyes met.

She stopped in front of me and asked, "You want your bill then?"

"That'd be great."

"Follow me." She took off at a fast clip, but I didn't speed up to catch her. I knew where the front desk was, and it wasn't like she would be able to settle my bill without me. There was no need to rush just because she was pissed about going home alone. When I arrived at the register the server was glaring at me but said nothing as she put my bill in front of me. "I'll take the one with the redhead in the other room too."

"I guess that's the least you can do since you're taking her friend home," she said, slapping down another tab in front of me.

I stilled, the pen in my hand poised over the receipt paper. "She's my fiancée," I said. The lie came easy. I heard the sharp intake of her breath, but I didn't bother to look up at her as I went back to signing the bills. Bills that I still fucking tipped on.

"I told you he was paying the bill!" Tiffany shouted from behind me. I turned, seeing Tiffany and Honey making their way towards me, arms around each other's waists. Tiffany was grinning, Honey was looking anxious. I shot an easy smile her way and put the pen down with a snap.

"Come on, ladies. Night's over."

Tiffany pouted but came along, dragging Honey behind her who looked like she wanted to be anywhere but here. When she was close enough to me, I wrapped an arm around her waist and pulled her into my arms. "You good?" I asked her.

She gave a quick nod of her head. "Yes, but Lawson, you don't have to take me home. I can get there on my own. I'm just a few blocks away and I'll be fine getting home, really." She gestured towards the door with an umbrella and I almost groaned when I saw the flash of pink pastel. Of course she had a big bubblegum pink umbrella. I forced my brain to focus on the words she was saying and led them both to the door.

A few blocks? That fixed the logistics of everything. I'd send Tiffany on with Taylor and take Honey home myself, he could swing by for me after he had dropped Honey's friend off. I snagged the umbrella from her and unfurled it the second we hit the sidewalk. I still had my arm around Honey keeping her close to me while Tiffany skipped behind us.

"You're both so cute. I hate it," she told us.

"Thanks. I get it," I told her honestly, because I did. I really did. I was right in the middle of it and I hated it too. Taylor exited the car and jogged over to us with an umbrella of his own. He held it over Tiffany's head as soon as he was close enough and looked my way, waiting for instructions.

"Taylor, I'm going to have you take Tiffany home. I'll be taking Honey home on foot. I'll text you the coordinates as soon as we arrive. I'll wait there for you."

He nodded at me. "Understood. I'll make good time. Nobody's out in this storm."

"Wait, am I getting a private driver?" Tiffany squealed.

"Looks that way," I told her and a second later the woman was launching herself into my arms with an excited laugh.

"This is awesome! Thank you so much!" She looked at Honey and winked. "Your man is amazing, Honey. Don't ever let him go."

Honey gave a weak laugh and a non-committal mumble that sounded something like, 'sure thing,' but I couldn't be sure since she was turned away from me, hiding her face in her sweater. She gave Tiffany a quick hug and they promised to text when the other was home before Taylor hustled Tiffany into the car, and we were alone on the sidewalk.

"You really don't have to take me home," she said, daring to look my way.

"I do," I said. "You're not safe with me, but you are safer from everyone else if you're with me," I told her.

"I think that's...good, right?" she asked, biting her bottom lip. The site of her teeth digging into the plump flesh made me want to be the one biting her lip. I turned away from her and gestured with the umbrella, that goddamn umbrella that I could see was covered in fat pink bows now that it was open. What was a woman doing with an umbrella like this? It looked fit for a little girl, which just...I imagined her walking in the rain with it, the fabric of it bouncing along through the gray of the city streets, Honey holding it tightly in her hands looking like a sweet treat.

A sweet treat that I wanted to sink my teeth into.

"It is," I said and then jerked my chin down the street. "Which way?"

"That way. It's just a little bit of a walk," she said, extending her arm to point down the street. "Not long at all."

"Then let's get a move on. Want to get you out of the rain."

She bobbed her head and stepped forward, but it only took a few steps before she was stumbling slightly. I sighed, watching her struggle. How much had she had to drink before she'd walked into my private room? I should not have poured her that damn last drink. This was my fault.

"Stop," I told her, my voice sounding strained to my ears. I fucking hated that I had had a hand in what I was seeing.

"What is it?" she asked, turning to look at where I was standing and shook her head. "Oh no, you're getting wet!" She tried to pull me in closer to her but were already standing toe-to-toe, pressed together under the umbrella. Not that it phased me. I'd had a lot worse in my life than getting rained on while having a beautiful woman pressed up to my side.

A lot fucking worse.

CHAPTER TEN

HONEY

"You're getting wet. You have to come closer." I pulled at Lawson's sleeve but the big man didn't budge.

"I'm good. Come on," he said pointing at his shoulder. "I'm carrying you."

I knew I was buzzed but I could not have heard this man correctly. He was what? "Sorry?" I asked. The rain hadn't let up for a second since I'd gone into the restaurant and I could feel it splashing up against my rain boots. I glanced down worriedly because I knew for a fact he was not wearing the right footwear for this. Rain boots didn't exactly fit the tall, dark and broody, in a bespoke suit look Lawson was currently sporting.

"I'm carrying you. You're stumbling all over, Honey."

"No, I'm not, that was just a little bump in the sidewalk, I swear," I said, gesturing towards the pavement. "I'm okay, really. I'm fine. I swear, I'm fine to walk."

"You know when people have been out having a good time and they swear they're good, they never are," he said, tilting his head to the side to look at me. The gesture got him a splash of rainwater on his face, which should not have made him look hotter, but it did. God, I'd kill to be a water droplet on Lawson's cheek.

"Lawson, look-"

He shook his head. "Law. Call me, Law. Now, come here."

"Just when I didn't think you could get any hotter," I muttered. "You go and ask me to call you Law."

"I don't like Lawson, that's my legal name." He said with a face that made it sound like legal names were...well, *bad*.

"What's wrong with a legal name? Mine's Honey and you don't hear me bitching."

He laughed, and I finally got why there was that stupid internet poem that said something about storms being named after people or some melodramatic shit. I loved melodramatic shit, so obviously I had saved the poem on an internet board or five. At the time I'd liked the imagery, but now I got it. Law's laugh affected me more than any rolling clap of thunder ever had, there wasn't a sound the storm had made that could touch the laugh the man had just let out.

He was intimidating, though I was drawn to him. But his laugh? His laugh was like the powdered sugar they put on beignets in the French Quarter. It was light, fluffy and sweet as any dessert I'd ever had on my tongue.

But at the same time it was strong. Just like Law. I could feel it in my bones. When he laughed it meant something. I could tell it was rare, but god, when he laughed, it was real, free, and precious. I counted myself lucky to have heard it.

I was still thinking about that, struck blind by this man's laugh and savoring the sounds when he bent and pushed his shoulder into my waist, folding me over at the hip and tossing me over his shoulder like I was a sack of potatoes.

"What the hell, Law?" I screeched, clutching at the umbrella. I couldn't lose it on the first day Juana had given it to me. I struggled to hold on and stay upright, which meant my hand went to his ass. "Shit! I'm sorry, I'm sorry!"

"It's fine. Relax, Honey."

"How the fuck am I supposed to relax hanging over your shoulder like a sack of root vegetables?!"

He laughed again and I had to press a hand to my mouth to stop the moan that almost slipped out of me as I felt the rumble of his deep laugh right against my thighs. I was only a woman, after all. Powerless against the savage type of beauty Law wore as easily as the suit he donned.

"You're a funny girl, Honey," he said, adjusting me higher on his shoulder as we passed a couple. They looked surprised but then shrugged, because this was New York, and it wasn't like a man carrying a woman in the rain was that big of a deal. Especially when I waved a hand at them to know I was all right.

"You know what's *not* funny? Being carted around like this," I told him, even though I was lying through my teeth. I was loving every second. I didn't understand why he was doing what he was doing or how it seemed that everything the man did seemed to have a direct line to my fantasies, but here we were. Who was I to turn a blessing away?

"Sure, sure."

I was quiet for a second before I said, "You're going to take a left at the next light. My building is the third one on the right, it's a blue metal door."

"Got it. Blue metal door." He pressed his hand to

the back of my thigh and I bit my lip to keep quiet at the intimate touch. I knew he was doing it to keep me steady as he crossed the street, but damn if it didn't feel so good to have him touch me like that. Now wasn't the moment to indulge in that, not when I had an apology to make.

I sucked in a deep breath. "I'm sorry, I lied to Tiffany about us being engaged. I know why you did it in the shop, but I didn't have to keep it going."

For a minute Law didn't answer me. He just kept walking, his stride even and smooth. I wasn't sure if he heard me or not but just when I was about to repeat myself, he spoke.

"We'll talk about it once you're home." He said in a way that left no room for arguing and I gave a quick nod before I realized he couldn't see that.

"Okay."

We walked the rest of the way in silence and all too soon I was sliding down the front of him and onto my feet. It was when I was on my feet that I realized my predicament.

I was pressed up against Lawson Sokolov's front for the second time that night, my back to the door. I stood too close to him for just a second too long before I took a deep breath and whirled to face my door, my hands fumbling with the keys that were in my sweater pocket. I tried a key and swore when it wasn't the right one.

"Sorry, I'm just a little-"

"Drunk? I know." He didn't sound happy about that and I bit the inside of my cheek, holding back the retort that might have slipped out. I was a grown woman, a regular big girl, and I didn't need him brooding about me having one too many drinks that night. He'd even poured me two, a beer and a shot, so I didn't think he had much room to complain. I slid the right key home and threw open the door.

"Right, thank you for getting me home, Law. I can make it up on my own," I told him, pointing over my shoulder with my keys.

He leaned past me and looked up the dimly lit stairwell that showed the two flights of stairs leading to my apartment. They were normally no big deal but tonight seemed darker, steeper and generally far sketchier than I remembered them ever being. Law seemed to be of the same opinion because he shook his head at me.

"I'll walk you up. No trouble."

"But-"

"You wanna get carried up the stairs too?" He asked me, and I knew he would do it if I pressed the issue.

"Fine, fine," I sighed, standing back and letting him into the building. It wasn't like I was opposed to him carrying me, but I knew it would cause quite a stir if my neighbors caught sight of it. Jesus, if Juana saw? I'd never hear the end of it with her. I could already hear her tutting and saying, "I thought it was just a friend, mija? That don't look like no friend to me."

That being said, it was far easier to have Law follow me up the stairs than the scene we might attract if he carried me up them. When we arrived at my door I glanced back at him to see he was peering up at the lights and rubbing his chin. He didn't look like he liked what he was seeing in the slightest.

"What?" I asked, making sure to keep my voice down. I didn't want to alert Juana that I had gotten home.

"Need brighter lights," he said, but didn't go on and instead nodded at my door. "Let's get you inside, you're soaked."

"Not as bad as you," I countered, but I did as he asked and opened the door.

"Not worried about me. I can handle it."

I rolled my eyes at him and watched as Lawson's eyes narrowed at the gesture, but he didn't say anything, just followed me inside of my place. I swallowed hard and closed the door gently behind us. I was safe with Law, wasn't I? He'd been nothing but good to me, saving my ass not once but twice in the week we'd met.

I was definitely safe with a man that carried me

home in the rain. I had to be safe with one that laughed so big the sound of it lit up the sky for me.

"You're not."

His words, not mine, floated back to me through my foggy memory and I fidgeted as I shook out my umbrella and deposited my keys on the kitchen counter. Why had he said that? I glanced his way to see he was looking around my apartment with an assessing sweep. It wasn't curious, but cataloguing, and I knew he was making a mental note of what he saw. Not because he was nosey but because he might need to use that knowledge later.

What the hell? I shivered and wrapped my arms around myself, suddenly feeling unsure of what to do around him.

"Thanks for walking me home."

He nodded, hands going to his hips. "Go get changed into something warmer. I'll wait here and then we can talk." He took a seat at my kitchen counter and I blinked in surprise at his order, because that's what it was. I wasn't used to hearing anyone speak that directly to me outside of the Cairn. He was all business right now, the laughter I'd earned from him on our way back from the restaurant, the way he'd held me in that night, all of it seemed to be evaporating like steam in the sunlight. There was a wall going up around Law. I could see the bricks of it forming, one-by-one, as they fell into place. The lines of his body were growing hard, shoulders hunched, hands flat on his thighs as he sat looking like an immovable object. The only thing that hadn't changed was the way he was looking at me. The intensity was there. The focus made me nervous but also had me drinking it up as fast as I could. When Law looked at me like this it made me feel like I had power.

Power was something that had come and gone, slipping through my fingers like grains of sand or rushing water so often that I had become conditioned to its absence. I lived my life in flux, knowing that however much power I had at the moment there would be moments when I had none at all. Lately had been a season of scarcity but all of that came to a screeching halt when Law was looking at me like this.

The man's stare was like an overflowing floodgate let loose in the desert, and like a fool I reveled in every drop of it.

"You're not."

Even with as little as I knew about Law, I could tell one thing. The man didn't lie, or use his words carelessly. He was unlike the other business men I'd waited on as a barista. The kind that came in throwing their money around and flashing their expensive watches at me when they collected their orders. The sort of man that was eager to share about their latest success when they asked for my number. No, those men were a dime a dozen in this city, actually they were probably a dime for two dozen. All of them eager to make a name and claim whatever part of the city they had managed to sink their teeth into.

I was used to those men. I could handle that sort with a practiced hand, but Law? This man was different and I wasn't so sure I knew how different. This man's attention came at a price. What that price was? No clue. Which meant I should not be as happy as I was to be on the receiving end. Writing checks my ass couldn't cash. But I couldn't help myself.

We stared at one another for a minute before I nodded. "Sure. Be right back."

My answer had him relaxing, it was just a slight softening of his body but I would take it. Listening was a way to get him to gentle, if even just a bit. I made a note to listen to what he said, but also not to go too far. He was a man in my apartment who had told me I wasn't safe with him, and it was in the middle of the night and I was still buzzed from dinner. I needed to be cautious, even if I wanted to throw myself at him and see what happened.

I closed my bedroom door and shook my head. "Not smart, not smart at all," I whispered to myself. Leaping without looking was not the way to spend time with Law, especially when the talk we were about to have was about me lying to my friend about our relationship. I blushed hot, a wave of embarrassment sweeping over me that not even the drinks I'd had could beat back. I went to my closet and snatched a dry hoodie and sweatpants to change into. It wasn't the sexiest, but it was probably my safest bet if I was going to remember to keep my distance from the man in the next room. I stripped, dressed quickly, and darted over to my mirror to dare a look at myself.

"Oh, fuck," I whispered at my reflection. Yes, I was trying to keep my libido in check, but that didn't mean I wanted to look like this. My hair was damp from the storm, the natural curl released in a way that was wild, not styled like I normally preferred. I tried to smooth it down but it was no use, a quick ponytail was going to have to work for now. The light makeup I'd applied had completely worn off and my mascara had run slightly, smudging sooty circles beneath my eyes and making me wince. Law in all his collected perfection had seen me like this.

No wonder he'd asked how much I'd had to drink and who I was at the restaurant with. He was probably worried that I was going to do something reckless. But then again, he'd pinned me against the wall and touched me like he hadn't wanted to stop.

"If you were, and you chose to get this drunk, you wouldn't be able to sit down for a week."

Damn that server. Why had she chosen that moment to come into the room? We'd just been getting to the good part. Although...I glanced towards the door and folded my arms over my chest. He was in my apartment now waiting for me, and that had to count for something right?

Yes, he wants to talk to you about the lies you told, my tipsy brain yelled at me. Not spank you, or have sex.

"Right, right," I whispered, giving my head a gentle rap. How had I already forgotten about that? All it had taken was half a memory of Law touching me and my body was ready to go. I blew out a deep breath and approached the door. I hesitantly put my hand on the knob and took another deep inhale. I could do this. I could talk to a man that I was lusting after, a man that had fueled more than one of my solo fantasies, and keep it together. I would not make a fool of myself and jump him. I would be friendly and courteous and the talk we'd have would be good. Maybe I'd end up with a new friend on top of it.

I plastered a smile on my face and opened the door. It took half a second and one foot outside the room for me to remember one very important fucking thing.

"You're not."

He'd said those words. The one that I had to watch was the man sitting at my kitchen counter and watching me like I was his prey. He'd told me I wasn't safe with him.

"Hey," I greeted softly and padded slowly into the room. I cleared my throat and gestured at the sofa beside me. "Do you wanna sit here?"

He gave a quick shake of his head. "I'm good here." His body was back to being rigid again and his eyes were slowly sweeping over my body from head-to-toe, like he was assessing me for damage. Cataloguing everything meticulously in his memory like he had when he'd entered my apartment. I couldn't think of why he would need that information for later.

"Yeah, okay." I sat down on the couch and turned my body so that I was facing him. "So, about the lie…" I began, my voice trailing off when I saw that he was frowning. He frowned a lot.

I wish he didn't.

"Yes, about that," he said, voice husky. He cleared his throat and leaned forward on the stool slightly, body pitched forward enough that his elbows were resting on his thighs as he spoke. "What does your friend think?"

I blinked at him. "What? My friend?"

"Yes, your friend from dinner. Tiffany? What does she think is going on between us?"

I nodded, licking my lips and feeling stupid because of course, Tiffany. We had just seen her all of twenty minutes ago. How had I forgotten about her already?

"She thinks we're engaged."

"And why does she think that?"

"Because I-" I broke off, face going hot because I hated what I was about to admit to this man who was still such a mystery, even if my body screamed that it knew him in all the ways that mattered, "because I told her that."

"Why did you do that?" He asked. His voice was low, interest unmistakable. Curious.

"I liked it when you said it," I told him honestly. I bit my lip and looked away because it was embarrassing. But the alcohol I'd drank that night was still buzzing in my blood and I was nothing if not forthcoming when I was drinking.

"In the coffee shop?"

"Yes, I liked it then." I dipped my chin and looked away from him. "I didn't want to tell her the truth when she asked me about it."

"How does she not know you aren't engaged to me? You work together." I knew he really meant *How could she not know you had a fiancée? How could she believe it was him?*

I lifted a shoulder in a shrug. "I'm a private person," I told him. "Plus, I move around a lot for work."

His brow furrowed. "For making coffee? You don't work at A Different Brew?"

I shook my head. "No, I just sort of moonlight, I guess. I have an app on my phone I use to get shifts. It's like, you know one of those dating apps, but for work."

He sucked on his teeth and I could see he was thinking about something, but I couldn't tell what. The wall he'd built around himself was too damn high for me to get a clear look over. Watching Law was like trying to get a glimpse of a big tree over a privacy fence, you could see the tops of the strong and beautiful tree, but all of the limbs, the foliage and any fruit it might bear was lost to you. Hidden away from view on purpose.

Why did he feel like he had to hide from me? And what was he hiding?

"Do you like the work?" He asked once it seemed like he had settled on something.

"Yes, I like moving around. Been doing it all my life," I told him. Outside a lightning strike flashed and the room was illuminated which was helpful given the faint light in my apartment was at Law's back and his face was almost all shadows. If it were any other man I'd be afraid, but I wasn't with him. Stupid really, given that he had told me I probably should be.

"So you've moved a lot then? Not from New York?" He asked.

I gave a quick shake of my head, wet ponytail sticking to my neck in a way that had me sighing and undoing it to pull it into a high bun. So what if I looked raggedy right now? It was late and I hated wet hair sticking to me. If I was going to be trying to figure this man out I wanted to be comfortable while I did it.

"I'm from South Texas," I told him, "but I moved out here about a decade ago and I love it. You can go every single day without seeing the same person twice, if you really wanted."

"And yet we've seen each other twice in a week," he said, clasping his hands in front of him. "Funny isn't it?"

"Yeah, I guess it is," I said, hesitantly, because I didn't know what else to say. Did he think this was happening on purpose? I hoped not. What if that *was* what he was thinking right now? That I was some crazy stalker that got in at a shop he frequented and was running around lying about being his fiancée to anyone that would listen. Fuck, I hoped he didn't think that.

"I'm sorry about lying," I blurted out. "I just, it got away from me when she asked and I didn't really know how to tell her it wasn't true. I forgot about it, and then we had dinner tonight and she just...she ran with it."

He held up a hand and I stopped talking. "I just have a question," he said.

"What?"

"When you lied about us being engaged, did you just tell your friend or have you been telling everyone?" His voice was almost emotionless, monotone, each word succinctly spoken so there would be no misunderstanding his meaning.

"I haven't told anyone but her," I said. "And technically, I didn't tell her, you did."

He nodded. "That's true," he paused and then continued on, "did you let her think that because you liked the power?"

I blinked in surprise, my resolve to make it through Law's interrogation broken before I'd really gotten started. "The power?" I asked, unsure if I'd heard right. "I don't understand what you mean…"

"The power that would come with someone looking at you and knowing you belonged to me."

A tendril of warmth bloomed in my belly at his words, but it had nothing to do with talk of power, and everything to do with Law saying *I belonged to him.* My body had liked that a whole fucking lot.

I shook my head. "No, I—power, or clout isn't why I let her think I was-," the warmth grew in my body until I felt it tingle in my fingers and toes, "why I let her think I was yours."

Law's body gave a slight jerk and he stood from the stool. "Then why did you do it, Honey?" He had his hands in his pockets now and was standing beside my kitchen table, body angled towards the windows and I sucked in a breath when a lightning flash illuminated his features. He was just as beautiful as ever.

"Because I liked that someone thought I was yours," I said, standing and walking towards him. My feet sounded soft on the hardwood, imperceptible in the almost deafening sound of the rainstorm. It sounded like it was coming down harder now, the dull roar of it blessedly filling the silence that had descended between Law and I. I walked towards him, acutely aware that Law was backing away even as I closed the space between us.

"I wanted it to be true, even if it was just for a little while."

"You shouldn't want something like that. I'm not a good man."

"I've got no use for a good man."

Law's jaw clenched, his eyes were moving over my face, then down to the sweater and sweats I'd put on. I was suddenly wishing I'd chosen something, anything else, than the zero sex appeal outfit I'd gone for. Why the hell hadn't I wanted him to touch me? I didn't care if I wasn't safe with him-- because I didn't want to be safe from Law. He moved then, a hand reaching towards me, and I took it without even thinking.

"Get on the table."

I stumbled at his order. "What?"

He jerked his chin towards my dining table. "Ass on the table."

"But-what are you-"

"If you want this, you'll do it now, Honey." That was all I needed to hear. I hustled towards the table and like Law asked, got my ass on the table in record time. We stared at each other for a beat before Law sighed and came to stand in front of me. "If I was smarter, I'd stay away from you."

"Me too," I said quickly, "I mean probably, right?'

He cracked a smile, just a lifting of the corner of his lips, but he nodded. "You really would. You're better off staying away from me, Honey. You know that, right?"

"But I don't want to stay away from you," I said with a pout.

He reached out a finger and trailed it up my arm. "I don't want you to stay away from me either. That's why this is all fucked, Honey. We can't do this ever again."

"Do what?"

He sank to his knees in front of me. "This." He

reached out and went to put his hands on my thighs, but he stopped and looked up at me. "Can I touch you?"

"Fuck yes. Please touch me."

His heavy hands landed on my thighs the second I said the words and I moaned, scooting closer to the edge of the table, but Law's fingers flexed on me. "Don't move. You get more when I give you more. Do you understand?"

I swallowed hard, the steel in his voice striking the right chord in me and reminding me once again that Law had a direct fucking line to my libido, and my clit. "Yes, sir," I whispered, the title coming out of me as naturally as breathing. Law's eyes darkened, nostrils flaring as he bent his head close to me and inhaled. I gasped when I felt his lips graze my thigh. The touch was slight through the material of my sweats but it felt fantastic. My fingers flexed on the edge of the table but I did as I was told and didn't move a muscle. I was used to following orders when it came to sex, but what I had never anticipated was doing the same with Law. I'd do what he said and maybe, just maybe, he'd drop all this talk about us never doing this again. I could already tell that I wanted to do it again and again, even if he'd barely touched me.

"That's a good girl," he murmured, turning his head to brush his lips against my thigh. His lips were warm through the cotton of my sweats that were suddenly too hot. I needed to get them off, but I already knew that was going to have to wait until Law decided they came off. I swallowed hard, watching him as he reached up and loosened his tie.

"What are you doing?" I asked.

He looked up at me with an arched eyebrow, tattooed hands yanking his tie off. "Give me your hands."

Automatically, I held out my hands to the man and watched in stunned silence as he wound the silk material of his tie around my wrists. Being tied up wasn't new, but I hadn't expected this from Law. Holy shit this night was an unexpected surprise in the very best of ways. It had been months since I'd had an encounter with anyone, there were no lovers to speak of, and I had been so focused on work and the everyday rhythm of life that sex and orgasms that didn't come from a battery operated toy hadn't really registered. It's why I'd been so excited about going to the Cairn this weekend, of blowing off some steam and getting under someone in the delicious trappings that submission offered me.

But now here was Law on his knees in front of me with my hands bound in his damn tie. This seemed like a dream come true, a regular fantasy that had been served up special to me by the universe.

"Please touch me," I rasped out, because I was seriously getting dizzy from need. I was horny and the man I wanted was within reach. God, I needed his hands on me.

"Patience," he murmured, but he was already dropping my hands into my lap and hooking his fingers into the waistband of my sweats. "Hips up, these are coming off."

"Thank god," I whispered, moving to help him pull my sweats off.

A low chuckle from Law. "You're eager, aren't you?" He asked, but I didn't feel embarrassment at the question because fuck yes, I was.

"Of course, I am. Have you seen you?" I asked, because my whole no filter problem was still rampant and in the driver's seat.

"I could ask you the same thing." Law drew my sweats down my thighs with agonizing slowness, fingers brushing against my skin as he went. He dropped my sweats on the floor beneath the table and surprised me when he reached forward, putting his hand on my thighs and pushing my legs apart. I adjusted on the table when his shoulders nudged against the inside of my knees but Law said nothing about the movement. Good, so I could do that.

He put a hand on my chest, palm warm and pleasant on me. "Lie back."

I did what he asked, with my bound hands in front of me. "What are you going to do?"

"I'm going to eat your pussy." The bluntness of his words made me squirm and I might have moved closer to him if I wasn't trying to follow orders. I had to prove to him he wanted to do this with me again. "And you're going to lie there and enjoy yourself."

"But I can't touch you?" I asked, lifting my hands above me. I craned my neck to see him shake his head at me, eyes on my face.

"No."

"Why not?"

"If you touch me I won't be able to stop, Honey. That's for your own good."

I bit my lip, unconvinced by Law's words, but I wasn't going to push it. "Okay. I'm good with that."

"With what part?" He wasn't looking at me anymore, he was focused on my thighs, lips brushing against my skin as he began to explore the area. I gasped when he turned his head, nose dragging across the top of my pussy. My clit throbbed and I held my breath waiting for him to touch me where I really needed it, but the man was bent on torturing me in the most delicious way and showed no signs of speeding up.

"All of it. I want it. I want this with you," I said,

making sure to tell him exactly what it was that I craved. "Please touch me."

Law didn't say a word, just did as I asked. I gasped at the first stroke of his finger. It was just a light pressure, thumb against the thin fabric of my underwear, pale pink brushed cotton that rode high. I looked good in them, which made me glad I'd gone with something sweet, even if it was understated. The last thing I wanted him to think was that I had planned this. But I was just as shocked to be where I was as he was at finding me stumbling into his private room at the restaurant. He pressed his palm against my core, the heavy feel of him against my flesh made me moan and this time I did move slightly, just a clenching of my knees against him.

"Ah, ah, ah," he chastised, pulling his hand away, and I swore at my movement.

"I'm sorry," I said quickly.

"Sorry, what?" he asked, breathing warm on my inner thigh.

"I'm sorry, sir."

Law rewarded me by pressing his mouth against my clit, his tongue warm and hot against it. The little bud of flesh was getting harder, pushing up against its hood as he began to touch me, pet me more like. There was no other word for how his fingers were gently stroking me as he tongued me.

"These are not coming off," he told me, sliding a

finger into the crotch of my underwear and giving it a tug. "Do you understand?"

A thrill went through me at the gruff tone in Law's voice. This man knew what he was doing to me. "Yes, sir," I whispered, my eyes closing. But they shot open when Law gave my pussy a light slap. "Oh!" I cried out, my back arching off the table, but a hand on my stomach from Law forced me back down.

"Hands above your head. Keep them on the table." I did as I was told, but stayed silent, the breath stolen right of my lungs from the slap he'd given me. He bent his head close to me, I could tell he was close from the warm breath against my skin and underwear.

"You're wet already, Honey," he said, grinding the palm of his hand against my core. "Soaked through these little cotton panties of yours already, aren't you?"

"Yes, sir." My voice was shaky and breathy, and a light sheen of sweat had broken out on my forehead from the effort it was taking not to throw a leg over his shoulder and pull him to me. He was teasing me, warm breath, a trail of his fingers or press of his lips against my sensitive flesh before he was gone again. "Sir, please, I-I need it."

"What do you need?"

"Your mouth on me."

"And what do you want me to do with my mouth for you, baby girl?"

"Eat my pussy."

He practically purred at my answer. "That's my girl." His voice was hoarse, the only indication that our little play time was taking it out on him as much as it was me. When he slid my panties to the side and licked a slow stripe up my lips I almost sobbed from relief. "That's what you need isn't it?" he asked, splaying a hand over me, fingers over my mons pubis, holding my underwear to the side with his big hand. My underwear was going to be destroyed, stretched out beyond repair after this, but it was worth it.

"Yes, sir," I moaned, head turning to the side. I opened my eyes to look out the window at the storm that was still raging, the one that was suddenly matching how I was feeling. I concentrated on following the paths the raindrops took on their journey down the glass of my window. It helped hold off the orgasm I knew was poised to sweep me under. An orgasm from Law was going to be divine, but I did not want to prematurely arrive there. Every second I spent under this man's attention was too perfect and I wanted to stretch it out as long as I could. If I had the willpower I'd stay spun up in my current state all night. This man could keep me here until the sun came up and I would still beg for more.

He turned his head, the scrape of his stubble against my skin making me gasp. A second later his tongue soothed the area, making me sigh with pleasure.

Light struck again, the rumble of the storm shaking the window panes in my apartment but it didn't phase me. All of my attention was centered on the man between my shaking thighs. My lust and pleasure kicked up with the same fervor as the thunderstorm. Law's tongue touched my swollen lips once more before it dipped inside in an almost lazy thrust.

Jesus Christ that was amazing. He did it again and I bit my lip, forcing myself to stay focused on the damn rain. I'd almost come just from that one thrust. I pushed my hands into the table, a move that I knew would showcase my breasts in a fantastic way, if he was watching me. Law struck me as a man that liked to watch while he got a woman off.

"Mmm, you're sweet, but I should have known that." His voice was rumbling against my pussy, and I felt myself get wetter. "Shouldn't I?" He asked, and I whispered in response. Law pressed his lips back to my opening and thrust his tongue into me, this time with more force, the sound of my arousal and his tongue filled my ears even with the deafening rain pounding overhead. Law's finger circled my clit, pulling back my hood, and then he was blessedly putting his mouth exactly where I wanted him to. He drew methodical circles around my clit, each time getting closer with increasing pressure until I was practically sobbing from frustration.

"Please," I begged. "Please, I need you." His lips tightened on my clit and his tongue pressed flat against my over sensitized nerves. "Law!"

My thighs shook when he slid his fingers, two from the stretch of it, inside of me. "Oh god," I gasped when he began to pump his thick fingers in and out of me. The added feeling of fullness from his fingers made me dizzy and it wasn't long before I felt my orgasm starting to get away from me. I'd held it off as long as I could, there was no getting away from this. He crooked his fingers and hit the spot that always made my knees weak.

My eyes squeezed shut. "Oh, Law…"

Again he thrust, and again his fingers massaged my g-spot. It only took another minute before I was coming on his fingers with a sob.

"Law, Law, *Law...*" The last utterance was pulled from me with all the reverence of a prayer because this man did not quit. He continued to work me until my orgasm was done, my body relaxing and when I went limp against the table, he stopped.

"Good girl." His hand was warm on my stomach. He touched me lightly as if I were made of glass and then he was leaning over me and undoing his tie from around my wrists with the same light touch.

The tie came free in a whisper of silk and I opened my eyes to look at Law.

I grinned up at him. "That was good. Really good."

He put a hand down beside my head, holding himself over me. His other hand moved and my smile broadened when he touched my bottom lip. He swiped his thumb along my mouth, pressing lightly at the center of my lip.

"You deserve better than this," he said. His voice was hoarse, but there was a sternness to it that told me a truth I didn't want. He was saying goodbye. It had been good, really good, just like I'd said. But it wasn't stopping Law from leaving.

I could also tell by the way he was touching me that there wouldn't be a next time. The afterglow of my orgasm was fading as fast as it had come into being, and I pushed myself up onto my elbows. Law moved back, his hand falling away from my lips when I opened my mouth to speak, and I hated that the ghost of his touch lingered. My tongue darted out to the spot he'd touched me and Law's eyes narrowed before he turned away and began to do up his tie.

"You're leaving," I said quietly. It wasn't a question. Just an observation. I heard the distinct sound of a phone buzzing and I knew it was his driver calling.

He glanced back at me over his shoulder and gave me one nod. "Yes." He set off towards the door and I hated how I was now shivering without him. My body wasn't done with him. *I wasn't done with him.* I needed him, needed more of this, and I could feel the ache of losing Law replacing the pleasure he'd given me.

I wrapped my arms around myself and nodded back at him. "Thanks for bringing me home." Law was already at the door and he stopped there. His tie was back on, suit set to rights, and his hands were back down by his sides as if none of this had ever happened. As if he hadn't just had me screaming his name with his damn tie wrapped around my wrists while he ate me out like I was his last meal.

I shivered again watching him. He turned and I saw that I was right, he was completely and utterly back to his normal sophisticated, if a little brooding, appearance. A cool breeze ghosted over the tops of my thighs and I squirmed, acutely aware that my panties were hanging off one of my ankles and my sweats were in a pile on the floor. I didn't even want to think about how I looked naked from the waist down and sitting in my own cum on my kitchen table.

Law's eyes moved over me, I could see it even at this distance and with the poor lighting. Another lightning flash punctuated by the incessant buzzing of his phone. His driver must be getting impatient.

"You were lovely, Honey," he told me, voice husky and low, but with the same commanding note of finality to it that I was quickly coming to hate. I opened my mouth to reply but Law was already turning and opening my front door. Just like that, the man I had been obsessed with, the man that I wished I belonged to, the one I had stolen a moment's passion with tonight was gone.

The door slammed behind him and Lawson Sokolov walked out on me.

CHAPTER ELEVEN

LAW

I slammed the door to my apartment behind me and stared into the silent dark space. "What the fuck did I just do?"

Outside the storm was raging. The rain falling in rivers that made it seem like Manhattan was being swallowed up by the sea. Like a modern day Atlantis meant to sink beneath the shit colored muddy waters of the Hudson. I closed my eyes and forced myself to breathe deep. In and out. In and out, and then once more before I opened my eyes back up and groaned.

I put out a hand, steadying myself against the door. I'd been in enough brawls, outright put my body to the limit situations, and had never in all those years felt this heavy sort of sick feeling in my stomach. This was dark in a way that had my knees threatening to give, like I'd just been sucker punched. *What the fuck?*

"What the fuck did I just do?" I repeated. No answer came. My high rise apartment in Manhattan was empty and silent as a tomb. It always was. I wasn't one to have company over, didn't throw dinner parties or invite family because there were none. I was a man set apart, and I'd made it like that on purpose. Each and every connection that meant anything that could be used against me I'd severed for their own good.

"You mean for yours," I gritted out between clenched teeth. "You did it for you." I stared out into the darkness, the faint city lights giving some relief to the inky black of my living room. I'd had friends once, a family that I called every Sunday. Used to have family dinner weekly. Hell, I'd even used to play pickup games in the park in Queens on the block I'd grown up in. It'd been a different place than it was now. The neighborhood Honey lived in was familiar but not, like looking at my past through frosted glass. I knew what it was at a distance, but up close?

I didn't recognize it.

Just like myself. I was a different man now. I'd cut my friends, limited my family time, and ditched the games when work had become my focus. When I'd started getting my hands dirty a little too frequently and I knew it was only a matter of time before a capo or some fucker with something to prove came after the people I cared about. I'd seen it happen one too many times to the guys who'd started out doing the same shit as me when we were teenagers.

Ivan's mother got spooked by a car that tailed her and sat outside her work, Steve's girl got stabbed on the E train. Tommy's granny had her front window knocked in by a brick with a shitty misspelled threat tapped to the side of it.

It went on and on, and on, distracting the main target from their work, pushing them closer to losing their cool until they ended up making a mistake and paid for it with their life. Or even worse, until someone, their grandma, ma, or girl got dead. I made myself care about no one and nothing. I didn't need the complications of it, and there had been that one time...

Now, I knew I could go back, but it was hard to remember just how a man went about playing at being a functioning member of society when he'd been feral for far too fucking long. I'd tried, once, to give someone more. A woman who wanted me, a sub that had wanted it all from me, but it'd been a goddamn disaster from the start. I hadn't been able to give it. A sour taste settled in my mouth thinking about it, about her, about how we made the other into a twisted anxious version of ourselves.

Jane.

That year with Jane had been hell for both of us, even if she'd been too stubborn to see it. We had been bad together, better apart, and I'd decided then that I was better suited to focusing my restless energy into boardrooms and running numbers, not socializing. Not trying to resurrect a man that didn't exist anymore. Hadn't for years now.

I wasn't a man that worried about feelings or people because that distracted me. Because it put them in danger from shitty men who had no right putting their hands on them, much less knowing they existed. So I'd put distance between me and everything that meant something to me to protect them. But now I was at the top. Now I was legit and free, and I had no one to show for it.

It was better this way.

A clap of thunder made the room as bright as daylight and it reminded me of Honey's apartment. I pushed away from the door and went further into my apartment, turning on a lamp as I went. It was a big place, not just an apartment but a penthouse, with floor-to-ceiling windows, white and grey marble fucking flooring that was a bitch for my cleaners to keep clean. Not that it mattered. The floor hardly had time to get dirty with the amount of time I actually spent here.

I leaned against the back of the leather couch and

turned my head, looking into the dining room from where I stood. The whole place was luxe, top of the line with the newest appliances and a pricey zip code with a door man trained to keep the paparazzi at bay. The building was exclusive and it didn't matter if you had the money, you had to have the name, the sway in the city, to be given the privilege of cutting the fuckers a check every month.

I'd bought my penthouse outright for 15 million. It was worth it for the peace. The second I stepped inside the brightly light lobby and nodded at the door man, my world narrowed down to nothing. Everything was simpler. Peace was mine. A thing I had chased for years and finally found. But then why did it feel so empty in now? Why were these big open rooms, the ones with the high end finishings and furnishings suddenly not enough?

Why the fuck did I want to be in a drafty barely furnished apartment with a boiler that rattled and windows that shook every time it thundered? I crossed my arms, pissed that the place I wanted to be wasn't my home.

"Honey, that's why." It was her. It had been for a week. I licked my lips and groaned when I picked up the faint taste of her. She'd been sweet and wet for me, pussy eager as anything for my mouth and hands. She would have taken my dick if I'd let myself offer it to her. If I'd let myself stay with her.

But I hadn't.

I'd left as quickly as I'd arrived. I'd left her.

I could still see her face scrunched up, the way she'd looked impossibly small and lost sitting on her kitchen table with my spit still wet on her pussy lips. She hadn't wanted me to leave. I'd known that, and I'd still fucking done it even if every part of me had wanted to rush back to her. I'd wanted to gather her up in my arms and take her to bed, to kiss her and undress her. Take my time with her. But that didn't excuse the fact that the sex I wanted, the way I wanted to touch her, how I wanted her to respond to me, was more than what we'd done.

It was more than most casual encounters ever fathomed. It was a kink, a dynamic that had to be explained and explored with clear boundaries and safe words.

I hadn't had that with Honey.

I had a drunk girl with a big beautiful smile and a mouth that I wanted to claim, so I'd done what I would allow myself. God, the way she looked when she laughed, her head thrown back, dark curls bouncing over her shoulder and spilling down her back. She was a woman, but she was cute, and that was what sparked my interest. I had a soft spot for cute, for pastels and soft lace. For sundresses, and pink umbrellas with bows bigger than they ought to be. But Honey wasn't mine to keep, and I wasn't hers to have. So I'd given her an orgasm. Laid her out and eaten her pussy on her dining room table like it was the finest delicacy, because it was. And something was a delicacy if it was rare, right? I wasn't going to get another go at her, which made her pussy a meal no chef could ever come close to replicating. I'd eaten her like a starving man. God, she'd been good, naturally following directions and making me question if this had to be a one time thing.

If she could learn why did I have to stay away from her? She'd listened when I told her not to move, her thighs shaking as I went down on her, she'd let me wrap my tie around her and kept her hands glued to the table like I wanted.

She'd been a good girl.

A very fucking good girl.

"Fucking damn it." I pushed away from the couch and strode towards my bedroom, yanking off my jacket and tossing it onto the couch as I went. I needed to get out of my suit. It smelled like her, light and flowery, whatever perfume she'd been wearing had rubbed off on me and I could scent her all around me. I licked my lips again and there she was filling up my mouth, dancing across my tongue and making my dick hard.

I entered my bathroom, flipped on the light and balked at the man staring back at me. I looked like I did when I'd been put on the tail of a group I needed to shut down. Like I'd been up for thirty hours but wouldn't be slowing down anytime soon, an edge of manic light had entered my eyes. When I was like this, I was obsessive, I was unstoppable. A woman had never made me like this. It wasn't that there hadn't been opportunities. Of those there had been plenty. But I knew that what I had to offer a woman had to be given to the right woman. A woman with a darker side, a kinkier side. Smart, capable, engaging in her everyday life. But sweet, submissive, a little twisted in her desires when it came time to let her walls down.

A little girl just for me.

I blew out a breath and willed away the image of Honey laying splayed out on her kitchen table with her bound hands above her head. She'd been fucking gorgeous. Perfect. If I had an artistic bone in my body, I would have sketched it to have it somewhere outside of my brain. But I wasn't, so a memory would be all that I had. One that would fade and twist until it was too hard to recall. The thought pissed me off. But it was better this way. Better it be a misremembered moment than to go after her, to push for another night with her, a night I knew she'd easily give if I asked. I'd gone down that path before and there was nothing good there, not for either of us.

My thoughts strayed to Jane and I leaned

forward, bracing both hands on the cool marble of the sink and hung my head. When we had met at the Cairn it seemed like we might be a good fit, but she'd been too insecure and possessive, and I'd been quick to give up, my patience short when it came to a relationship that existed outside of the Cairn. What Jane wanted was a 24/7 dynamic and that was not something I could give. Not something I wanted to give, anyone, ever. The lines of the intimacy we explored within the safe space of the Cairn had been blurred, fucked over and twisted when we'd tried to bring it outside of the club.

In the light of day, our faults were exposed, all the worst bits of us bubbling and rising to the surface. The result was a big fucking mess that I couldn't end quick enough. Jane had tried to dig her feet in, but when I was done, I was done. She was still a member of the club, but I hadn't seen her during my visits. I wasn't concerned if we did happen to choose the same night to play. I'd faced down men not knowing if I'd get out alive, I'd also gone toe-to-toe in enough billion dollar deals and gotten my way that a run in with an old flame wasn't high on my radar.

But it did make me think about what it might be like when I found a woman that interested me. It was on my mind right fucking now, because I'd met Honey. And I was very fucking interested, even though I knew chances were she would want nothing to do with the sex and play I wanted from her. She'd called me sir and that had gone straight to my dick, but that wasn't the title I wanted to hear come from her pretty mouth.

What I wanted to hear was Daddy, and I didn't want her to just say it, I wanted to hear her scream it. I wanted her to mean it. It was concerning. I hadn't been able to give Jane what she wanted and we were on the same page when it came to sex and kink, so how the hell was I going to give Honey what she wanted when I didn't even know if we were reading from the same book?

Although...what was I doing worrying about a relationship with a woman that I'd only met twice?

"Honey, what are you doing to me?" I shouldn't have left. The dark thing that had started to grow in my stomach the second I left her, had kept growing on the ride back to my place, and was now wrapping itself around me, threatening to choke off the air I was breathing. It was screaming at me that I shouldn't have left her.

I flipped on the sink tap and let the cool water rush over my hands. "She wanted you to stay." I splashed some water on my face and unbuttoned my dress shirt. The cold water dripped down onto my skin and it cut through the fog of want Honey had left me sitting in. "I wanted to stay with her," I said, admitting the thing that I hadn't wanted to say out loud. Now that I had I knew it was going to be running through my mind for the rest of the night on a loop.

"I wanted to stay with her," I said again, lifting my eyes to the glass in front of me. I looked like shit, the light in my eyes only more intense. Wanting Honey was like a drug and I'd left my fucking fix sitting alone and half dressed, eyes pleading for me to stay. The Dom in me was riled and it would be easy to blame it on that, my natural instincts to care for a sub. A role Honey had played with, flirted with, but hadn't taken on in truth. She wasn't my submissive, but we had enjoyed a taste of the power dynamics that colored my sexual appetite. Honey had been sweet and willing, eager to do as I asked without question, even in the restaurant when I'd lost control for a second and threatened to spank her.

I'd seen the intrigue in her eyes. But how much of that was from alcohol and how much was from the woman? That was the entire problem with all of this. I wanted to stay away from her and give her more, but I couldn't when she was like she was-—a little too drunk, a little too clueless. It couldn't be like that. She needed to know what I wanted, what I craved from her. And tonight was not the night to introduce her to that.

So I'd given her what I could. A damn good orgasm, and me leaving her for the night. I'd only been able to do that by keeping her hands off me and her panties on. If I'd let her touch me it wouldn't have worked. I would have kept going. The thin cotton of her panties had been the slightest of barriers, but it had been enough for me to keep my resolve to not fuck her on her kitchen table.

If I'd done that I would still be there. If I'd done that, if I had claimed Honey, she would never be free of me.

She deserved better than that, so why the hell did I feel like shit for leaving her the way I did?

CHAPTER TWELVE

HONEY

After Law left my apartment I sat in my empty dining room for a long time. I kept replaying the last moments we had and then cringing at them before I replayed them one more time just to make it sting extra. Finally, when the cold had set in and I couldn't feel the ghost of his hands on my skin anymore I slipped from the table and onto my feet, scooping up my underwear and sweats before I headed to my bedroom. Cleaning myself up and getting into bed had been…difficult, but I'd done it. Part of me had wanted to keep waiting where Law had left me. Any second I was convinced he would come back, knock on the door and stay with me. He'd sweep me up in his arms and carry me into my bedroom. But that hadn't happened and now I just felt stupid for wishing it would.

I showered, changed again and got into bed. I laid in bed for a very long time, eyes on the window, trying not to think about much I wanted him to come back. When I finally fell asleep it was in the early hours of the morning. I'd seen the first glimmers of the sun peeking over the buildings when I'd finally dozed off. The storm was over when the pinging of my app woke me up. Bleary eyed I swatted at it when another ping sounded.

"Shut up," I whispered, even as I was turning my phone over to look at the screen.

BaristApp has 12 new notifications.

"Shit." The shops in the city must be desperate if they were all posting shifts at sunrise. With this many notifications I'd have my pick of any shift and location. And it was a Friday and people always tipped more on Friday. I bit my lip, hovering over the screen, not swiping open on the app. As nice as it was, I wasn't sure I wanted to take any jobs today. For one, my head was pounding. The previous night's drinks had made themselves known by way of a slight hangover, and two I felt like shit because the man I wanted had left me alone when I desperately wanted more.

He didn't even have my phone number so I couldn't even pin my hopes on the long shot that he would text me later. When Law walked out of my apartment that had been it. The man was gone, in the wind. The only thing I knew about him was that he was the CEO of Law Acquisitions, liked Korean Barbeque and got coffee at a shop that I sometimes worked at. It wasn't a lot to go on, but maybe I would see him if I took a shop in Hudson Yard? I tapped the screen, opening the notifications and scanned the shift postings hopefully. But no dice. There were no postings in Hudson Yard. There was however, a posting in Tribeca which would be perfect for what I had planned that night.

A night at the Cairn.

If I took the job in Tribeca I could walk the short distance to the club and take my time. It would be easy breezy before a night of possible play. I was sure even if I didn't find anyone to my liking that me showing up earlier would give me a pretty great shot at getting a room for myself so I didn't have to take the train back to Queens. I never liked taking the train back home at night after spending time in the Cairn. There was something about it that didn't feel good. When I spent time at the club I let my defenses down, I embraced a softer more vulnerable side of me when I indulged my little side. Public transport at night in the city wasn't the best place for a little trying to get home.

I shivered beneath my covers, remembering the

time that I had tried to do it and had been left scared and running from a group of catcalling men that had followed me the length of my platform before the train had arrived. I'd tripped and bloodied both of my knees before getting on the train. It had taken everything in me not to burst into tears on my way home, but I'd managed it.

Now I didn't take the train home. I stayed at the club even when I wasn't sure I would meet anyone, which was fine. I could decompress and relax after what was usually a grueling work week. I didn't take many days off, just my regular one day a week, but when I went to the club I took two. The extra day added a bit of luxury to my time off. I always came back well rested and happy even if I didn't find a partner I fit well enough with to play. The time to be myself as I wanted to be at the club was enough all on its own.

I pushed myself up and hit accept on the Tribeca posting. It was a short shift and didn't start until noon. I had plenty of time to try and get myself together before I needed to be there. Plenty of time to try and shake off my hangover and the funk that had settled over me when Law walked out of my apartment, and my life.

"Why didn't he stay?" I whispered, wrapping my arms around myself. It had been good. He had enjoyed himself, or so I thought.

"I don't want you to stay away from me either. That's why this is all fucked, Honey. We can't do this ever again."

He'd said that. I knew he had enjoyed it, I knew that he had wanted me as badly as I wanted him. But if all of that was true when why had he said we couldn't do it again? Why had he left me the way he had?

"You were lovely, Honey."

I felt tears well up in my eyes. Lovely. Law had called me lovely. He'd given me his laugh. He'd carried me home in the rain, and he'd noticed my hallway lights were too dark.

The man was paying attention to me. There was no way he'd wanted it to be a one time thing, but even so...

"He still left. Respect it," I told myself, swinging my legs and standing from my bed. It didn't matter if my paths crossed with Law ever again. I would give him his space. I would pretend that last night hadn't happened. Even if it sucked. Okay, it was mostly definitely going to suck. I knew that every cell in my traitorous body was going to want to go to him the second he came into my field of vision but I wouldn't do it. I'd maintain my distance and give him a bland smile, the kind that you gave to people you recognized in passing but weren't really sure if you knew them or not.

I went to the sink and brushed my teeth, glaring

at myself in the mirror. My eyes were red-rimmed from crying, my hair was wild from the rain and from my time with Law, I could see bags under my eyes from the lack of sleep. In short, I looked like shit. Just fucking great. I spit and rinsed my mouth putting away my toothbrush with more force than necessary. I blew out a deep breath and considered myself. I was going to need makeup today for sure if I wanted to roll into the shop looking human. It would be necessary for the club as well.

I couldn't show my face there looking like I had cried the night away over a man. I turned the sink on and washed my face. I hated that I had spent the night crying over a man.

I applied my moisturizer and began applying my foundation, my mind wandering while my hands worked. My mind wandered a lot when I was stressed. Daydreams had always been my escape when I was younger and it hadn't changed the older I got. After last night, it was second nature to vanish into a daydream, but I normally vanished into a happy daydream where everything was perfect and I guessed this was sort of that.

This daydream featured Law.

I'd be walking down the street window shopping and he would see me from across the street. I wouldn't notice him, I'd be drinking a coffee and enjoying the perfectly sunny day, eyes on the shop's offerings when he would approach me. He'd call out to me and I'd turn, not seeing him right away. But then there he would be walking towards me through the crowd. We'd lock eyes and he'd smile at me, a real genuine warm smile and he would tell me that he was happy to see me, surprised that it was here and now, but happy. I'd be happy too and I'd tell him that, and then before we could say anything else he would apologize for leaving.

"I got scared," he'd say.

"It's okay. I'm glad you're here now," I'd reply.

Law would take my hand in his and we'd walk down the street, hand-in-hand window shopping and ducking into a little restaurant down the street for a place we could just talk. We'd stay there for hours before we moved on with no destination in mind, the only thing on our agenda for the day would be spending time together.

The day would be perfect.

"You're pathetic," I whispered, stepping back from the mirror and grabbing my curling iron. I flipped it on and began to brush out my hair. "What the fuck, Honey?" The day dream was too much, even for me. A man like Law wouldn't say he was sorry. He wouldn't say something like he 'got scared.' This wasn't a romance novel where the hero was just too overcome by his feelings so he ran.

This was real life, and men like Law did not run.

He'd left because he'd wanted to. He'd been good to me getting me home, and the orgasm? 10/10 wished it would happen again. Law had treated me right, even if I'd spent the night crying. That was on me and not the man. I took a section of hair and began to curl it, eyes on the strands as they heated.

"Pathetic," I repeated, the word echoing in my ears with the same kind of finality of the door shutting behind Law. I had heard that sound as sure as the thunder that had kept me company until I'd managed to fall asleep. I did my hair, focusing on getting the curls just right, spraying them with extra hairspray because I didn't just need my hair to last through my shift, but also the night that I was going to spend at the Cairn. When my hair was done I went to my closet, grabbing the leather tote I used when I stayed overnight at the club, it was a dark brown, the leather of it buttery soft and I loved it. It had been a splurge for me to buy. A purchase that I reserved only for when I was indulging the side of myself I kept hidden from the world. I fingered the soft leather and stared into my closet, the smoothness of the bag beneath my fingertips calming me, reminding me of where I would be in as little as twelve hours.

I might feel like shit right now, but I wouldn't then. I pulled an emerald green dress, floor length with a high slit and thick straps that did fucking wonders for my modest cleavage. It would be a change for me, but the dress had been another impulse splurge. It made me look like a greek goddess, the draping of it, the flowing skirt that moved behind me when I moved. It was pure elegance and I hadn't been able to resist buying it when I came across it at the consignment store down the street.

The club seemed a fitting place to embrace my inner goddess. She would not be phased by a man like Law giving her an orgasm and walking out the door before she'd even stopped trembling from the aftershocks of it. The woman that would wear this dress would push it to the side and hold her head up. I snagged a pair of strappy gold heels. The strap wound it's way delicately up my leg ending below my knee, a detail I loved. The best part was the heel was thick enough that I wouldn't be in danger of falling over after eight hours on my feet from work. I stroked my hands over the delicate material of the dress and blew out a heavy sigh before packing it and the heels away. I added a few undergarments in case I really wanted to impress, not that it mattered because the only one I wanted to impress was myself.

"This is for me," I said, but I wasn't quite convinced. I could hear it in the slight tremble of my voice. When I went to the club I normally opted for pastels, softer colors and dresses—mostly sundresses and ballet flats with hair bows and ribbons woven through my hair. But not tonight.

I had to be different tonight. I had to act different tonight.

It was the only way I would be able to put myself back together after my encounter with Law. An encounter that should not be affecting me like this. It was one night with a man I'd spent maybe two hours with tops, but *still...*

That time spent with him had changed me. I didn't even really understand how or why, but it had woken up the need and want to belong to someone —*to this man*. I hadn't felt that in so long.

Truthfully, I hadn't felt much when it came to the opposite sex unless it was within the negotiated boundaries of kink. The men I met in my day-to-day never piqued my interest. Mostly because I knew they would not be able to give me what I wanted. I bit my lip, tossing a few beauty products into my bag before hitching it high onto my shoulder and slipping into my sneakers on my way out the door.

What I wanted was unique to the patrons of the Cairn and not the men I came across in New York City. It was better that way. Less complicated, or at least as much as I could make it. Because there had been that time with...him.

I frowned, not liking how easily I could recall his

face. Christian. All smug brown eyes and shining golden hair. He'd been handsome and charming when we met at the Cairn. His personality big and open, warm in a way that had me interested in learning more about him. Interested in seeing who he was outside of his role as Dom, outside of the club.

I had never wanted that before. We'd met the previous year when I had been eager to date. The itch to have a familiar face, a body I knew waiting for me in bed, had started to grow until it was all that I thought about when I crawled into bed at night. A girl could get by on her own, and I usually liked it, but sometimes the feel of another body was the only way to satisfy exactly what I needed.

It had been that craving for someone else's hands on my body that had pulled me into Christian's gravitational force. He was like the sun, pulling everyone he met into his orbit until they revolved around him. Until he was the focus of their world. It hadn't taken long at all for me to fall into the same holding pattern, the same obsession as everyone else when it came to Christian O'Hanon.

He was a good Dom. An exceptional one, really. That was how I'd fallen so quickly for him, mistaking the sure way he carried himself, the deft hand as he guided us through our scenes together, the absolute confidence he invoked when he was a

Dominant. All of it had snowballed together. Blinding me to the fact that we were not compatible. We were living two different lives, on two different timelines, with Christian insisting on an engagement ring I kept refusing. A whirlwind romance that would end with me married to him and us moving in together, even if we had just met two months before.

The way he pulled at my walls and boundaries, shoving his way and his will through them had left me reeling. It felt wrong. Just like every place I had moved before finding New York. All of it, so much so that I had almost pulled up stakes and left the city. But the thing was, I loved New York City too much to leave it. I had no family and few friends, but the one thing I had was the city.

I had New York.

I wasn't going to give up the place I had earned for myself to run from a man that didn't understand no. We had begun in a place that insisted on consent and trust, boundaries and limits, as its most tried and true tenets. Christian was a man that wanted what he wanted, when he wanted it. And I was, for all my faults and mistakes, what he wanted.

A good man would have understood my hesitation and given me time, but it turned out Christian wasn't a particularly good man. He was, however, an incredibly selfish one. When I'd broken it off with him he had stalked me for weeks. Juana had taken to yelling at him and shaking her broom, making sure he knew he was no longer welcome in our building. Elaina and her kids made sure to keep an eye on him, glaring at him until he left when he parked across the street waiting for me to return from work. They'd called the cops on him more than once when I was out. Christian for his part stopped coming around my apartment and made a game of trying to find me at my jobs. Thanks to the random nature of BaristApp's offerings he had only succeeded twice in nailing down exactly where I was that day. Both times I'd felt my heart in my throat when I saw his familiar handsome profile in line.

"You have to stop," I told him.

"I won't, I love you. This is what you do when you love someone."

He was wrong. I knew that, but some part of me started to believe it. That I deserved this for letting him fall in love with me. That it was my fault somehow. Until we'd run into one another at the Cairn.

Christian had been there with another submissive. They'd been tangled up in one another in the great room. The submissive giggling in his lap while he toyed with her hair, leaning into to whisper in her ear. It was harmless in a place like the club, but seeing them together had been like a bucket of cold water being thrown on me.

She hadn't even looked a thing like me. Blond hair, blue eyes, fair skinned and slight. My exact opposite. I think that had hurt more, somehow. Knowing that he was putting me through hell, making me look over my shoulder when I was out, making me wonder if I would have a day of peace or end up running from him, and yet...yet, he was choosing to play at the club and with a woman that could not look further from me.

It was sick how I hated that she looked nothing like me.

I'd gone straight to Connie and told her everything. The woman who manned the front desk was not just a receptionist. She was the right hand woman to the club's owner, Zeus. Yes, weird name, but the man was god within the walls of the Cairn, so no one really questioned it. No one had ever seen him either.

My money was on Connie being Zeus, because no sooner had I told her about my split from Christian—the stalking, the police reports, the unwanted visits at work, than Christian suddenly vanished from the club. When I re-entered the great room he was nowhere to be seen, his blonde though? She was there and looking pissed, but alone. I was glad her night was ruined.

How fucked was that?

The answer was very fucked. *Very, very fucked.*

"Eight months probation. If you so much as think he's following you, I want to know," Connie said, holding up a finger.

I nodded, barely able to hold her piercing gaze. "Sure thing."

She pointed her finger at me. "I mean it, Honey. You so much as think you see him and you tell me. He'll pay."

"But-"

She waved a hand, already turning on her heel. "Enjoy yourself. You're safe here."

And that had been that. Connie had taken care of him even if I didn't know the particulars. I hadn't seen Christian since that night. The woman had power. She had to be Zeus.

I went to the club then freely, letting my guard down enough to slip into little space. Enough to take my pleasure with other Doms. But when the eight months mark of Christian's probation came and went I wondered what had happened to him. Whatever it was he hadn't reappeared in my life and that suited me just fine.

"You shouldn't want something like that. I'm not a good man."

"I've got no use for a good man."

I shut my door, the words Law had spoken to me the night before ringing in my ears. I'd told him I didn't want a good man, but it was a lie. After Christian, *all* I wanted was a good man. Someone to be good to me. But that seemed to be impossible to find even in a city like New York where anything was possible. Or at least possible at a price.

I paused, knowing the lights Law hadn't liked were overhead. I didn't have to look to know they were off now, light pouring in from the windows that lined the third floor far better than the old fluorescents provided and all for free. The building super fucking loved free. I was about to go down the stairs when Juana's door flew open and the old woman poked her head out, looking at me.

"I thought you said you were meeting a friend."

Fuck. She'd heard us.

"I did meet a friend," I said, playing it cool.

"You said it was a woman," she said, wagging a finger at me and I blushed hot. I shifted my bag higher on my shoulder and ducked my head.

"I ran into that friend after dinner." Was all I said, but Juana's eyes narrowed at me and I knew she'd probably heard way more than I would have ever wanted her to. God, this is why I went to the Cairn and didn't bring men back to my apartment. Juana would have a fucking heart attack if she knew what I got up to. Last night had been tame. My skin prickled and I remembered Law ordering me to keep my hands flat to the table. Okay, last night was tamer than some, but not all.

I backed away towards the stairs wanting to be anywhere but standing around chatting to my sweet neighbor lady who had probably heard me cum on Law's face last night. And all of it during a thunderstorm that should have let me scream bloody murder and get away with it. Shit. Just how fucking loud had I been? "I gotta run, Juana. I have a-"

"Well, he must be a good friend if he got the lights fixed this morning, mija," she said, and I froze, one hand reaching out to steady myself on the banister.

"My what—he did what?" I managed to splutter out. Juana padded out into the hallway, wearing a lilac housecoat and fuzzy funny slippers that swished when she walked. She pointed a bony hand above us towards the lights and I followed her finger to see that the old fluorescents and their cheap metal coverings were gone. In their place were sleek new LED track lighting that ran the length of the hallway. I turned to see that not only were the lights replaced in the hall but also all down the stairwell.

"Holy shit," I whispered, leaning over the banister to see that the lights went all the way down to the ground floor. "He couldn't have."

"He did. He must really like you," Juana said, coming to stand beside me. She smiled hopefully at me and patted my shoulder. "Tell him thank you, will you? It was so nice for him to do it. They came early and were very quiet."

"How do you know my, ah, that my friend did it?"

"Because the work men asked for you when I wanted to know what was going on." Her hands went to her hips and she drew her small frame up, making me laugh. Of course Juana had wanted to know just what the hell was going on and who had ordered it, even if it was an improvement to the building. She was always in the know about stuff like that. "Said that it was for Honey, courtesy of," she paused and scrunched up her face, biting her lip, "Ay, mija, como se dice el nombre de su novio?"

Novio.

Fuck. Why was she pushing for me to get a man so badly? Didn't she know that relationships were just a mess? That they could leave you scared and looking over your shoulder? Questioning your own perception until you were so messed up you were angry his new woman didn't look like you?

Didn't Juana know?

"He's my friend," I replied, batting away her word choice with the deftness of a tennis pro.

Juana rolled her eyes. "Friend. Novio. He sounds Russian."

Yup. It had been Law all right. Sokolov was as Russian as it got around here.

"A mister Justice Soko-love?" she tried.

I burst into a belly laugh. "Close."

She shrugged and looked up, giving the new lighting a happy smile. "Tell him thank you," she said again, hands clasped against the pretty lilac of her house dress.

I nodded and gave her a fake smile, because I didn't have the heart to tell her that I was never seeing Law again. She looked too happy for me to tell her the truth.

"Of course. I'll tell him."

"Bueno, bueno." She clapped her hands and then gave me a push. "Go on, or you'll be late for work. You're always rushing around. It's bad for you."

I leaned down and kissed her cheek. "I'm fine," I told her, but I let her fuss. I liked it when she did. She waved me off and I hurried down the stairs, my eyes on the lighting the entire way down so much that I almost fell twice because I missed a step. I don't know why I was so focused on the new lights. It's not like there was going to be a note from Law attached to one of them. I pushed open the door and stepped out onto the sidewalk, phone out and checking the directions to my shift in Tribeca. It was only a five minute walk from the Cairn which would make tonight easier.

Thank god.

The walk to the subway was quick, the routine of the transit lulling me into an almost meditative trance. It was easy for me to zone out, go on autopilot and I welcomed it, letting the calm rush over me. My thoughts seemed to be nothing if not obsessed with bouncing between Law and Christian. The less I thought about either man the better.

When I arrived for my shift at the coffee shop, a trendy little spot with zero counter space but a steady supply of heavy tippers from what I remembered, I was happier. My smile was still brittle during my shift but as each hour crept by it relaxed some. The knowledge that my escape was that much closer edged me towards manic. At the end of my shift, I was practically bouncing off the walls, my blood singing in my veins with energy. My smile was infectious and all of the customers I spoke to left with more pep in their step. I knew I'd be getting a direct request through the app the next time the owner, Sally, needed a fill in.

"Always a pleasure, Honey." She smiled at me in the genuine way someone did when they wanted you around, and I liked that. It made it easier for me to imagine what it might be like if I did take the job with Tiffany at A Different Brew. I pulled out my phone and glanced at our messages from the night before. She'd let me know she was home and we had texted for a minute or so before she'd most likely fallen into a drunken slumber. I, on the other hand, had just really started my sobbing and brooding for the night.

'How you feeling today?' I texted her.

She replied nearly instantly. *'Amazing. That driver was smoking hot and that car drove like butter.'*

I smiled down at my phone while I walked. *'I'm glad you enjoyed the ride home.'*

'It was fucking awesome! I can't wait to get plastered around your fiancé *again ;)*

My smile faltered. I still hadn't told her the truth. I wasn't sure if I would, because how did you bring that up? Everything seemed more tangled now that Law had played along for the night. My phone buzzed with another text from Tiffany and I tabled my thoughts.

'You think on my offer to come work with me?'

Shit. The other big thing from last night.

'Kind of. Still thinking.' I sent back, because at least I was telling the truth there. I was still thinking about it. Still didn't know what I wanted to do when it came to putting down more roots in New York. You'd think after a decade that it would come easier to me, but it didn't. My little relationship blowing up with Christian hadn't helped...and thinking about him when a permanent job was being offered wasn't exactly doing wonders for my decision making.

'BOO! Okay, fine, I'm not gonna nag but I love you

and want you to come work with me. I'll drop it though. What are you doing tonight?'

My belly tightened. Yet, another secret I would have to keep from her. Another lie I would have to tell because I just didn't think she would get it. Get what I was doing by going to the Cairn. Then again, it was New York, maybe she *would* get it...My fingers hovered over my phone. I didn't want to lie to her, but I also wasn't sure, so I took the conservative approach.

'Got a book club, then helping my neighbor lady cook dinner.'

That seemed safe. It also seemed like a thing Tiffany wouldn't ask to come along to.

'So you're basically 85?' She sent back and I knew I'd picked the right activity to keep her from wanting to join.

'LOL. Yes, I am tonight and I'm loving it.' I looked up and saw that I was only a few doors down from the club, my feet had brought me here without much input from me, but now I had to go. *'Gotta run, just got to book club!'*

'You're such a nerd. Have fun!'

'Love you too.'

I shoved my phone into my pocket and sucked in a deep breath. The doors of the Cairn were imposing. They looked like they belonged out in some ancient

European city, or on the set of a movie where the explorer reaches paradise. They were huge, carved from dark stone that made me think of obsidian or jet. They seemed to suck in the light of the city, absorb it rather than reflect, which always gave them a bit of an edge. A little bit of a dark and scary fairy tale touch that made me think of the Grimm's brothers stories I'd read as a kid. Copper handles extended out, a patina of grey and green coloring the metal, and I hesitated for a second, fingers reaching but not touching.

Behind me a car passed by honking and a kid shrieked with laughter across the street. I could hear two women talking, their heels clicking on the pavement as they walked past me. All of it was mundane, so perfectly normal and at odds with the doors in front of me. The ones that looked like they'd been plucked from a dark fairy tale, but in this story the prince didn't save the princess or slay her dragons. She did it.

My fingertips touched the handle and then I was gripping it and pulling the door open. I did not have a prince charming, and I probably never would, but that didn't mean that I couldn't and wouldn't save myself. I slipped inside the club and closed the door firmly behind me, shutting out the normal world. The world where my power was fleeting and passing. I traded that world for the Cairn. And here, in this place, I had all the power—and that included saving myself.

"Hello, Honey," Connie greeted me from the desk she sat at. It was a polished black hunk of obsidian that gleamed in the gold-hued lights of the anteroom. The color of it was a perfect match to the dark hardwood floors of the club and the desk gave the appearance that it had seemingly sprung up from the floor. The lines of the desk were sharp and jagged but they added a touch of feral to the room that reminded me precisely what it was that I was surrendering myself to when I crossed the Cairn's threshold. The room was beautiful, at complete odds with the apartment I lived my life in. Where my home was sparsely decorated the Cairn was sumptuous in its furnishings. The walls were covered in wallpaper colored a shade of red so dark it was nearly black, gold gilt was brushed across some parts of it as if a painter had taken it to mind to brighten it up but then gotten distracted. The effect was beautiful and chaotic. Heavy crimson curtains ran floor to ceiling along the windows I knew to be black out. The effect created an inviting space that made you want to linger and appreciate the art on the walls, or the elegant furniture, a chaise lounge and a few leather backed chairs arranged around a fireplace with an obsidian mantle at the opposite wall.

Above us a sparkling chandelier glittered, casting

a golden light on everything, but mostly the black as night desk that seemed to absorb the golden light right into it as if it were a living breathing thing, and not a piece of furniture.

And then there was Connie. The woman I thought was Zeus.

She was sitting behind the desk with her hands pressed flat to the surface with a smile on her face. It wasn't a big inviting one, but it was a smile. One that softened her angular face enough that I knew I was welcome. I'd seen her cruel smile before. That one was a step above a snarl, features pulling into a mask of intense focus and bared teeth that left no meaning to just how very unwelcome the recipient was.

I hoped she'd used that sharp as knives smile on Christian.

"Connie, hi," I greeted her back with a wave. I walked forward, my sneakers hardly making a sound on the hardwood floor. "How have you been?" I asked.

She inclined her head and tapped the mouse beside her, the screen in front of her springing to life. "I've been well. It's been a few months since I've seen you. I hope everything is good for you."

We met eyes. I could see the unasked question there. Has Christian been bothering you?

I gave a slight shake of my head and then said, "It has been. A lot of work, but it's all been good. I'm happy to make some time for a visit though." I put my bag by my feet and stood awkwardly in front of Connie's intimidating as hell desk. I never knew what the fuck to do with my hands when I was standing here.

"Are you staying the night?" She asked, eyes sliding from me to the screen.

"Yes, if there's a room available."

"There is. Shall I book it?"

"Please. That's wonderful news." The weight I'd been carrying with me slipped off so suddenly and subtly that I almost pitched forward from its absence. My shoulders had been hunched since Law had left, the memory of him leaving pulling at me until every step I took felt as if I carried a thousand pounds on my back. Today had not been easy, even if I'd pretended it was.

"Wonderful." She smiled even as her eyes were still on the screen and she gave it a few clicks. "I've added it to your account, but before I do that I need to tell you one very important thing, Honey."

"What is it?" I asked on high alert.

She looked at me. "Christian is here tonight."

I sucked in a breath and took a step back, the weight that I'd shed suddenly all around me and in danger of suffocating me. I shook my head and snatched up my bag. "I don't-he's here? Now?" I asked, looking around me.

She nodded and looked remorseful. "He made his booking a month ago. I hadn't seen you through, so I assumed accepting the reservation would do no harm." Connie paused and leaned forward, one hand extended towards me though it lay flat on the desk. "I can see that I was wrong by the look on your face."

I tried to force my face into something that resembled calm even as my heart was racing. "No, I'm fine," I said automatically.

Connie arched an eyebrow at me. "You don't seem fine. I can deny his reservation, Honey. It's no trouble at all if it would put you at ease. Although, if he has held up his end of the probationary period, I would have to reach for a reason to send him away. So I will ask you once again, has Christian paid you unwanted visits or reached out to you? If he has, that would be a direct violation of the rules laid out by Zeus."

I wanted to lie. I wanted to say the bastard had, but I knew better than to lie to Connie. To Zeus. She —they—would find out the truth and then I would find myself on her bad side. I never wanted to end up there.

"No," I said quietly. "He's left me alone."

Connie fell silent as if considering her next move and she glanced back at the screen briefly before her eyes were trained on me once more. "I can still come up with something if him being here makes you uncomfortable."

I licked my lips and thought. Did it matter if he was here? He had left me alone since she'd spoken to him. Did I want to ride the train all the way back to Queens and then what? Spend the night and the next day moping that I had missed my chance at relaxing in the Cairn?

"Nothing will happen to me here though...right?" I hedged as I weighed my options. I couldn't run from Christian and get the rest and respite I needed. I'd been working so much lately, focused on what, I didn't know. It wasn't setting up a life, not really. I had one, but I did my best to stay loose and as untethered as I could. That wasn't normal. It couldn't be normal.

Somehow it had gotten worse lately. The evening with Law had just been the tipping point that had left me feeling low. I was grateful I had an evening planned here, and had done it before my night with Law. If I hadn't had it to look forward to I would still be crying my eyes out in my empty apartment.

I needed this place. I needed to hold onto my power for as long as I fucking could, anywhere I could find it. I wasn't going to be leaving, which meant I was going to need to know what I was walking into if I was sharing the halls of the Cairn with Christian O'Hanon.

She gave a slight tip of her head. "Nothing at all. You will be watched 24/7. Christian will be escorted off the premises if he steps out of line."

"What would constitute stepping out of line?" I asked.

She was silent for a beat before she answered me. "He is not to touch you. If he speaks to you and you do not consent to the communication, one of our team will end it immediately. Your boundaries will be enforced."

"And if they aren't?" I whispered, my voice small in the big room. At my back the fireplace crackled and I knew it was magical looking without even turning my head to see. The flames would be lively and warm, dancing against the black onyx of the mantle, so at odds with the cold feeling in my chest as I negotiated my stay with Christian's presence.

"Then he will be permanently banned from the establishment. I will also, of course, ensure that you are taken home in one of our private cars following your visit."

"If he steps out of line?" I asked, confused at her offer. It would make sense that I not have to head back out into the world with Christian now angry and on the loose.

"No," she said, giving me a kind smile, "I expected that seeing him would be intense for you. I know things can be overwhelming already given the nature of our club. You will be seen home even if he minds his manners and behaves himself."

Her offer was surprising, but I was glad for it.

"Thank you."

"Of course, your comfort is our concern." She stood from her seat and then gestured for me to follow her. "I'll show you to your room then, if you are ready?"

"I am."

Connie said nothing else just started walking, her steps were smooth and sure. She could have been fucking gliding like one of those movie vampires in comparison to how I was stumbling after her. I felt unsure on my feet, even in my sneakers. She glanced at me when I stumbled around a corner and pursed her lips.

"You have no reason to worry."

"I know. I'm not," I lied, hitching my leather bag higher on my shoulder. The smooth leather beneath my hands was reassuring. I focused on stroking a hand along the side of it and said again, "I'm not."

Connie gave a soft sigh of annoyance but she kept walking, pulling out a set of golden keys from her pocket. "Zeus has noticed you, Honey. You will be well taken care of during your visit."

That time I didn't just stumble, I nearly face planted. "I-what? He what?" Zeus didn't just notice anyone. I was barely convinced he was real.

She smirked, eyes still forward so that I could barely make out the expression by the upturn of her cheek. "You sound surprised." She was enjoying this, I could tell by the laughter I heard in her voice. That was...surprising. Connie was all business, but laughter?

What the hell was going on?"

"Well, yeah. It's Zeus," I said, as if she didn't know. As if the woman wasn't him when I swear she had to be.

"He's not that great," she muttered, stopping at a door and turning to face me. "But at times he can be useful in his interest, and you, Honey have caught his interest." She handed me a golden key. "This is on the house."

My mouth dropped open. The room we were standing in front of was not the normal one I was used to, which was a simple affair. Clean and simple, but still as elegant as the rest of the club with it's furnishings, even if it was small. Normally the room I took was just a bed and an ensuite bathroom.

Nothing more. Those doors were black wood, the same as all the other short term stays.

This door was golden to match the key she held out to me.

I'd heard about the rooms with the golden doors. Christian had told me about them, but we had never stayed in one. They were for VIPs, those Zeus favored. And try as he might Christian could never seem to break into their good graces. It had irked him to no end. A giggle bubbled up in me as I took the key from Connie.

Christian would shit bricks if he knew I was here and where I was staying. Good.

"Thank you," I said, because you didn't say no to a gift from Zeus. You took it for yourself with both hands and didn't bother to worry about the price. Whatever the cost it would be worth it for the brief moment in time that the world was yours. Zeus could give you the world within these walls and after the tumultuous night I'd had, the feeling of being adrift in my own life, just all of it…

I would take the world for my own, even if it cost me everything.

Connie winked. "Of course, Honey. As always it's a pleasure to see you," she started forward but paused beside me and turned her head to look at me in profile. She was so close I could feel the ghost of her breath on my neck and I shivered, suddenly aware of how close Connie was to me. Her shoulder was nearly brushing mine and if I reached out my pinky I would be touching her hand.

I stayed still, not daring to breathe.

"You will be safe. I promise you. Nothing will happen that you do not want." Her voice had dropped an octave, it was huskier now and I shivered under her unwavering attention. The woman was intense, but I liked that so I met her gaze as best I could while I waited for her to continue. "That you," she paused again and I could hear the pounding of my heart with each passing second. Connie moved, leaning closer to me, so that she was whispering in my ear, "do not ask for." I sucked in a breath, eyes closing at her last words. "Do you understand?" she asked.

"Yes," I whispered, eyes still closed, my fingers clutching the golden key so tightly I knew my palm would be sore and bruised when I let it go. Connie chuckled, the sound of it making me squirm. She had a good chuckle, the tone of it low and husky, practically reverberating through my body from my head to my toes. I heard her let out a soft sigh and for a second I thought she might touch me, but reason told me she wouldn't. The rules of the Cairn were strict. There was no touching unless it was agreed upon. This was a safe place, and Connie was at the helm of it. She would not touch me unless I asked her.

My insides warmed and shifted, arousal sliding over and through me like honey, coating it all in a sticky sweetness that nearly had me opening my mouth and asking her to touch me.

She could be Zeus. She's probably Zeus. My brain screamed at me, and I bit back the words.

As comfortable as I was in the Cairn and the lifestyle I would not and could not fuck around with someone as powerful as Zeus. I had survived Christian, but Zeus? If that went wrong, there would be no coming back from that for me. I needed to keep my mouth shut. But with the way she was standing, so close, the heat from her body radiating out and warm on the back of my hand that was nearly touching hers, the smell of her—a scent that was a mix of jasmine and sandalwood, floral, sensual and rich, and the sound of her voice...it was hard to remember that I needed to watch myself around Connie. The woman knew her way around a submissive, she was experienced and deft in the lifestyle. I knew that if I did spend time with her, ask her to touch me, that she would make it a weekend to remember.

Thankfully, I didn't have to put the limits of my self-discipline to the test. Connie ended it by moving away. I opened my eyes to see her grinning at me, eyes openly moving over my face and then down my body before she gave me a wink.

"Good girl." She turned and set off down the hallway with the same ethereal grace that made me feel awkward and tripping over my own feet to catch up. "Have fun tonight!" She called over her shoulder, wiggling her fingers in a goodbye.

I nodded but said nothing, eyes glued to her

figure until she was out of sight and around the corner. When I was sure she was gone, I sagged against the golden door. "Holy fuck," I whispered, forehead against the cool surface of the door. "Holy shit."

I let myself into the suite as soon as I had recovered enough strength in my legs to stand. I shut the door with more force than necessary and winced at the loud slam. "Fuck." I was off to a great start in my fancy VIP room, all right. I turned to survey the room and once again felt my knees go weak. I was used to rooms that were functional, meant for a stay and a night of play, but this?

This was luxury.

"It's beautiful," I said to no one, but it had to be fucking said. The room was open concept with the same dark flooring of the anteroom. A fireplace was here as well, a dark mahogany mantled thing that made me think of the historical museums I'd been in as a kid when on a road trip with my mom. We used to duck into the old houses and pay the couple of bucks to wander around while we waited for whatever club she was moonlighting in to open its doors to performers. In front of the fireplace was a green velvet settee with leather straps I could see folded across the length of it.

Across from the fireplace was a huge four poster bed made of dark wood. The posts of the bed were beautiful, less for function than for aesthetic, and I walked towards the bed to get a better look at them. The posts of the bed were works of art, like wood made lace, airy and light but undeniably strong. I could see the metal fasteners at the base of the posts made for straps or whatever rope its occupant might care to employ.

A forest green bedding that made me think of relaxation and indulgence. I reached out a hand, smoothing it over the impossibly soft bedding that would, if I had my way, see a fair share of action.

"This is fucking awesome."

To the left of the bed was a heavy desk that looked as antique as the rest of the room. But even from where I stood I could see the glint of an electronics hub peaking out at the side. It was meant for work. Not work that I did, but the kind of work someone who stayed in a golden room might do. I dropped my bag onto the seat in front of the desk and kept walking, through an archway and into a chef quality kitchen and dining room.

I clapped my hands excitedly at the sight of it. I opened the fridge and was hit with another wave of surprise when I saw it was fully stocked with food and drink. I reached in and pulled out a bottle of sparkling water and took a deep drink, enjoying the quiet of the rooms. I turned, seeing that glass lined this room treating me to a stellar view. It was beautiful now with the sun setting and coloring the room in hues of pink and gold. This was exactly what I needed. I reached back into the fridge and grabbed what looked like a fruit platter. I spied strawberries, blueberries, pomegranate seeds and kiwi slices all artfully arranged on a golden plate.

Who the fuck kept a whole fruit platter on hand just in case someone stayed in a room? Who kept a whole stocked fridge for that matter, on the off chance a guest might stay?

Zeus. That's who.

The contents of the fridge were easily more than I ate in a week. I was frugal with my purchases, buying in bulk, shopping in season and locally as much as I could in the weekend markets, and I cooked at home the majority of the time. I licked my lips, mouth watering at the sight of the fresh fruits arranged on the plate I held. It was beautiful, the dull golden gleam of the platter shone in the light of the sunset. I looked up from the plate and my mouth fell open when I saw that the windows lining the room were not just windows, but doors. I walked forward seeing handles on each windowed door and saw that they could be folded open to create a roomy balcony.

"Holy shit, yes," I murmured, making a beeline for the doors, sparkling water in one hand, my fruit platter in the other. There was a chaise lounge out on the balcony centered in a space that looked made to relax. It would be chilly with the rain from the day before but it could be freezing and I would have still spent my afternoon on the balcony. I toed off my shoes on the way and made myself at home. Whatever I was going to pay for this night of luxury, it was probably going to be a lot, so I might as well make myself at home. Zeus always collected, and I wasn't naive enough to believe my little slice of paradise would come at no cost. I would pay for this luxury down to the pomegranate seed, but I couldn't think of any better way to rack up a debt to Zeus than on a balcony in Tribeca treating myself at sunset.

CHAPTER THIRTEEN

LAW

"Well, well, well, look at what the cat dragged in..."

"That's a terrible saying, Connie."

She lifted one delicate shoulder in a shrug with a sunny smile. "A lot of things are terrible sayings, but that doesn't make them any less true."

I raised an eyebrow at her but said nothing, walking across the anteroom to her desk. "I'm glad you're in a good mood," I said. Connie was...lighter somehow. She was a calm and collected woman, but I knew she was prone to severity. I'd seen her joke and smile, been on the receiving end of both from time to time, but Connie was usually business. If she was making use of bad sayings and smiling at me there was a reason.

"What can I say? I woke up on the right side of the bed today."

"There's a reason. What is it?" I asked without disguising my curiosity. There was no need to hide anything from an old friend like Connie, and even if I tried she would figure me out if she had the motivation to do so. And besides, I had fuck all to hide here. The Cairn was one of the few places I let my guard down, and Connie was chief among those that I chose to be myself with.

If I was curious about her good mood there was no point in hiding it.

Connie leaned back in her chair, a huge monstrosity of angles and iron that I knew she would claim was avant-garde but just looked...uncomfortable. She somehow sat as unbothered and serene as any one had the right to. She shifted, one hand going to the iron armrest and drummed a red painted nail against the metal with a light tap.

"Oh, maybe because a person of interest has checked in. You know how I have my favorites."

"Is that so?"

She nodded. "Well, she's a favorite of mine but she's caught Zeus' eye. So you know how that goes."

My eyebrows went up. "Zeus?" I asked, unable to hide the surprise in my voice. "I thought he was just a front to keep the masses in line."

"A front? Like he isn't real?" She asked, and I

knew it was time to hide a little something from Connie. When Zeus came into play, there was always something to hide even when it came to a man like me. I was no fool.

"Never really crossed my mind that he was real," I lied.

She smirked. "Now why would you think he isn't real?"

"No one has ever seen him, that's why."

"Oh, plenty of people have seen him. But they're all smart and follow directions like good boys and girls." She rose from her seat and motioned for me to follow her. "This way, Law. I've got your rooms ready." She was clearly done with our conversation.

Interesting.

Who the fuck had ever seen Zeus? The club had been around since the 80's and I'd heard Zeus had never been spotted, even though this was his domain. It was a classic mob move. Keep the King hidden while the pawns kill themselves to gain clout, lose their real momentum to small wins and petty ploys that wouldn't get them a damn place while they convinced themselves they were real players. The King would watch it all unfold from a safe distance while his people took care of the day-to-day.

It was a game of strategy. One that was only successful with the right people working for him and I knew Zeus had that in spades. He had Connie, for one. The woman was formidable, smart and capable. She was more than enough to keep the idea of Zeus alive and looming over the club members. She was the perfect person to serve as a reminder of the absentee king none of us had ever seen or heard from.

"You know, come to think of it...you might like our VIP as well. She's a sweet thing." Connie was still walking ahead of me, not bothering to see if I was following, so I let my face show my surprise at her words.

"Who are you talking about?"

"Now, if I told you that would ruin the surprise, wouldn't it?"

I shrugged. "Depends. You know how I feel about surprises."

She laughed and pushed open a set of doors leading me down a hall I knew well enough. It was the wing I normally stayed in. All the doors here were a dull gold color, these were the rooms reserved for only the most connected of members. The utter lap of luxury available with full service and the power of the Cairn's own concierge to make your every whim possible. I saw the room I normally stayed in come into view and began to automatically slow but Connie did not. She kept right on walking as if she hadn't noticed a thing, but

I knew she had clocked my slowed steps when she spoke.

"We have a very important guest in that room this weekend."

"Oh, is that so?"

"Yes," she said, glancing at me over her shoulder then, "but don't you worry, we have a beautiful room waiting for you."

"Even though I'm not as important as the 'very important guest'?" I asked, giving her a wry smile.

"Zeus does have his favorites, but you will always be one of mine," she told me.

I chuckled and nodded at her. "Then that's all that really matters. I don't know Zeus."

"There are others who would give anything to have his favor."

I shrugged, making a show of looking nonchalant. "I play by his rules and respect his world," I gestured out at the hallway and the golden doors we were still walking past, "I know my place here. Respect the order and him. I think that's enough for a man like Zeus."

She hummed. "It is. He's very fond of order."

"I understand that." It was true. I did. Order ruled supreme in my world because order bought you peace. Peace I valued above all things.

"This is your room," she said, stopping at a door and holding out a key to me. "We have no planned events for tonight, but there may be an exhibition once I hear from the couple that was set to debut. I'll have dinner sent for you within the hour."

I took the key from her, nodding my thanks. "Thank you, Connie."

"Always a pleasure, Law." She made to move away but stopped and gave me a considering look.

"What?" I asked.

"I'll introduce you to the person in your room tonight. I have a feeling you'll both be...*suited*." The way she said suited made my stomach tighten. She had an eye for the types of subs that I favored. If Connie thought we would be a good match, chances were that she was right. "Would you like that?" she asked.

"I think we both know the answer to that," I said, opting to let her make her own inferences from my answer. The truth was I was suspicious. Why would she want me to meet this guest? Why would she be thanking me? That screamed set up. I'd worked for the mob for years. I knew a set up when one was shoved down my throat.

Connie's eyes glittered, but she didn't call me on my answer. Instead, she grinned. "Right then. Enjoy yourself and I'll make introductions after I've made sure she's settled in."

"Thank you," I said again and Connie waved me off.

"Don't thank me. You're the perfect little treat for our guest of honor tonight. It'll be me who's thanking you by the end of the night." She wiggled her fingers in farewell and turned on her spike heel. "Catch you later, Law."

I smiled but said nothing, just turned and entered my room. She had my curiosity working overtime. "A gift, huh?" I mused, entering the suite and shutting the door behind me. I glanced around, barely registering the details of this suite. Exposed brick and dark wood floors were the bones of this one. A large bed with white comforters and pillows took up the center of the room which was a far departure from the suite I normally stayed in. That suite was built for the comfort of a stay. It was meant to be lingered in and enjoyed, but this one seemed to be about functionality. There were no frills to it even if everything in it was luxe and tasteful. The walls that weren't brick were wallpapered dark grey with a raised brocade pattern. There was art on the walls, all of it oversized and bold. Studies in the Chiaroscuro style of art that heightened the dramatic focus of the room.

The focus on the big, fluffy white bed that looked like a damn cloud sitting in the middle of all of this darkness.

I turned my head, walking further into the room to see a room to the left, and glimpsed a shower head through the open doorway. So that was the bathroom which meant the other doorway that was currently shut would be the kitchen or dining room. I dropped my bag on the floor and started for the bed, pulling out my phone when a work email pinged through. The email would be a good distraction from the inkling of apprehension that was settling into my belly like acid.

The details of the room weren't important to me, but what the room said was. And it wasn't just speaking, it was practically screaming bloody murder at me.

If the focus was the bed, which from where I was now standing beside, it was one hell of a bed. I dragged a finger over the top of the comforter and then tested out a pillow. The comforters and sheets were all made of the finest material. Plush and buttery soft to the touch. It would be a dream for anyone that spent the night in it.

You're the perfect little treat for our guest of honor tonight.

Very fucking interesting, Connie.

What the hell was she up to? This room was little more than a space to play, to explore the limits and boundaries of a new play partner Connie clearly thought a lot of. Not just Connie, but Zeus. Why the hell were the two of them offering me up to someone?

I felt a wave of unease hit me. They were serving me up on a silver platter to a sub, and that didn't sit well with me. There were reasons they might do this, the biggest among them that they owed the sub something. A debt to be paid, some score they wanted to settle, and Connie had decided I would work as payment. I sighed and took a seat on the bed, fingers tight on my phone. I had pulled up a work email to scan through. Work was a good way to relax, it made sense to me, there was order to be found in the figures and deadlines that waited on me.

But this?

There was no order here. Not anymore. I'd come to the club to unwind. My night with Honey had left me so keyed up that I was going to be nothing short of a monster in the office on Monday if I didn't find a way to let some of the tension that settled into my bones out. I needed someone who understood my needs. A submissive that could hold my attention long enough for me to forget about Honey.

If I didn't I'd run the risk of ending up on her fucking doorstep by Saturday night. Worry, unfamiliar and powerful settled over me washing away the stress Connie and Zeus' meddling had stirred up. What if Honey didn't let me in? I had left her sitting with my goddamn spit and her own cream on her thighs without so much as offering to help clean her up.

I didn't leave women like that.

Not ever.

And now there was a woman I wanted, well and truly wanted, and I had walked out like a piece of shit.

"God fucking dammit," I growled out, tossing my phone to the side. There wasn't going to be any work getting done tonight. If I stayed tonight I was going to have to suck it the fuck up, grit my teeth and see what Connie and Zeus had up their sleeve.

We have a very important guest in that room this weekend.

Don't thank me. You're the perfect little treat for our guest of honor tonight. It'll be me who's thanking you by the end of the night.

My mind raced. I turned over Connie's words and stood from the bed to pace around the room. Who the fuck was that important? Why would they want me? Not only that, but why would Zeus and Connie be thanking me for it? I wasn't an idiot. I'd caught that little admission. An admission I knew was meant to butter me up.

In this world, a favor from Connie and Zeus was like winning a golden ticket.

I'd be a fool not to take it.

That didn't mean it didn't come without risk. I

had known Connie for years, considered her a friend and was comfortable enough to trust her with who I truly was, but that didn't negate the fact that I understood the games she played, or that her loyalties were to Zeus first.

Anyone else came second to Connie. It had always been that way. Always would be. If he'd taken a shine to someone and I had been brought into the game it was for a reason. I pulled off my suit jacket and walked to the closet beside the bathroom and hung it up. I was undoing my tie, thinking over the plausible reasons I'd been dragged into this mess when there was a rap at the door.

A spike of adrenaline shot through my body at the sound. What the fuck was this? I stalked towards the door, not quite ready for games no matter who was playing them. If it was something from Zeus or Connie, or even had a whiff of having to do with their VIP sub, then I was checking out. I'd been here all of half an hour and I was already more tense than when I had arrived.

Golden ticket or not, I was not going to be toyed with from the get go. At least let a man relax, shake the dust off himself. I reached the door and opened it with a jerk, fully ready to tell Connie I was done for the night, but there wasn't a person in sight. Only a cart with a tray topped with a golden cover, a bottle of whiskey, ice bucket and a glass sat on top of the cart.

Dinner. That's right. Connie had said she would have it sent up. I'd forgotten that with how wrapped up in my head I'd been. I relaxed slightly and pulled the cart in with one hand while I shut the door with the other. It was when I had the cart in the room that I saw a single sheet beside the bottle of whiskey. It was folded crisply in half, the ends of it held down by the bottle.

LAW was written across the top in a slash of ink, as if there would be any mistake of who the letter was meant for seeing as how it was delivered right to my door.

I let out a sigh and decided to pour myself a drink before I opened the letter. Leaving the club was still on the table for me, but the letter was feeding into one massive flaw that I had always suffered from.

Curiosity.

Connie knew exactly what she was doing. Knew that I was probably considering leaving the Cairn. I wasn't one to be played with, preferring to set the terms. And while that was my world outside of the club—it was not my reality here. The well timed delivery of dinner accompanied by the note was Connie's chess move to keep me exactly where she wanted me. I opened the bottle of whiskey and poured myself two fingers worth, adding ice to it before I picked up the letter. I stared down at the paper, it was heavy cardstock and I rubbed my thumb along the top of it for a second before I took a healthy swallow of my whiskey and opened the letter.

Law, it began in Connie's familiar handwriting.

The submissive you will meet tonight is under Zeus' protection.

"Fucking hell." I was right, there was a larger plan in motion tonight. This was not simply about a VIP's visit. But still. Why me?

You are truly the only Dominant in the club tonight to be trusted with her. You will be introduced in confidence by myself. Trust that I understand your tastes and she will be precisely your flavor. I have no doubt the pair of you will enjoy yourselves tonight.

I felt a prickle of irritation wake up in me. Had the submissive picked me out? Was this Zeus fucking hand delivering me to a submissive because I'd caught her eye? I didn't like the thought and took another deep drink from my whiskey, the ice tinkling in the glass when I set it down on the cart with a thud.

This submissive will be under stress tonight and for that reason you would be the perfect company for her to keep. You will, of course, be compensated heavily by Zeus for your presence.

"Of course, of course," I muttered. I poured myself another whiskey, not even bothering to measure. I must have filled half the glass and picked it back up with a weary sigh. I'd come to the club to relax, to burn off the fire Honey had given me, not play fucking babysitter.

I know you hate games.
Sorry about that.
Connie
PS: Give the girl a chance!

I stared at the exclamation point for a beat. That one slash and a dot at the end of her postscript annoyed the hell out of me. She knew exactly how my mind worked and that I was ticked about this new development. When I'd been the eyes, ears and fists of New York's mobs and gangs I'd played babysitter plenty of times. A mafia princess trying to assert her independence, a spoiled daughter on her quinceañera, the Bratva's oldest fuck up son on a bender that needed drying out.

I'd done it all at some point.

The reason for that was because I could be trusted to do a job, any job, keep my cool and keep my mouth shut about it. It had all been for the greater cause of getting my freedom and getting the fuck out of the life. Babysitting had been low stress, even with the biggest of tantrums thrown by my charge, or whatever fuckwits had thought they could make a name for themselves by coming after what was mine. My fingers tightened on the cool glass of my whiskey and I glared at the stupid painting in front of me. A woman half bathed in light, beautiful face half obscured by the dark. She wore a deep green dress that flared out behind her as if caught by a gust of wind, the skirt of it melted into the shadows giving the appearance that she was running. She had to be running, or in motion of some kind with the figure that was behind her. Only an arm was visible against the verdant green of her skirts, the fingers seeking but missing her as she ran forward. I'd been good at my job because I thought of who I was paid to protect as mine. They weren't just a job, or a payday, they were mine.

No one fucked with what was mine.

Connie knew that. And she was using that knowledge now to her and this VIP's advantage. She and the almighty pain in my ass Zeus were asking me to think of the submissive as mine for the night. If I took this on, tonight would not be about relaxing or finding release, but about protecting what was mine. My fingers twitched and I swirled the whiskey in my glass around, staring into the amber depths of it.

"You don't have to do this," I told myself. I hadn't taken a job in years. This wouldn't be the same as it had been when I was working to go legitimate. I knew that. But a job was still a job, and that's what this was. I tossed back half the contents of my whiskey glass and lifted the lid on the platter to see a dish of pasta with red sauce, a steak sat on another plate alongside fresh bread and a side dish of salad, and I hummed in approval. At least I wouldn't be going hungry if I stayed.

"You can leave," I said, even as I already knew what I was going to do. I closed my eyes briefly and tossed back the rest of the contents of my glass before I rolled the cart towards the dining room. The familiar adrenaline that had always accompanied a job that I took was already surging through me, the high of it reminding me that even if I had talked myself into accepting boardroom conferences and multi-million dollar deals as substitutes, there was nothing like this.

This reminded me I was alive. The unknown, the thrill of that had my heart thudding in my chest, blood pumping through my veins like a damn freight train. Connie had played her hand right.

I was taking the job.

Whatever Zeus was willing to offer me had better fucking be worth it.

CHAPTER FOURTEEN

HONEY

The fruit had been delicious even if I'd stained my jeans by way of an errant pomegranate seed that had fallen between me and the chaise lounge cushion I'd been laying on. It had stained the damn pristine cushion as well. Fuck.

I'd flipped the cushion and made a hasty exit from the balcony, content to pretend that I hadn't been the culprit even though the suite and every single thing in it was perfectly kept. There really wouldn't be any hiding that I'd been the one to make a mess, but I figured a pomegranate stain was small potatoes to Connie and Zeus.

"She has to be Zeus," I whispered even though there was no one else in the room. Until I saw the both of them together, Connie and Zeus, I wasn't going to think any differently on the matter. It would make sense that Connie was Zeus—she'd been the one to personally tell Christian to fuck off, after all. She wouldn't like knowing her order had been defied. But her concern went deeper than that, or at least I thought so.

Connie was formidable but I'd seen how she treated club members she had no invested interest in. Impersonal. Detached. Polite? Of course. Civil and professional? Always. But with no more personality than if they were getting checked in for a dentist appointment.

I set the platter down in the sink, rinsing it and drying it, my thoughts wandering. I remembered the heat of Connie's skin against my hand. The low sound of her chuckle, the way she'd practically had me begging her to touch me.

Connie liked me.

I wouldn't be in this room if she didn't.

The almost...the almost, I frowned, walking from the kitchen and into the bedroom. What the fuck had that even been in the hall? The almost seduction? The unspoken offer from Connie to be the one I chose tonight.

I flushed and licked my lips. I hadn't thought she'd noticed me like that, but now that I knew I couldn't shake the knowledge. It was a heady thing to be wanted by a person like Connie. She was a switch, but her tastes leaned far more towards Dominant. I'd seen her with her ex-lover, an idiot model that had somehow charmed her. But the relationship had been fleeting, coming and going as quickly as an early morning frost. Connie was highly selective in her partners. To be chosen by her was a mark of pride among the submissives and I only knew one or two that had enjoyed the privilege of it. There was no mistaking the fondness in their eyes when the woman entered the room, face impassive until it landed on one of them and she smiled. When Connie smiled it had the power to warm the entire room, the focus of her expression transforming into the personification of joy and desire.

On the nights that Connie smiled at a submissive was the night they became the most sought after partner in the club. Everyone wanted to know what it was that had pulled Connie towards them, everyone wanted a taste of it, even if it was second hand. I was flattered she'd shown interest in me, even if it made me nervous. Even if I knew better than to play around with a woman like that.

Christian is here tonight.

I sucked in a deep breath and held it tight. I counted to ten and then slowly let it out before doing it again. I'd picked up breathing exercises to keep myself calm after Christian had stalked me. The anxiety of those months had grown until nothing it seemed could bring me back down. Nothing really had, not until Connie had interfered and Christian had disappeared altogether.

And now he was here and I was fucking doing breathing exercises like I was practicing for Lamaze.

I let out my last breath and balled my hands into fists by my sides. "I'm not going to let him ruin this for me. You'll be protected," I reminded myself. "Connie said so," I added, hoping it would give me the confidence I needed. The truth was I was shaking like a leaf, even if I had the protection of the club to make sure I was safe tonight. I held out my hand and grimaced, seeing my fingers trembling. It was going to take me seeing Christian for this to wear off. Otherwise I would be jittery and anxious in the lead up to it.

"Find him first thing," I ordered myself, crossing the room to the closet where I had stored my things. "Rip the bandaid off as fast as you can. And when you see he's nothing to be scared of, you'll relax."

Maybe it was all in my head. Maybe I had made Christian out to be worse than he was, I tried to reason with myself while I got ready, shaking out the curls I had made earlier and brushing them into something softer. Maybe Christian wouldn't even take notice of me if he was there with someone else. I couldn't imagine he would set foot in the club otherwise. He wouldn't risk the embarrassment after the last time. I dressed in the gown I had packed and smiled, feeling it's silky fabric swishing around my legs as I walked into the bathroom to apply my makeup.

I would go with drama. Tons of drama. Smoky eyes, false eyelashes, thick eyeliner, contouring to accentuate my already high cheekbones. A bold red lip that would say 'fuck you' to any and all that glanced my way. Not that I needed to say it to many people, just one in particular. Just one asshole I wished had never been a part of my life.

Maybe tonight will be good. *Maybe, maybe, maybe...*

I rolled my eyes at my reflection and focused on my makeup. I knew all the maybe's in the world were really just wishful thinking.

Your boundaries will be enforced.

Christian was here. It was going to be a weird night. Even if he wasn't allowed to harass me, or touch me.

"Connie said," I told my reflection moving on to my eyelashes. The words had power in the Cairn, but here in the emptiness of my suite, where I stood alone, barefoot in a dress far too fine for me, and painting my lips crimson for armor, the words sounded painfully weak and paper thin.

What would it really do if Christian set his mind to something? He was obsessive. I knew that. It was one of the reasons I had fallen for him. The drama and intensity of his desire had been intoxicating, and I had grown up with mommy issues. I craved that sense of belonging and care from another person even if I did my hardest to ignore it. Christian had fed those needs until I was his and then he'd changed.

Everything had changed.

I shook my head. "We are not going there. Not now. Not tonight." I put down my mascara wand with a snap of my hand and snatched up my perfume bottle, spritzing myself and then turned heel and left the bathroom with a slap of my fingers on the light switch. I pulled out the strappy gold heels I'd brought and went about putting them on, forcing my brain to focus on the straps of it, delicately and securely tying them up. When I was done, I gave myself a final once over in the gilded mirror propped up on the wall beside the bed.

The heels added just enough height to me that I became statuesque in the best of ways, the dress's color accentuated the tan of my skin, my makeup the right blend of drama and simplicity that insisted I belonged anywhere I chose to go, my long dark hair fell in soft waves, spilling over my shoulders and back, a lovely contrast against my dress.

The woman staring back at me was beautiful. She was perfect and serene, or you'd think so, if not for her eyes. If you didn't look at her eyes you'd think she was a goddess returning home. I swallowed hard and looked at myself, looked right into my eyes and saw the fear in them.

Christian is here tonight.

I closed my eyes and took in a shuddering breath. The man still had a hold on me that sent a blast of fear straight through me, nearly rendering me immobile. I hated feeling like this. Hated knowing that a person was responsible for it. I opened my eyes and looked back into my reflection. Yes, I looked perfect and confident, except for my eyes.

"Fuck."

Was it too late to tell Connie I needed to leave? Could I make a hasty exit, or maybe just not leave my room and-

There was a sharp rap at the door and I let out a yelp, jumping slightly at the noise. I stared at the door in silence, eyes wide and the only thought that came to me was 'what if it's him.'

"He doesn't know you're here," I insisted, and forced myself to start moving. "He can't." I said the words out loud because a long time ago I'd had a therapist teach me that anytime my thoughts got too loud, made me start to panic, that I needed to look at where the fear was really coming from. Was it being told to me by the outside world, or was it coming from me? From my own thoughts? If it was the latter, I had to remind myself the only fear I was responding to was from inside my head. If the only threat were the words I was repeating then the threat wasn't truly there, was it?

Talking out loud was a way to break the loop of anxiety that had a tendency to spin out of control when I was stressed.

"He doesn't know you're here," I said again, forcing myself to say it louder. "It's not him." I moved then, crossing the room and making for the door. "He isn't there. It's not him," I said, heart racing. I reached for the door and opened it quickly before I lost my nerve. A cart greeted me, not a person in sight. A nervous giggle escaped my lips. I'd been worried and there wasn't even a staff member to be seen.

There was nothing on the cart save for a note with Connie's familiar handwriting on it but I wheeled it into my room all the same. I shut the door and stared down at the letter with big scrawling black lines that simply said *Honey.*

I reached out and picked up the crisply folded paper. It felt creamy and luxurious beneath my fingers, because of course it was just like everything else in this place—-the very best. I unfolded it and bit my lip, eyes scanning the paper.

Honey, it began, and seeing my name in Connie's

writing helped me relax slightly. She'd taken the time to do this herself.

I know you're nervous but you have no reason to be. I've arranged company for you to enjoy yourself. Tonight will be utterly beautiful. Trust me.

Yours,

Connie

I re-read those last two words. Trust me. She knew I was nervous and she was assuring me that I had no reason to be because she had taken care of it. I wiggled my bottom lip between my teeth, not caring that I was probably ruining the lipstick I had just carefully applied. What did she mean by company, exactly?

PS- There's champagne in the fridge. I insist you enjoy a glass before tonight.

I smiled seeing the postscript and dropped the letter onto the cart. I walked to the fridge and opened it taking a clearer inventory of what was in it. Earlier I'd grabbed the fruit platter and not paid much attention beside that. But now I saw that there was not just a single bottle of champagne, but there were several, alongside other food that I might want to try. "Is that a chocolate cake?" I whispered, leaning in to see that it was, indeed, a chocolate cake. I was going to eat at least half before I left. No doubt about it. I pulled a bottle of champagne from the fridge and took my time pulling the wrapping free and popping the cork. It made a satisfying popping sound and I dropped the cork onto the counter, snagging a champagne flute from the cabinet. Once I had poured my drink, I took a dainty sip and sighed. It was cool and sweet, bubbly in just the right way that woke up my senses and broke through the panic I'd been spiraling in.

I took another sip and then drained the glass, which I promptly refilled with more bubbly. I didn't normally drink at all when I came to play, but this was different. My nerves were jangling so loud I could practically feel them trying to burst through my skin. Liquid courage was essential if I was going to make an appearance at all outside of this room.

I wandered back over to the cart, heels clicking lightly on the hardwood and stopped beside it. The paper was laying where I had dropped it and I touched it again, smoothing it out with two fingers.

Yours, Connie

I didn't miss the yours she had included. Connie had never been overly sentimental with me and this was new. What if it was her that would be keeping me company tonight?

I flushed hot, skin going prickly with all the energy of a live wire. If it was her then tonight was going to be something all right. I took another hasty sip from my drink before I set it down and made a beeline back to the bathroom.

I needed to double check my makeup and get the hell out of my room before I drank the entire bottle and refused to come out. Or worse, actually, I could drink the bottle and show up ready to lay into Christian. I shook my head and carefully fixed my lipstick. I wanted neither of those to happen tonight.

For the second time that night I turned the light off and walked towards the suite's door. The gold key Connie had given me was hanging on a hook beside the door and I took it, looping the leather string it hung on around my wrist for safekeeping. I stared at the polished gold of it, my reflection dully visible in the smooth surface. I could see my outline, the shape of a woman that was, at this angle, unafraid and standing with her shoulders back and head high.

I could be that woman, even if it was a lie.

I lifted my head and reached for the door. I could pull this off and enjoy myself.

"No, you *will* enjoy yourself," I corrected myself aloud. I reached for the door and opened it. The hallway was empty when I left and locked my door, which was both a blessing and a curse. I had never spent much time in this wing and I was unsure of which way to go, but I more or less remembered the direction Connie had brought me from and turned left, setting out that way.

I only had to walk for a minute or two before I

heard the familiar din of laughter and voices echoing from up ahead. Adrenaline flooded my veins but I kept my gait slow and smooth. I would not panic. I would not fucking do it and give Christian the satisfaction of knowing he still had a hold on me. I exited the hallway and turned to the right, grateful to see that I was now standing in the Great Room which served as the heart of the club. Here there was a wide open space, the room dark like the rest of it.

High above us was a massive chandelier that bathed the room in a wash of golden light. It softened the hard edges of the room and gave it a romantic touch that instantly enticed you into wanting to explore. I stepped up out of the hallway I was in and into the room and walked slowly around the perimeter of it, glancing towards the bar at the left side of the room. There was a series of hallways from the other guest suites and all of them emptied into a longer passageway that circled the Great Room that rose above it. I could see people milling about in the lower corridor, their curious eyes on who had already claimed space within the Great Room. All around the room there were groups of couches and seats for people and couples to enjoy, and at the center of the room was a small raised platform which told me there would be an exhibition of some kind tonight.

That would be fun. It would also be perfect for

blending in with the rest of the crowd. No one would be looking my way if they were all focused on the stage. I tried to be discreet in my search for Christian, but when I saw that I had caught more than one person's eyes in my quest, I stopped and took a seat on a plush pouffe looking thing at once.

I would stay here and regroup, then make for the bar and order myself a drink. Something to hold and an opportunity to do another scan of the room. I was sure Connie would find me soon, but I wanted to get my bearings as quickly as possible. Best to not be surprised if I could help it. I took in a deep calming breath and lifted my head, taking care to meet the eyes of anyone that looked my way. I gave them a slight smile and turned away again, hoping it came across as pleasant. I did want to meet people tonight, but given the circumstances…

It was going to be rough.

After a minute more, I rose from my seat and made my way towards the bar. When I got there it was busy and I stepped to the side preparing to wait my turn for a drink when Connie's voice was suddenly in my ear.

"Why do you look nervous?"

I jumped with a jerk. "I'm not nervous."

She snorted and gave me an assessing look. "Then why did you jump just then?"

My hands went to my hips and I tossed my hair

over my shoulder. "Because that's what any reasonable person does when someone is suddenly talking in their ear. You surprised me is all."

She grinned. "Good. I meant to."

It took everything in me not to roll my eyes at her. "Gee, thanks."

"Why are you waiting in line?" She asked, brushing past me and towards the bar. "I gave clear instructions that you were not to wait tonight."

"Well, I mean, I don't know. I just sort of-" I began, but Connie was already at the bar with people stepping quickly to the side and a bartender hurrying towards her. She bent close to them, a finger motioning in my direction. The bartender's eyes flicked towards me and they gave a slight nod at whatever order she was giving. Then Connie looked back at me and hit me with a dazzling smile, gesturing for me to step forward.

"Honey, come here, won't you?"

A hush fell around us as other club members noticed me. I came forward, feeling the weight of every person's eyes on me as I did so. Shit, shit, shit. My plans to stay out of view and not attract attention were out the goddamn window now. Not with Connie's smile on me like that. It was like a spotlight, and now, now she had me at the bar and was introducing me to the bartender as if we were long lost friends.

"This is Stephan, you'll take care of my lovely Honey, won't you?" She asked.

"Of course, anything." He met my eyes and winked at me. "Anything," he said again, and there was a heat in his eyes that hit me square between my thighs.

"Ohhh, I don't think he just means drinks," Connie purred, leaning towards me. I flushed but said nothing and nodded my hello to Stephan with a quick 'thank you.'

"What will you have?" He asked.

"He definitely doesn't mean to drink," Connie informed me, but for all her commentary she was leaning against the bar looking bored as anything. That is until she was looking at me. Then it was the full strength of her smile and attention. Jesus, this woman could knock you off your feet and you would thank her for it.

"A Cosmo, please," I ordered quickly, because it was the only thing that I could think of with Connie staring at me like she was.

"Coming right up," Stephan said, and he looked away then, making the drink for me. I was grateful he did, because I wasn't entirely sure how I was supposed to manage both his and Connie's attention at once and remain upright.

"Did you get my letter?" Connie asked.

I nodded. "I did. Thank you."

"And did you have champagne?" She wanted to know.

"I did."

"Well done, lovely girl."

I flushed under the praise, even if it was for something so minor as having a glass of champagne. "I didn't do anything, though…"

"You followed directions," she said, with a shrug. "It doesn't matter the task. You know that, Honey."

She was right. I did.

"What was it about company for tonight?" I asked, choosing to follow that thread.

"Ah, yes, that." She pushed up from the bar and stood taller, turning her head to scan the crowds.

"Yes, that, what do you mean by that?"

"It's not a that, *but a him*," she told me and then tutted, clicking her tongue against her teeth. "He hasn't arrived yet, I'm afraid, so you'll have to make do with little old me until then."

A him. What the fuck did she mean by that?

"Sorry?" I asked, leaning towards her. I was dimly aware that Stephan had returned and placed my drink in front of me with probably a drop dead gorgeous smile on his handsome face, but I wasn't here for that. I wanted answers and Connie had them. "What do you mean a him?"

"For your company tonight, Honey," she said,

glancing towards the bar and reaching past me to slide the Cosmo my way. "Thank you, Stephan. This looks lovely." She inclined her head in a way that was very clear. Move on. A second later Stephan glided away, but I still didn't turn my head to look, nor did I take stock of the cocktail Connie was placing in front of me.

I shook my head still not understanding. "But when you sent the letter I thought-"

She moved so that her front was to the bar and her side was to me. "What? That it was me that would keep you company tonight?" She asked, turning her head to the side, tilting it just enough to give me a little smile.

I blushed hot and snapped my mouth shut. "I-I, it's just that..." I was stammering. I sounded foolish, I knew this, but it was hard not to when Connie was expectantly looking at me for an answer to such a loaded question.

"It's alright if you did. I would be honored," she said, when I only managed the semblance of a sentence that sort of came out as a breathy 'no, no, not that. Sorry.'

I dropped my eyes to the bar at her answer. I was still looking down at the bar when she slid the drink next to my hand. "Drink up, darling."

"I don't know if I should..."

"You'll have eyes on you and a chaperone, so to

speak. There's no worries about what might or might not happen."

I lifted my head and stared at her. "What do you mean a chaperone? I thought you said it was company."

She raised her hands in a placating gesture. "It is, it is."

I felt a finger of apprehension slide down my spine and I picked up the cocktail, eyeballing the contents warily. "Why do I feel like something is going on and you're trying to keep me out of the know?"

"I would do no such thing," Connie replied, lifting one hand to her chest and giving me what I supposed she thought was a look of honesty. It wasn't. She wasn't fooling anyone. The woman was far too steeped in the foundation of the Cairn to play innocent. I was right, but what the hell was going on? I had thought it was her, but now that I knew it wasn't my earlier anxiety began to flood in around me.

"And speaking of your esteemed company for the night, I see him now."

I whirled, the cocktail in my hand, the contents spilling over the side as I did so, splashing my toes when it hit the ground. I winced at the messy gesture. I lowered my eyes when I saw the club members milling about us had also seen it. Fuck. A man leaned in to whisper to his partner about it, eyes on my feet. A woman dressed head to toe in leather pursed her lips at the wasted liquor and turned, walking away with her partner who gave me a reproachful glance.

They thought I was drunk.

I wasn't drunk, I wanted to scream. I was nervous. I was a ball of anxiety and barely holding it together because I knew that somewhere out there my stalker ex boyfriend and Dom was waiting for me. But not only that, I was nervous as hell because Connie had a plan sprung and I was the idiot that had walked right into it. I had to admit that my plan to pay the price for a night of luxury had made a lot more sense when it was just me and a balcony eating fruit like a hedonist.

But now that I was smack dab in the Great Room and Connie was talking about *a him* and there didn't seem to be a pair of eyes that hadn't moved my way and lingered at some point in the handful of minutes I'd been here, I wasn't so sure. It no longer felt like I was being gifted a beautiful evening, but that I was a pawn in someone else's game.

I didn't like it one bit. Not even a little half of a bit.

"Connie look, I can handle myself tonight. I promise you won't need to-" I began while scanning the room again, the sticky cold feel of the spilled

Cosmo coating my fingers when I took a hasty sip, because I had no other idea what to do with the damn thing now that I was holding it.

"Ah, about time you joined us, Lawson."

I nearly spit the half sip of Cosmo that I'd just taken when Connie interrupted me. Lawson. There was only one Lawson that I knew, only one that I wanted it to be, but there was no way it was him. *There couldn't be.*

"Honey." It was one word, gruff and disapproving, and I knew that voice, would know that voice from anywhere. It didn't matter if days or years had passed between the last time I had heard it and now. I wouldn't mistake it for anyone but the man I had been left wrecked by within the last 24 hours. He stepped out of the crowd as if by magic and was there in front of us, in another impeccable suit, this one dark blue. A perfect shade that matched his eyes.

Eyes that were on me. Eyes that were angry.

Why was he so angry?

"What the fuck is going on?" He asked, looking at Connie and immediately. I missed his stare. Even if he was angry, I wanted Law's eyes on me. I didn't care what his eyes were saying so long as they were on me.

Connie gave a breezy shrug. "Exactly what I told you in your letter, Law. This is our VIP guest that we need you to keep company tonight." She gestured towards me with a flick of one red tipped nail and then inclined her head to look at him. "Or is there a problem?"

"The problem is I didn't come here to play babysitter," he bit out.

I jerked back as if he had slapped me, because that was exactly what it felt like. "What?" I whispered, fingers squeezing the Cosmo glass stem.

Law's eyes were back on me and I realized that maybe I had been wrong. Maybe I didn't want this man looking at me when he was looking at me with contempt. What had happened to make him look at me like this? Hadn't he eaten my pussy like a dying man? He'd had all the lights in my building changed because he'd thought they were dangerous, for fuck's sake!

You were lovely.

He had told me that, so why was he looking at me like this?

"You're drunk," he said as if that explained everything.

"No, I'm not."

"The drink you practically spilled all over yourself says otherwise," he told me, pointing down at the floor with one of his stupidly well formed thick fingers. I licked my lips looking at that finger. I knew what that finger felt like pumping inside of me. What it could do when he used it against my clit.

I squirmed, pressing my thighs together and forced myself to match his gaze even though I half felt like throwing my drink in his face.

"I'm not, so save your concern for someone else, Law."

"Ohhh, I see you two know each other?"

I gave a shake of my head. "We don't."

Law's jaw squared and he stepped in closer to me, boxing Connie out. "We do."

"I don't know this man," I said, turning my head and ignoring him. I raised my glass to take a sip but Law's hand shot up and he snatched it from me, placing it on the counter behind me with a jerk of his arm.

"You've had enough, little girl."

My mouth parted and I sucked in a sharp breath. *Little girl.* I looked up at him, which was hard with how close we were, I had to crane my head back to do it. "You don't tell me what to do," I told him, even though my body was waking up at his behavior. My brain was screaming that Law was into what I liked, that what I had wished and hoped for last night was true. Why else would he be here?

"What the hell is she doing here? You did this, didn't you?" He asked Connie, as if I hadn't spoken.

She held up her hands. "I did no such thing. Honey made her reservation of her own volition. Same as you, Law. Same as anyone in attendance.

And I can see that you two know each other, so what's with the conflicting stories, hmm?"

"I'm sorry, I know Lawson Sokolov. Not this man."

"Honey, I swear to god..."

I moved away and tried to get past him, but he moved in front of me barring the way. "Get out of my way, Law."

"That's not happening, Honey."

"Honey, darling," Connie said, breaking in between us with one arm that forced Law back a step, "this is your company for the night. Your chaperone, as I told you."

"I don't want him. He can keep his company."

"Oh, believe me, I'd love nothing more than that."

Tears stung my eyes at the acid I heard in Law's voice, but I refused to let him see how he affected me. "You're a real asshole, you know that?" I said instead, and was proud my voice only slightly wavered.

"And you have no self control when it comes to making sure you're safe. If you think I'm going to let you walk around here sauced and looking like you do, you're out of your mind."

"I'm not drunk," I hissed at him.

"The fuck you aren't. I can see a pattern here, Honey. You're irresponsible and you drag other people in to clean up your shit. That's what I'm doing tonight, isn't it? I'm the fucker on clean up duty courtesy of Zeus. What did you do? Figure out I came here and cash in a favor to make this happen? You knew who I was last night, didn't you?"

I gasped, a hand raising to cover my mouth and I looked at Connie. "I have to step away. I can't listen to this anymore."

Connie gave me a nod. "Move it, Law."

His blue eyes went to her and I could tell he didn't like being told to move not once, but twice. He clenched his jaw, but said nothing and remained exactly where he was standing, which was right in front of me.

Connie's eyes narrowed. "Now."

There was a tense moment where I didn't think the big man would move, but then he was, even if he looked like he hated every second of it. When he was far enough back I darted forward, hurrying through the crowd and looking for somewhere quiet to put myself back together. How could he have said that to me? I wasn't irresponsible. I was highly independent to the point of veering on isolation. I had never brought another person down with my shit, as Law called it. Even if I had known who he was and where to find him I would have never resorted to forcing him to spend time with me. I wasn't drunk now, I was nervous and god, who wouldn't be? And last night?

Last night I had needed to blow off some steam, and I hadn't been alone. Tiffany and I had been having a great time until, until...until I'd gotten lost on the way to the bathroom and this whole stupid thing had started.

I hurried through the crowd and it parted in front of me. Connie's sway was useful in a moment like this, but it also meant they had seen the whole thing. I blinked back against the tears that had once again welled up in my eyes. I wouldn't cry. I wouldn't do it just because an idiot who had given me an orgasm mouthed off to me. I had done a lot of stupid things in my life, but crying over Lawson Sokolov twice in 24 hours was not going to be one of them.

Down the steps I went, down into the corridor that ran along the perimeter of the Great Room and it was only there, when I had ducked into an empty alcove beside a potted plant, that I sagged against the wall with a gasp that told me I was wrong.

I was totally crying because of Lawson Sokolov, and there was just no helping it.

"Fuck," I swore, dabbing at my eyes with the backs of my hands. My make up had taken time and effort and I was ruining the whole damn effect because Law had what? Told me shit I already knew he thought about me? There was no way what he'd said hadn't crossed my mind while I lay in bed staring at the rapidly brightening sky. I'd known it then as surely as I knew it now. He'd told me exactly what he thought of being with me the minute he walked out of my apartment with no intention of coming back.

I just didn't expect it to hurt this much hearing it come out of his beautiful mouth.

"Fuck," I whispered again, sniffling. I put one hand on the cool marble of the pillar beside me and forced myself to stand up. I wasn't going to cry in the corner tonight. I was going to get it the fuck together and keep my head high. I was going to enjoy some of the clout Connie's attention had gotten me in the club and I was going to---

"Well, well, well...what do we have here?" A voice drawled, and my eyes went wide. "I didn't think I'd see you tonight, but here you are and looking pretty as a picture."

For the second time that night I was hearing words from a man that I could have just fucking done without.

I took in a shaky breath and pushed away from the wall, turning to face the man that had sent me into the anxiety spiral I was currently slipping away in. Law's bullshit had been the icing on the cake, but this man? This man was the cake, and that cake was made of shit.

"Christian," I said, crossing my arms over my chest.

The man that I had once thought I loved, or maybe even did but had learned not to, was standing nonchalantly in front of me. Not even five feet away, he was so close I could see every bit of him in hi-def. He looked good. His blond hair combed neat, gray eyes cool and indifferent, though they weren't looking anywhere but at me. He was attired like he usually was when we had been together. Tailored slacks, designer dress shoes, impeccably pressed dress shirt with the sleeves rolled up, this I knew he did to show off the expensive timepiece he normally wore.

It was a well put together outfit that showed his wealth without implying he was trying too terribly much. Christian was always a fan of making sure everyone knew just how unimpressed he was to be in their presence. He would never go all out for the Cairn. I watched him consider me, eyes moving slowly over me from the top of my head down to my gold heeled feet and he let out a low whistle.

"You're looking delicious."

I shivered and tossed my hair over my shoulder. "What do you want?"

He raised an eyebrow. "You know what I want, but I'm not sure you're game to give it to me.'

I felt my blood turn cold. "What the hell are you

going on about, Christian?" I dared to look to the side hoping I would see some of the protection Connie had spoken of, but there was no one in sight. There was a commotion in the Great Room and I knew whoever was having their debut tonight was taking the stage. All eyes would be on them. No one would think to look down here in the shadows for me.

Perfect timing for whatever this was, but I wasn't surprised. Christian had planned it this way. Of course he had. He'd thought of this and made his move at the perfect moment. The man with the plan. He always had one.

Why hadn't I thought of it? How could I have been this careless?

Because you were fucking crying like an idiot over Law, and maybe you are a tiny bit drunk, my brain informed me and I scowled, hating the taste of the truth.

"You shouldn't frown," Christian told me, taking a step closer to me. "You'll get wrinkles. You know that."

I took a step back mirroring his movement, and collided with the potted plant beside me. I took a wobbly step away from it. Christian had been forever trying to get me to get Botox as a 'preventative measure' because he liked how 'youthful' I looked. I'd almost done it before I remembered the way my mother had chased after her youth. She would have taken up an offer of free Botox at the drop of a hat. I refused to do it. The very next day Christian had begun policing my expressions.

God we had been so fucked up together, hadn't we?

"Christian, back off. I mean it." I held out a hand to him, palm facing him and shook my head when he came closer. "Now. Stop."

"Honey, you missed me. I'm sure of it."

"I can tell you she didn't miss your sorry ass for one minute," another voice said, and I almost tripped over my own feet in surprise.

"Who the fuck are you?" Christian asked, glaring at the person behind me that had spoken. I didn't need to turn my head to see who it was. I knew exactly who it was.

"I'm her man," Law said, coming to stand beside me. He crossed his arms and considered Christian. "From what I heard, you're not supposed to be this close to her."

Christian's eyebrows drew together and he opened his mouth to say something stupid. I knew it was stupid by the way he was drawing himself up as if he was going to have the backbone to actually threaten Law and do something about it. Thankfully, the arrival of a giggling dark haired woman broke the growing tension between the two men. She was oblivious and all smiles to the show down and threw her arms around Christian's waist.

"I was looking for you! You said you were going to get me a drink!" She exclaimed, giving him a hug and what could only be described as puppy dog eyes.

Christian's mouth pressed into a thin line. "I got caught up with old friends. Sorry about that, Love."

I wrinkled my nose at the nickname. What the hell? God, I hoped it was her nickname and not her real name. Honey? Love? What was he doing, going around collecting us for his twisted menagerie?

"Oh, that's all right. I just missed you so much and-" she turned and looked at Law and I with a puzzled expression. "Hi, are you some of Christian's friends?" She asked.

I cleared my throat, searching for an answer to her question that wouldn't sound totally suspicious. "Well…" I began, but that was as far as I got because Law was grabbing my hand and shaking his head.

"No," Law told her.

Her mouth dropped open. "Oh."

Law ignored her and looked at Christian. "Come near her again and I'll break your neck. Not gonna repeat it." He turned, pulling me behind him, and we left the couple standing in stunned silence. I struggled to keep up with him but after we had cleared the corridor and made our way back up into the Great Room, I yanked on his hand.

"Stop dragging me around like a fucking caveman."

He looked over his shoulder at me, eyes still narrowed in a glare. "Then walk."

"I am, but some of us are wearing heels. I can't keep up with these shoes on." I gestured down at my feet and returned his glare with one of my own.

"Wear better shoes next time."

"I wasn't exactly planning on needing to run when I picked these out," I muttered, yanking on my hand, but he held fast.

"Wasn't planning on baby sitting either, but here we are."

I gave my hand another yank and this time managed to free myself from his hold. "If you think for one hot second that I want to be here with you, you're horribly mistaken."

He rubbed a hand across his jaw and chuckled. "Oh, is that so, princess?"

"Fuck yeah, it is."

"Wasn't the story last night when I left your place."

My breath left my body as surely as if Law had punched me in the gut. "Fuck you," I whispered, because he was right. I hadn't wanted him to leave. I hadn't said it, but he knew. He'd known and he'd still gone. He'd known and he'd still talked to me the way he had tonight. "You're an asshole."

He nodded, hand still at his jaw. "I know."

"Why are you even here?" I asked, taking a step back from him. But it was no use because Law came right with me.

"I came here because I'm a member of the club, princess."

"Don't call me that," I snapped. "If you're a member of the club, then why haven't I ever seen you here before?"

"Works a bitch, can't get away as much as I'd like. Which means when I do make time I want to enjoy that time how I want, not how Connie or Zeus fucking thinks I need to," he told me, with a bite to his voice that I was quickly growing accustomed to. His meaning was clear. He had wanted to come to relax and I was here messing up his plans.

"I didn't know she was going to ask you, or ask anyone to watch me. I swear," I told him, holding up my hands and shaking my head. "She just-I mean, I thought it was going to be her tonight that was with me, not someone else." I sat down on a couch, this one covered in a pink satiny material and I frowned when my ass slid to the side, the slip of my dress not doing much to keep me in place. I glared at Law when he chuckled and placed my hands on either side of me, holding myself in place. I gazed out at the floor where the couple debuting tonight had taken the stage and were making their introductions to the crowd. "I thought it was going to be Connie," I said again, "It never crossed my mind it would be you, of all people."

Law hummed and moved close, standing in front of me and blocking my view of the Dominant that had just picked up a flogger. I glared at him. "You're blocking my view."

"You telling me you wanted Connie?"

I blanched and shook my head. "No, of course not. She's scary."

He crossed his arms and I noticed he looked annoyed. "And I'm not."

I snorted, crossing my own arms in response and immediately regretted it when I slid to the side. Fucking stupid satin ass couches. Who the hell made these? Why was it here if you couldn't even sit on it without fighting to defy gravity? I planted my feet firmly, widening my stance to do so and met his eyes.

"You're not scary. Not one fucking bit, Law. But I'll tell you what you are."

"What is that?"

"A pain in my ass."

CHAPTER FIFTEEN

LAW

She was mad. Honey wasn't sweet anymore. She was a wildfire that was bent on consuming any and everything that had the misfortune of crossing her path.

I fucking liked it more than I should.

She looked like an angry goddess with her legs spread open just an inch too much, thighs soft and inviting, god, if I wasn't so pissed at her I would sink down onto my knees and taste her. Worship at her pussy until she screamed my name and came all over my tongue. I'd done it before, I could do it again, even if this time it would be in public with her sitting on a gaudy bubblegum pink couch.

Who the fuck ordered this thing?

I liked pink, but this? This was nauseating in its

Pepto Bismol shade. Plus, it didn't look stable by the way Honey was fighting to stay upright. It made her arch her back slightly, pushing her tits out and I liked the way she looked like that, even if she got a glare on her pretty face.

She wasn't having any shit tonight. I could tell when she told me I was a pain in her ass. I never dreamed my reason for coming to the club would be waiting for me wrapped up as pretty as a Christmas present. She looked good in the dress she chose, the dark green of it made her tan look all the more tantalizing. I knew her skin was soft, I've had my hands on her, but with the way the material is flowing over her thighs, trailing like water down her legs…god, she made me want to touch her.

She made me want.

My hands clenched. I shouldn't be wanting a damn thing from Honey. If I did, I could take it all from her.

"That's a nice story, princess," I told her, not breaking her stare even though the heat behind her eyes would be enough to make half of the people in this room seek cover, "but I know different."

She glared at me for a second more, eyes narrowing before her bottom lip trembled and I saw her eyes dart to the side. She was looking at someone else. And I knew exactly who the fuck it was without turning to look. Her shitty ex, the guy Connie told me about before I took off after her.

Christian O'Hanon. Fucking dipshit.

I knew him, or of him, but not enough to care to learn anything other than he was a shithead. Lower level hanger on with a lot of his daddy's money he used to get himself into exclusive places, places like the Cairn. But he didn't go too far here. Zeus had a thing for people earning their stripes, and Christian was still a novice.

But he was one with a mean streak.

Honey swallowed hard, her eyes following his journey across the room. I didn't like the fear I saw in her face. She was afraid of him. Did he put his hands on her? The thought made me feel light headed. Anger hit me like a tidal wave and I clenched my hands into fists. I'd rip his throat out with my bare hands if he so much as touched her. The fire was dying in Honey the longer she watched that asshole and it cracked something open in me to see it. The strength that had flared bright in her rapidly dying and shrinking, until I saw her shoulders slump and her hands shake as she put them down on the couch to hold herself steady.

I had to do something so I played the only card I knew would work to pull her out of wherever the fuck it is that her mind was going.

"Eyes up here, princess," I said, coming closer to

her and flicking a hand from her to me. "Did I say you could look away?"

Her dark eyes snapped to my face, just like I asked, and I saw the embers of her strength coming back to life when she did. "You don't tell me what to do," she said, but her voice was quieter.

"I think tonight that's kind of the point. Connie appointed me as your babysitter."

"Chaperone," she corrected.

"What's the difference?"

She rolled her eyes at me and then shrugged. "I guess there really isn't one," she said after a minute. When she looked away from me, I snapped my fingers at her and I watched the fire in her eyes go into a full blaze. "What the fuck Law?" She was pissed. Perfect.

"If I'm going to lose my whole night to watching your ass, I'd appreciate your undivided attention, *princess.*" I said the words that I knew would get a rise, they came easily to me. Princess a little too easily, and I tried not to think about that. I hadn't asked her what she liked and what she didn't, but I could see she was a brat. A submissive from what Connie told me, but one that liked mouthing off and pushing her Dom's boundaries. That was all I had been told so far, all that I had time to know while her ex lurked around the club like a bad dream.

"I can't believe I thought you were nice," she

whispered, but her eyes locked on mine. "Why the fuck did I ever want to go home with you?"

She might not understand it now. She might hate me right now, but this was all for her own good. I was doing this for her.

"Up," I said, gesturing for her to follow me and when she didn't budge, I said, "Unless you want to wait around for that asshole you call an ex to come calling?"

That got her up and moving, but not with a huff and a curse from her. I smiled in spite of myself. I liked that she was mouthy. It suited her far better than the wide eyed woman I'd rescued from the coffee shop, even better than the drunk girl that had fallen into my private room, but still it wasn't the Honey I'd laid out on her kitchen table and ate until she was sobbing.

I liked that Honey the best, but this one? She was all right in my book.

Honey stomped behind me, the heels she wore striking down on the hardwood with thuds so loud, I whirled on her and held a finger up. "Are you trying to cause a scene?" I asked through gritted teeth.

"Maybe."

"Throw a tantrum when there isn't a couple that demands respect. Do you understand me?" I jerked my chin towards the stage where a couple was in the middle of a flogging scene. The submissive was standing, hands clasped and secured behind her back, stance wide. The position forced her to arch her back, offering her tits up to her Dom who was circling her with a flogger in hand. He was bringing the leather down on her with sure and swift flicks of his hand, the snap of the leather meeting her skin mingled with the submissive moans of pleasure and pain. When Honey didn't answer me, I looked at her to see that she was watching the couple with rapt attention. Her eyes were wide and I knew she liked what she was seeing from the way her mouth parted, a soft inhalation in time with the swing of the Dom's arm. The leather cracked against his submissive's thigh and Honey licked her lips, her hands smoothing across her own thighs, fingers tightening in the lush material of her dress.

She was interested all right.

"Like what you see?" I asked, stepping in close to her when I noticed a man with tattoos and dressed in leathers notice her. I glared at him sending the clear signal that she was mine and I watched him retreat with a dip of his head. I looked around, eyes sweeping the crowd and saw that there were others watching Honey, like sharks in the fucking water. If this really was a job like I used to do, the kind where people got dead and their blood was on the line, I'd be on red alert. There was hunger in the eyes of the crowd we stood in, and I didn't like it.

They saw what I saw in Honey. She was magnificent, and they all wanted a piece. I should have known there was a reason Connie wanted me here besides Christian. She could have had that piss ant handled in no time. What she was focused on was who would be spending time with Honey. Not just Connie, but Zeus. Honey had attracted the eye of the all powerful Zeus, but what I couldn't figure out was *why?*

She was a beautiful woman. Striking with her dark brown eyes and the mass of dark curly hair that spilled over her shoulders and down her back. She had a great set of legs and her tits were, well, they were amazing. Not too big, just the right size for me to take in my hands while I ate her pussy. My palms tingled, and I remembered the weight of her flesh in my hands, how soft and willing she'd been then, moaning my name while my tie was wrapped around her wrists. I felt my cock start to harden and blew out a heavy sigh.

Right now was a shit time to get a hard-on for the woman I needed to be watching. The woman that I was purposely goading into getting pissed at me so she didn't notice her ex boyfriend, or the fact that she had more attention on her than the submissive on stage getting their ass turned black and blue.

"You know I do," she said, not looking away from the couple. She licked her bottom lip, tongue sliding along the plump flesh of her mouth.

"I don't actually," I said, even though she was right. I could tell from the arousal that was plain as day on her face, her body was practically vibrating with it. I knew if I dropped to my knees in front of her and pressed my face to the V of her thighs that I would smell it on her. My dick was hard now, balls starting to feel heavy, and I gritted my teeth at the familiar ache. I wanted this woman.

It didn't matter. I wasn't going to touch her. Not until she asked me to. Not until we had a very big talk, and not until she was stone cold sober. I frowned, glancing towards the bar where Connie was still lounging. She had an elbow up on the bar, lines of her body lax and casual even though I knew she was anything but. The woman knew precisely who was who, and what was happening on the club floor. Nothing escaped her notice, which had me wondering what the hell she was playing at letting Honey's ex near her. Our eyes met and she smirked at me, raising the glass she was holding to her lips in what I knew was a toast.

Things were going exactly to Connie's plans. Plans that I still didn't understand. All I knew was that she'd offered me up as protection, made sure that I took the bait and now, here we were after I put on a little show for that fucker Christian. I glanced to the side, catching a glimpse of his profile. He was with the dark haired woman, the brunette that looked like a distorted knock off of Honey. They were the same height, similar build, their hair was close but not identical with dark curls and waves that made you want to comb your fingers through it. But the similarities ended there.

He had come here tonight with a Honey knock off, which made me think he knew my girl would be here. I flinched, not liking the *my girl*, but there was no time to figure that shit out now. I was done being out in the open with the club members circling Honey like she was up for grabs.

I didn't care if she was unattached. She was mine, if only for tonight. And I didn't like it when others thought they could take what was mine.

"We're leaving," I told her, turning back to face her.

She looked at me, dark eyes narrowed. "Why? Maybe I don't want to leave."

"Do you want to stay here where that asshole is?" I asked. "Or do you want to get comfortable?"

"No." She bit her lip and then looked away. "I mean, no I don't want to be out here where he is. He keeps watching me and I can't just-I don't know how to act like I don't care, because I do." Her voice wasn't steady now, not like when she was giving me shit. She was nervous again.

I grunted in acknowledgement, because I got being bothered by shit more than you liked to admit. Particularly, since I was looking right at the source of my being bothered, and she was infuriatingly beautiful. "Then move it."

"I swear to god, you order me around one more time..." She muttered, but she fell in step behind me and this time did so without causing a commotion. Good. I would reward her for that later.

"You like it," I said, not having to turn to look at her to know she was right at my elbow. I didn't need to have eyes on Honey to know where she was. My body felt it. Could point me in her direction by still semi-hard dick. Instead, I kept my eyes on the floor, sweeping them back and forth and making sure everyone kept their distance. She was overwhelmed. I could hear it in the slight tremble of her voice when she answered me.

"You're so bossy."

Again I grunted and concentrated on clearing a way in front of Honey. The crowd parted like the Red Sea, something I was sure had more to do with the interested look Connie was directing our way. Other club members could see she was watching us, which for the moment gave our movements more weight. The attention was a double edged sword. On one hand, I was glad for it, for the speed it gave us, we were halfway across the room with the hallway to my room in sight in half the time it had taken for us to leave the bar. But all that attention brought Christian O'Hanon's eyes among those trained on us, tracking our every movement. There was no way he wasn't watching us cross the room. That he didn't know exactly where I was taking her.

"Where are we going?" Honey asked, hurrying to walk beside me. We descended the stairs and were in the hallway before I answered her.

"My room." I glanced her way to see that she was frowning. Did she not like where I was taking her? "Is there somewhere else you would like to go?"

She sniffed but didn't say anything, just crossed her arms and shook her head. "No."

We were silent the rest of the walk to my room and I spent the time making sure there were no footsteps echoing behind us. There weren't any, which was lucky for whoever might have been stupid enough to think about following us. We came to a stop in front of my door and I paused, turning to look down at her.

"Are you sure you want to come inside my room?" I pressed.

Honey rolled her eyes at me and nodded at the golden door. "Of course, I do. If I didn't I wouldn't have left with you."

She had me there.

I gave her a quick nod, pulled out the golden key and unlocked the door. I held it open for her and Honey sailed into my room with all the confidence of a queen. That did something for the uneasy feeling that had started to take root in me at seeing her shaken. I didn't like knowing Honey was unsure, that she might be feeling fear or anxiety, a display brought on by the sighting of her ex. My hands curled into fists and I followed her inside of my room before I shut the door with a jerk of my hands. God, I didn't like what just thinking about Honey scared of another man did to me.

She was mine. Mine for tonight, and I took care of what was mine.

CHAPTER SIXTEEN

HONEY

Law's room was sparse. It was nice, every bit of the luxury the Cairn was known for but it was lacking the more indulgent comforts my suite featured. I didn't miss an opportunity to let him know that Zeus gave me swankier accommodations.

"I've got a nicer suite than this."

My arms were crossed and I faced away from him, staring at a painting to the right of his door. If I turned my head I'd see the only other thing that really demanded attention in the room. His bed. It was a massive affair of well formed dark wood and what looked like tons of fluffy, pristine white pillows and comforters. If a cloud could be turned into a bed, it would be this bed.

It was so at odds with the rest of the room, the darkness of everything else seemingly working to frame the bed as a bright spot to be focused on. It drew the eye easily and I wasn't too keen on giving my attention to it when the man at my back made me horny beyond belief. He made me as horny as he did angry and annoyed, and just...well, I had almost cried over him again, and I had spent the better part of the last night crying over him. Staring at his bed really didn't seem to be the move needing to be made after running into my stalker ex boyfriend.

"Like what you see?"

He'd known the answer to that question before he'd even asked me. He had to have, even if we hadn't so much as had a single conversation on my limits and preferences. I hadn't made a secret of how interested I was in the couple on stage. It wasn't so much that I was interested in them, but the act. The Dominant had handled the flogger with precision, the leather of it kissing the thighs and flank of the submissive, turning her skin a lovely shadow of pink with each bite of the leather. She'd taken each strike with pleasure, eyes closing, head tipped back and a smile pulling at her lips. It hadn't been a stretch for me to imagine that it was Law and me on stage. That it was me with my hands cuffed at my sides while he circled me, a flogger in his strong and capable hands.

In my version he was shirtless, the light of the dungeon moving over him and turning him into a work of art. All hard angles and muscle, the shadows and light playing over him until he resembled an avenging angel. The kiss of the leather against my heated skin capable of bringing me to my knees. I would promise anything to have him keep going, to have his mark in the form of red skin and bruises delivered via the flogger he held, because it was him.

What my angel decided to give me I would take gladly.

Or demon, the voice in my head whispered to me. I turned, looking back at Law who was standing in front of the door with his hands at his sides, fingers curled into fists. He was glaring. The man did not look happy. He was also avoiding looking in the direction of the bed, which meant he was staring straight ahead at the door that I was assuming was his bathroom.

When he didn't respond to my comment on the room I continued on, because if I didn't fill the space *with something* I was going to pop. "I've got a huge bed and fireplace, and you know, actual furniture. My bathroom is just about as big as this room," I said, waving a hand at his room.

"Strip."

I blinked, my mouth dropping open. "What?"

"Get in the shower. Now." He pointed a hand at the bathroom. "You need to sober up. A shower will do it. I'll get the water running while you get undressed. There's a robe in the closet," he said, nodding at the door behind me.

"I don't need a shower," I told him.

He didn't stop on his way to the bathroom. "You do. You need to relax."

"I'm fine," I said quickly.

"You're not fine. That shithead has you wound up, we need to bring you down again. I want you to have time to sober up too. I don't know what the shit that was, with Connie letting you drink tonight, but that does not fly with me."

I blushed hot because I knew why he was saying what he was. Drunk or tipsy submissives were never up for grabs, not when it came to play partners. I'd come here wanting to find a partner to play with, but Connie had insisted I drink. Why?

"I'm not drunk," I said.

"You were spilling your damn drink all over yourself," he shot back, pausing in the doorway to the bathroom.

I started towards him but he backed up a step and my mouth fell open at the movement. Did he think I was going to throw myself at him or something? "I was nervous, okay? I knew Christian was going to be here tonight and then Connie was teasing this big reveal at who she was going to have me with tonight, and then there you were," I threw out my hands, glaring in his direction. "What the hell was I supposed to do?"

"Not spill your damn drink."

I rolled my eyes, looking away from him and stalked over to the closet, because I knew he wasn't going to let this go. If I didn't get into the robe and let him force me into the shower we were going to argue all night. Besides, getting out of my shoes wasn't a bad idea, my feet were killing me. "Whatever."

"Get in the robe," Law snapped, disappearing into the bathroom.

"Yeah, I know, I know, bossy pants." I heard Law chuckle from inside the bathroom and I tried to ignore the warm feeling of pleasure that sound gave me. He'd said that I brought people into my shit, he'd gotten pissed about having to 'babysit me', and he had walked out on me 24 hours earlier. I did not need to be noticing his chuckle, or thinking about how nice that sound made me feel. I needed to be mad at him. I needed to be just as annoyed as he was with me, and that was that.

I leaned down, undoing the straps of my heels, and stepped out of them with a grateful sigh. I was pulling the straps of my dress down my shoulders when I heard Law clear his throat. I looked over to see that he was standing with his back to me, hands clasped behind his back and staring at the painting that I had just been making a study of.

"Let me know when you're ready." Was all he said before he fell silent and went about staring ahead.

"You're really killing this bodyguard vibe," I told him, slipping out of the dress and hanging it up on a hanger.

"I should, was one of the things I did once upon a time."

That was...interesting. Both the fact that he'd done it and the fact that he'd shared it with me. I hadn't really thought he would give me that much of his background, not with what he'd given me so far, which was nothing. Well, he'd given me tears and an orgasm, but I couldn't use either of those to get to know the man.

"Cool," I said quietly, because what else was I supposed to say to that? I didn't know, since I'd never met a bodyguard. All I knew about them was from movies or television. But straight back, the focused way Law was staring at the painting as if it were the only thing that existed while I knew damn sure he was aware of where I was made me feel protected. Not to mention the way he'd swept me out of the room and kept the others away. I'd played at not noticing all the attention, but it was hard not to look at Law, and each time I did I saw where he was looking and was met with another pair of hungry eyes.

I thought I would know what to do with the spotlight Connie had decided to send my way, but I was wrong. I hadn't known. In fact, it had almost been too much.

"I'm going in," I said, wrapping the robe around myself and padding towards the bathroom.

Law gave a grunt, but I watched his shoulders relax slightly. He turned so that he was in profile but his eyes were now on the wall to the left of me, still not on me. "I'll get you something to eat and drink. Take your time."

I opened my mouth to tell him I didn't need him to get me anything, but I stopped. Even if I was mad at him I liked knowing he was getting those things for me. After the unexpectedly intense night, knowing that anyone was getting those things for me—taking care of me—was a heavenly comfort.

"Thank you," I said instead.

Again, he grunted in reply, and when he didn't move, I set off for the bathroom. I closed the door and was taking off my robe before I heard his footsteps sound in the other room. I blew out a sigh and looked at myself in the mirror. The makeup I'd put on earlier had held up despite the night, and my hair? Still piled high and looking absolutely amazing, but me?

Not so much on either account.

My eyes looked tired. Worried. I could see that beneath the makeup I was pale and my shoulders were hunched up. No wonder he had wanted to get me in the shower. I sighed, hating that he was right, and approached the walk in shower. I held my hand out under the spray and found that it was a delightfully warm temperature. It was going to do wonders for the way my muscles were bunched. Of course Law had picked the right temperature, just like he was doing the right thing in the other room by making sure I had food and drink.

As far as babysitters went, he wasn't a terrible one. I stepped into the shower and sighed in relief at the first warm spray of water. I closed my eyes and stood there, letting the water clear my mind of the worry over Christian and the anxiety brought on from being the focus of so many club members. I was used to blending in more at the club, I was noticed, but only when I wanted.

Tonight had been an entirely different animal. Attention had come fast and unbidden, as easily as breathing, and I didn't know what to do with what felt like an overabundance of energy that was currently coursing through my body. I took in a deep breath and held it for a second before I let it go in a deep exhale. Again, I took in another breath and let it out, and then another and another until I felt myself start to mellow. Down the drain went my fear and anxiety, and by the time I reached to turn off the shower I had lost track of how much time had passed. I turned off the shower and stepped out, breathing in deeply once more while I dried off and pulled on the robe. This time the fluffy softness of it felt good, really good. I hadn't registered it the first time and I smoothed my hands over it with an appreciative sigh.

I paused in front of the steamed up mirror and thought about swiping a hand over it to see what I looked like but I didn't let myself. If I did that I would get in my head again. I patted at my hair which was still up and pushed the damp tendrils that had come loose away from my face before I opened the door. The cool air of the room was sudden and it made the warm air at my back all the more appealing. I hesitated on the threshold, not really wanting to walk forward and leave the warm comfort of the bathroom, but also desperately wanting to see what Law had gotten me. I could see the telltale cart beside the bed and swallowed hard when I caught sight of him lounging in the one and only chair in the room. It was leather and high backed, angled towards the bed and sitting just off to the side of it. His big body was taking up every inch of the chair and he had a mug in his hand.

Was he drinking tea?

"Hey," I said quietly from where I stood.

"Come on out, Honey."

"But it's cold in here," I told him.

He frowned and glanced towards the door where a blinking thermostat was on the wall and stood. "I'll turn on the heat. Get in the bed, it'll be warmer there."

My feet were moving before I could think. "Yeah, okay, but where…" my voice trailed off and I looked at him again, "where are you going to sleep?"

"In the chair," he said, as if that were obvious. He was already at the thermostat and was punching buttons to kick on the heat. "There, that should do it. I don't want you getting cold. In the bed. Now."

"Bossy," I muttered, but did as I was told.

"Seems to be the only thing you respond to," he countered, and I smiled even if I didn't want to.

"Fair point," I said, pulling back the covers and getting into the bed. It was cold now but I knew the sheets would warm within a few minutes. "Are you drinking tea?" I asked, looking at the mug he had set on the cart.

"Yes, we both are."

"Are we now?"

"We will be as soon as you tell me how you like

yours." He came to stand beside the cart and gave me an expectant look.

I bit my bottom lip and then, because I did love tea and the cloying smells of jasmine and bergamot were too much to resist, I said, "I'd like a splash of cream, that's it."

Law didn't say anything, but that seemed to be his default setting. I watched his hands while he worked. They were inked, the tattoos I'd seen before, the ones that had pulled my attention in the first place that morning in the coffee shop had my attention once again. The bold black lines of the ink were pretty...in a savage way. Just like Law.

"Here you are," he said, holding the cup out to me.

"Thanks." I took the cup and inhaled deeply, letting the familiar smells of the tea calm me further. This had been exactly what I'd needed. I sipped the tea and nodded at him. "Thank you. I mean that."

"It's my job," he said and I felt my chest get tight. I didn't want him to say that. I wanted him to want to be here with me. But that Law didn't exist. He pulled the dome lid from the tray on the cart back to reveal fruit and cake. The cake was chocolate with thick luscious looking frosting over the top of it. I focused on the fudge dripping down the sides, preferring to think of the cake than dwell on the fact that the Law I wanted, the one I wished was real, wasn't.

Why did I want a man that didn't want me? What was wrong with me?

Different man, same old song and dance.

"What's wrong?" He asked, squatting down so that he was looking up at me instead of standing above me.

"Nothing's wrong," I lied. "This looks great. Can I have the cake?"

"Not until you tell me why you've got that look on your face."

"What look? I don't have a look." I hid behind my tea mug and avoided his eyes. "Hey, do you think that's a real painting, like an original? Or is it a print? I thought it looked like something famous, but I didn't really pay the most attention in school." I was looking at the painting now and rambling, but it was the best I could do given my current situation.

"Honey…"

"It looks like it could be an original, but they make fakes all the time that have the brushstrokes and crap like that, so you never know."

"Look at me, Honey."

"The Cairn *would* have a million dollar painting in one of these suites. They just would," I insisted, while I did everything but what Law asked. I kept my eyes fixed on the painting while Law shifted closer to the bed.

"Honey." Law put a hand on the bed, not

touching me but close enough that I had to pay attention. "What is wrong? I can't help if you don't tell me, princess."

The tightness in my chest spread. *Princess.* I had told him not to call me that, but it was a lie. I liked it when he called me that. I'd felt proud as hell that people had heard him call me princess. And now here he was again, saying it, but it was all wrong. It was all wrong because Law didn't want me to be his princess.

It was just a name.

"Nothing's wrong," I lied again. That was two times, and I wasn't getting any better at it. I could tell by the heavy sigh Law let out. He flattened his palm against the bed and then moved, sitting on the edge of it so that he was blocking the damn painting I'd been fixated on.

"I know you're lying," he told me, shifting his body so that it was angled towards me. "I don't know why though."

I let out a dry laugh. "Oh, Law, come on."

He shrugged. "I'm not a mind reader, Honey."

"I'm lying because you have made it abundantly clear you don't want to be here with me, which is," my voice tightened, coming out strained against the lump that was fast growing in my throat, "that is perfectly fine, because you don't need to want to be here with me. It doesn't matter if you don't want to be here with me."

"I didn't say I didn't want to be here with you." I frowned and forced my eyes down into the depths of my tea. Far easier than meeting Law's piercing blue gaze. I wasn't quite ready for that. No matter what my heart wanted. When I said nothing Law sighed, and went on. "You have to understand that I don't like it when things are out of my control. Connie made it a lose-lose situation for me. For us, tonight. This isn't about you."

I bit my lip and turned my tea mug in my hands. He had a point.

"I don't understand why she did it."

"I think I might," Law said, surprising me. I looked at him then and saw he was staring at me, his handsome face no longer hard or cold. He was again the man that had laid me out on my dining table, the one that had claimed me in front of a shop full of strangers.

I knew this Law. I liked him far better than the man I'd spent most of tonight with.

"What is it?" I pressed, leaning forward, elbows to my thighs beneath the thick comforter.

"She was up to something. We both knew that from the get go, but we didn't know what. Connie likes to pretend things just 'happen,'" he made air quotes with his fingers, "and when they do she takes advantage of a situation that was no one's fault. That way she can't be blamed or pegged for making shit go down that no one but her wanted."

"Or Zeus," I interjected, "she does whatever he wants."

Law inclined his head. "Very good point, Honey. She does exactly what her invisible master tells her to. Tonight it was focused on you, focused on me. I haven't figured out that part yet, but Connie is making more sense."

"I'm glad it's making sense to you, because it isn't to me."

"She got you drunk to make sure no one played with you. It's against the rules to play with a sub that's under the influence."

I rolled my eyes at him for what felt like the 100th time that night. "I already told you I wasn't drunk. I'm not drunk. Haven't been all night. I was nervous."

Law snorted but he kept talking. "She knew your ex was coming before you got here. Probably knew long before you made your reservation."

I nodded. "I didn't make one. I just decided to do it."

He rubbed a hand along his jaw. "Then that just 'happened,' and she ran with it."

"I guess so." I sipped from my mug, and then asked, "Did you make a reservation?"

He nodded. "I did. Couple days back."

"So she knew you were coming ahead of time. Not me."

"She must have made the decision then to have me with you. The other thing that happened was we already knew one another. Zeus couldn't have known that."

I shivered. "I wouldn't put it past him. The things he knows, or what I hear he's capable of. He's got his fingers in everything."

"And why would he want to saddle me with a traveling barista?"

A wave of embarrassment hit me. *Traveling barista.* Why did it feel like something I should be ashamed of? I'd never cared what other people thought of my job, because it paid the bills and I enjoyed it. It was honest work, which meant there was no reason to feel...like *this*. I swallowed hard, cheeks hot from his words. Aside from my embarrassment, I had no idea why that would be a move Zeus wanted to play.

"I don't know," I whispered, fingers drumming against the ceramic of my mug. "Matching us up doesn't make a lot of sense when you say it like that."

I felt the energy in the room shift. I knew Law was still as a statue and mostly likely focused on me with that unnerving stare he had.

"Honey, I didn't mean it like that."

I smiled brightly and looked up at him with fake cheer. "No, I know."

His lips pressed into a thin line. "If there's one rule we are agreeing on tonight it's no more lying. That's over, do you understand?"

My mouth fell open. "What?"

Law put a hand beside my thigh and moved forward until he was leaning towards me, lips only inches away from my face. "You are done lying to me, Honey. Do you understand me?"

"Yes," I whispered before I could think better of it. "I understand."

"Good girl."

"I shouldn't like it... but I really, *really* like it when you say that to me."

He smirked, eyes dropping to my mouth before he looked back up at me. "I know."

A finger of pleasure sparked in me and slowly, but surely, I felt my lust start to wake up. "What do you want from me, Law?"

"I want to know why they want us together."

I shook my head. "I don't know why. Same as you," I told him, softly.

"Then I want to stick close to you until I figure it out." He held out his hand to me, palm up, fingers open and waiting for me to touch him if I wanted. "What do you want?" he asked.

I stared down at his hand, the mug of tea in my

hands suddenly feeling ice cold from the heat that was now rising to the surface of my skin. I was heating up, every part of me on fire and that was all from Law giving me his hand. What would I do when he had his hands on me? My heart skipped a beat, because I already knew the answer to that. I would fall apart, piece by piece, part by part, letting each and every fracture fall into his waiting hands.

There was no world in which I would not fall to pieces under Lawson Sokolov's hands.

"I want that too," I told him, slipping my hand into his.

CHAPTER SEVENTEEN

LAW

She was fierce even when she was tired. Even when she was embarrassed and hurt, or confused. Honey was fierce in a way that I had seldom seen in people with far more power than she had. Not that it mattered. She took what she had and she wore with the grace of a Queen in command of herself. I could see the unbreakable parts of her, the parts made of steel that had her holding her head high and which let her walk through her every day as if she were untouchable.

She was plenty touchable, breakable, and every other-able there was that meant fragile. It didn't stop her her one fucking bit. I watched her where she sat sipping her mug of tea, eyes back on that fucking painting. I wanted to throw it out into the hallway so that she would be forced to look at me. I wanted her attention. All of it. I was hungry for it, and I knew that was bad.

Bad for me. Bad for her. Bad for the fucking both of us.

I was jealous of a goddam painting. What the hell did that say about us going forward? Probably nothing good.

"We have to negotiate, Honey."

Her eyes were on me then. "Negotiate what?"

"Us," I said, and watched her eyes go round as saucers.

"Us?" She whispered, the confusion in her voice ringing clear as a bell through the room. "What do we have to talk about? There is no us."

"You just said you wanted to stick with me until we figured out why Zeus and Connie are trying to shove us together," I reminded her. I looked down at my hand, my beaten to hell hand that had done more violence than anything else. Softness and beauty were things I didn't touch. But when Honey had put her hand in mine?

God. That had been all beauty.

And when I'd had my hands on Honey in her apartment the night before? Fucking bliss. I'd left because I wanted to keep her safe from me, because I knew that if I kept on touching her, let her put her hands on me, that we would have a big fucking problem. Because the second Honey touched me is the second she was mine.

When she had put her hand in mine she'd sealed her fate without even knowing it. I wasn't going to let her go after tonight. Sure, she was mine by order of Connie, but this was going to go beyond that. I was done keeping myself from what I wanted, and what I wanted as her.

"I remember," she said, eyes dropping back to her mug of tea. "I just don't get why you want there to be an 'Us'. You said it yourself–it doesn't make sense why Zeus would want us together. Why would you be saddled with a *'traveling barista'*."

I grimaced at the way she said the last two words. It sounded dirty, like something you didn't mention and not a job to be proud of. "I didn't mean it like that. I was just naming your job because I don't know anything else about you."

Her dark brows drew together and she looked up at me. "I guess that's true…" She said, voice uncertain and I knew I had an in there. I wasn't lying to her. I'd just told her there would be no more lying and that rule applied to us both.

"You do honest work. More honest than anything I do, or have ever done, to get paid. Why would you think I would give a shit about your job?"

She shrugged. "Because everyone in this town cares about that stuff. You know that. It's always who you know and what you do, not who you are or what you feel."

I smiled at her. "True, but fuck those people."

She laughed, the sound of it small, but it was a laugh all the same. "You should laugh more. It's...nice," I said, because I didn't say what I really wanted to say, which was that it was beautiful. That it sounded better than anything I could remember hearing or would ever want to hear. Words like that made me sound like a kid that didn't have his shit together when it came to women and love.

I almost made a face. Love. What the hell was I doing that 'love' was a word that managed to make it across my brain? Outside of the context of I loved her tits, or I loved the way her mouth felt on my dick, or I loved eating her pussy? What did I know of love?

No, this had fuck all to do with sex and her body, or how she made my dick feel. This went to what Honey was making me feel inside. The emotions she was waking up in me were big, too big for me to make sense of this early, but I was going to have to try if I wanted to keep my head in the game.

"Thanks," Honey said, smiling at me. It was small, thin, but like her laugh, it was there. "You have a good laugh too."

"When did you hear me laugh?" I asked, because I couldn't think of doing it around her.

"You did it twice," she told me without hesitation. "Well, twice but... the same time, you know?"

I shook my head because I didn't know. "No."

She sighed at me as if it was my fault I wasn't keeping up with her half formed thoughts. "In the rain, you laughed twice then."

"I don't remember doing it."

She shrugged as if that didn't matter. "I still heard it. I liked it. You sound different when you laugh. A whole different man."

"That's good, I guess," I ventured when she didn't explain.

"It is. You sound like a man you can make–" she stopped and then shook her head, cutting herself off.

"Like a man you can make what with?" I asked, interested now that she was looking like she wanted to be anywhere but here. "What were you going to say, Honey?"

"Nothing."

"What did we say about lying?"

She grimaced and then said, "What I was going to say was that you sound like a man you can make a life with when you laugh.

We both froze. Honey because I knew she was nervous at the honesty she'd given me, and me because I'd never been told I was the kind of man that could make anything. I was a man that broke things, people, and lives. I took. I had always taken, right from the beginning it was how I earned my place on the streets and at the table beside mafiosos. I broke people and names with my hands. Even my corporation was focused on taking companies apart bit by bit until there was nothing left. My hands did not create. Not ever.

But now this woman...Honey, thought I was a man she could make a life with and all from the way I sounded when I laughed. I wished I could remember laughing around her because I wanted to know what she looked like when she thought that about me.

It had to be beautiful. I bet it was. Would bet half my damn fortune on it. I grunted when she gave me a curious look.

Honey rolled her eyes at me. "What's that supposed to mean?"

"It means I've never heard that before."

"Maybe you should laugh more."

"Could be."

We stared at each other and then she was grinning, a giggle coming from her lips. "I like that you don't really. Laugh, I mean. And...and I like that I got to hear it."

"What else do you like?" I asked, switching the topic to something that mattered a whole lot more to me than my laugh. Though I could see from the pinched look on Honey's face that she thought my laugh was plenty important.

"Nice conversation switch," she sighed, setting her mug down on the cart beside the bed and stretching out like a cat in the sun. Arms over her head and leaning back on the down pillows the bed was piled with. I swear I'd never seen a more overstuffed bed than this one. I was surprised she wasn't swallowed by the blankets and sheets when she climbed in, but I did like seeing her surrounded by soft things. Things I knew were comfortable and delicate, just like her. I wanted to keep her like this where nothing and no one could hurt her.

But in order to do that, I needed to know exactly what I was working with when it came to Honey.

"We were going to get here anyway. Might as well do it now."

"I guess," she sighed heavily from where she was laying on the pillows and then shifted onto her side, a move that caused her robe to gap, revealing her soft flesh to me. I could see the top curve of her breast right down to the swell of it, her nipple frustratingly hidden from me. She shifted, her arm moving beneath her breasts, pushing them up, and I forced myself to look away. I was supposed to be negotiating, or at least starting the conversation we needed to have, not trying to catch an eyeful of her tits.

"What do you like?" I asked again, giving her an expectant look. Honey licked her bottom lip and then bit the inside of her cheek, the gesture making her look young. It had me imagining what she must have looked like when she first moved to the city a decade ago. What would have happened if I'd met her then? Would I have been able to keep her like this? Happy, safe and surrounded by fine things where she didn't worry or work herself to death?

Would I have even had that in me then? No, I probably hadn't. I'd just gone clean and was focused on work. My drive and energy bent on rising to the top in the corporate world. If I'd met her then I would have been just as careless with her as any other man. I didn't want to be just any other man to Honey.

I wanted to be her Dom.

CHAPTER EIGHTEEN

HONEY

"What do you like?"

I blinked knowing I probably looked like a cartoon character, but giving a fuck was way beyond me right now. Lawson Sokolov, Law, this man, a Dominant from what I had put together so far, was asking me what the hell I liked. Not just that, he had held my hand. It had been for a moment, just the barest slide of our palms together, fingers touching, pressing close before I'd lost my nerve and pulled back, because I'd discovered a terrible thing.

I loved holding his hand. I loved feeling his big hand beneath mine, palm warm, rough thick fingers curling close against mine. That was bad, but life had been way worse than me telling a man his laugh made me think you could build something with him—not something, a life. *A life.* I might have melted through the floor from cringe if it wasn't true. We'd already covered the topic of lying. There would be none of it, and anyhow, Law had the annoying ability to know exactly when I was lying. That was going to bite me in the ass for sure.

"We have to negotiate, Honey."

And now he was looking at me like I was the only thing that mattered, which I guessed in a room with just a bed, a chair, and a painting that wasn't exactly hard….but still. *Still.*

Not only that, but he wanted to know what I liked. And I knew it was in the context of BDSM and intimacy. And, whether or not we had counted on it, a relationship.

But what kind of relationship?

I already knew I didn't want to just play casually with Law. I knew what I wanted. I wanted the whole man. I wanted a Dominant, a lover, a friend. God, I wanted him to look at me like this over the breakfast table. I wanted this man to hold my hand in the street and laugh like he was different, like we both were, I wanted him to…I wanted him to…no, it wasn't that I wanted him to do anything.

I just wanted him.

That was it.

"Honey?" He asked again, that low and rough tone in his baritone making my toes curl in the mountains of blankets I was currently buried under. "What do you like?"

I liked a lot of things. A lot of kinky things. I wouldn't be here if I didn't, neither would Law. I didn't have to be afraid of judgement or worry what he might think about the things I liked, because we just might be on the same page. So often potential lovers and I weren't even reading the same book, but now there was hope.

God. I hoped we were on the same page.

"I'm a submissive," I told him, finally finding my voice to speak, "but, I, ah, well, I'm into being a little bit of a brat."

He snorted and rolled his eyes. "Never would have guessed it," he said, the sarcasm evident.

I stuck my tongue out at him. "You bring it out in me. Lucky you."

"Better go buy a scratch off with this kind of streak."

I laughed, the lightness of the exchange making it easier for me to speak and tell him exactly what it was that I needed, because what I needed was exactly this. A mixture of intimacy, sexiness, and sweet all rolled up in a kinky package.

"I'm a Middle," I said, finally. Lawson sucked in a breath, the sound of it making me worry that maybe it wasn't what he wanted to hear. "What is it?" I asked, quickly, worry already starting to run through my body like ice water. What if this was how it ended between us?

"I think I'm getting why Zeus and Connie decided to play matchmaker," he muttered, but said nothing else and nodded at me to continue on, "keep talking, princess."

That name was going to be the death of me. I opened my mouth and kept talking like he'd asked. "I like Daddies. Soft Doms do in a pinch, or a sensual Dom, but I can't really handle a lot of the extreme stuff. I don't like pain, but spanking is okay. I do like floggers, canes, and whips, but mostly for the effect, not the pain. Shibari is good, some suspension, but not too much." When he gave me a questioning look, I explained, "I'm afraid of heights so it's a bad combo."

"Are you a pet?" He asked.

I gave a quick shake of my head. "No, but I do like collars."

Another quick inhale of breath. "You would."

I smiled in spite of my nervousness. "I'll take that as a compliment."

"How verbal do you like your Daddy?"

"Very," I said, ducking my head, chin to my chest, pulling my robe tighter. "I like it when he calls me bad names, but only when we're having sex, or playing."

"What about when you're not? What do you want him to call you then?"

I looked up and saw that he was watching me closely and the rush of having Law's undivided attention hit me again. It was addictive like a drug I couldn't get enough of. He'd been worried about me being drunk but the man severely underestimated how his attention had me twisted up and feeling like I was halfway to tipsy.

"Only sweet names then."

"Like princess?"

"Among other things," I said, playing at being nonchalant, but I knew he was reading me as easily as a book. He knew I liked it. I'd bet anyone twenty bucks he was going to be calling me princess a lot more after this talk.

He hummed, and leaned back in his chair. "You have a praise kink, don't you?"

I shifted uncomfortably because that was usually something a Dominant figured out during our play, not before. I guessed it was a bit obvious with how his few well placed 'good girls' had affected me. "Yes."

"I like that. I like that very much."

I felt that familiar warmth of pleasure spread through my chest even though I hadn't done anything, but still. Law was happy, he was pleased, and that gave me satisfaction.

"I don't like other partners," I told him. "I don't share well, and I don't want to be shared either."

"Good. If you're mine," My eyes practically fell out of my head at that, but they nearly rolled right off the bed and fell onto the floor when he said, "you're mine. All of you."

"Oh."

"Would that be a problem for you if we..." his voice trailed off and he turned his head, eyes on the floor for a second before they came back to my face, "decided we wanted a long term arrangement."

"Yes," I said automatically. "That's absolutely fine. It's perfect." Normally, I might have been worried that I was agreeing too quickly to something, but not this. Not with Law. Because if I agreed to this then I had all of him too, no one else would put their hands on my...on my...

"Are you a Daddy?" I asked when I realized I didn't know.

"I am. Been one for 15 years."

Fuck yes. FUCK. *YES*.

The breath punched out of my lungs because the thing I'd been wishing for, hoping for, ever since he'd said I was his girl, since he'd threatened to spank me in the private room at dinner, god, it was true.

"That makes me happy," I told him.

"Me too, Honey." He sucked on his teeth and then

sighed. "But as happy as that makes me, it's time for you to go to bed."

I pouted because I didn't want to go to bed, so I told him. "I don't want to go to bed. I want to finish this conversation."

"You're exhausted. Can hardly keep your eyes open." Law rose from his chair and was pulling off his jacket as he went. He stopped in front of the closet I'd pulled the robe from and hung it up there while he loosened his tie. "You're going to bed now. We can finish our talk in the morning."

I opened my mouth to protest but a yawn escaped me and I cursed silently. So much for trying to insist that I was fine. He was right. I was tired. The night had been a roller coaster of emotions from anxiety to fear, happiness and sadness, and now this.

This could only be described as sexual tension. No, frustration. That was it.

I knew Law was a Dom. A Daddy. And yet, I was too tired to do one thing with that knowledge and we both knew it. Law was doing the right thing by putting my ass to bed, but that didn't mean I was going to go willingly.

"I'm fine," I said again. "We can keep talking. Honest."

"Honey." There was a warning tone to his voice that told me I was getting close to the edge, the edge of what I wasn't sure yet. His patience? Being cute? The edge of getting my ass spanked? I didn't know. But it was there and I was walking right along it.

I liked it.

"Law," I tossed back, crossing my arms and met his stare with one of my own. I might have actually looked formidable if I didn't yawn again.

"Lay down, close your eyes. I'm turning off this light in five seconds."

"And what if I don't?"

"One," Law counted and I rolled my eyes.

"You're supposed to answer a question when someone asks you nicely."

"Two."

"Oh, you aren't going to really count us down, are you?" I asked, watching him while he walked to the light switch and stood there staring at me with an almost bored look on his handsome face.

"Three," he said, raising his hand to the light switch and leaning back against the wall. I noticed then that he looked relaxed. The normal rigid set of his shoulders, the way he looked like he was on high alert at all times, like he might have to spring into action had melted away and he looked...well, different. He looked like the man who laughed, and I smiled watching the transformation. He was happy like this, even as we were tentatively exploring the push and pull dynamic that could, and I hoped would, develop between us.

"I can't believe you're actually counting."

"Four," he said when I continued to stare right back at him.

"Oh, thi-"

"Four and a fucking half, Honey. Are you listening to me?"

"Yes, and I wish you were saying better things than a bunch of stupid numbers," I shot back.

Law's eyebrow shot up. "Fi-" he began but I hadn't missed the dark look that had slipped into his eyes, the one that replaced the easy and relaxed man that laughed and I threw myself down on the bed and yanked the covers over my head.

"Oh, all right! Are you happy?" I asked from the safety of the covers. If you were safe from monsters when you were covered by a blanket head-to-toe, then the same had to be said for being safe from Law, right?

"Very good girl," he said, and flicked the light off. I saw the room go dark from behind the blanket and only then did I peek out.

"Where are you going to sleep?" I asked, not sure what was about to happen. There were two answers. One of them was right and the other was not, but both would tell me what kind of man and what kind of Daddy I was dealing with.

"The chair. Where else?" He said, and my heart soared.

He'd picked right.

"I dunno," I hedged, pretending that I hadn't known he wouldn't pick any other answer, but the grunt and the sigh told me he knew why I had asked.

"Go to bed, Honey. Get some rest." I didn't have to see him to hear the weariness in his voice. Here in the dark the Law everyone else saw was gone. He wasn't strong or unfeeling now. He was just a man. A man that was tired, and I liked that he let me see that side of him.

It was easy to do things like that in the dark. I could feel my own walls sliding away. I didn't need to throw attitude or keep my distance. I could just want him. I heard him cross the room and then, he was sinking into the leather chair beside the bed, the sound of his clothing sliding against the leather making me smile.

I closed my eyes and I had a smile on my face even though I knew he couldn't see it. "Okay." I hoped he could, at least, hear the smile in my voice. It was all I had to give in the dark.

∼

I OPENED MY EYES SLOWLY. THE BED BENEATH ME WAS soft and nice, the blankets I was curled under far nicer than anything I owned. I knew I wasn't home from just the quiet stillness of the room. My apartment in Queens was noisy. The sounds of the city intruding on my space as soon as the city woke up, or in a lot of cases, never went to bed to begin with. My apartment was noisy a lot.

This room was quiet, peaceful, so much so that the silence descended like a solid thing that had weight and bearing. It pressed down on my shoulders, coaxing me back to sleep. I could rest for a while longer and not worry. Nothing would touch me here. I might have done just that, burrowed deeper into the blankets and comfy pillows and caught a little more sleep, if not for the pull in my belly that told me I wasn't alone.

For all the still and quiet of my room I could hear someone else breathing. I opened my eyes and nearly squeaked when I saw Law sitting in the leather backed chair beside the bed. I'd forgotten he was here. My brain had convinced me it was all a dream. Some really weird stress induced dream that had manifested itself by way of Lawson Sokolov, the object of my wet dreams and state of simultaneous sadness and arousal.

The man really could do it all.

But here he was, sleeping soundly and looking just like he belonged where he was, which was saying something, because I couldn't think of a single time I had ever slept sitting up and enjoyed it. Law's big body took up the entirety of the chair, his hands clasped in front of him, resting against his belly, and his head tipped slightly to the side, chin pointed down to his shoulder as he dozed. I licked my lips, propping myself up on an elbow and watched him sleep. He was pretty when he was like this. Eyes closed, eyelashes fluttering against his cheeks in a way that surprised me. I hadn't noticed he had thick dark lashes. I was always too focused on his eyes, or the way his mouth was moving, the slant of his body or the way his shoulders looked taking up a doorway. Too busy wondering what his hands would feel like on me again to notice his lush and downright pretty fucking eyelashes.

I curled mine and coated them with my tried and true mascara to achieve what he had naturally. Figured. I rolled my eyes at him and kept watching him. His lips were full and I knew they were softer than they appeared, or at least how they normally did when he was awake. Now his mouth was relaxed, just like the rest of his body. He looked just as soft and easy as his mouth did, and I wanted to kiss him, or at the very least touch him. My fingertips itched to trace the line of his bottom lip, to follow the swell of his mouth to his cupid's bow, but I knew better.

A man like Law would have a problem with me doing that.

And besides we were in the Cairn. I couldn't go around touching him when he was asleep. I'd ask first. But that would mean he would have to wake up first and I would have to be here when he did. I frowned and shifted, sitting up and shaking my head. I had no intention of being here when he woke up.

That was too awkward after the night I had gone through. All my best laid plans of relaxing for a night swept under the rug and forgotten. I'd been an anxious mess that had been dumped in Law's lap by Connie and here I was. I pushed the covers back and moved slowly, not wanting to wake Law. But the second my toes hit the hardwood floor I knew I had failed.

"What the fuck, Honey?"

My eyes flew to him to see he still had his eyes closed, but he was frowning now. The softness of his mouth gone, melting away as he woke up to the familiar hard lines I was used to. The rest of him was taking on those angular and sharp planes too and I frowned seeing it. I had liked him relaxed.

"Go back to sleep," I said.

He opened his eyes then and glared at me. "You first."

"It's too late for me to be sleeping," I told him. "I'm used to being up early.'

"Do you even know what time it is?" He countered, and that stopped me. I didn't. Not even in the slightest, because this room did not have windows and it was dark, the only lighting coming from the dim lighting of the room's LED track lighting that shone from one side of the front door. It wasn't a lot, but it was enough light to find your way if you woke up in the middle of the night. I chewed my lip. It could be the middle of the night for all I knew.

Shit.

"Not exactly," I hedged. "But my body does. I know it's morning."

"It's not even close," he said, and moved then, hands going to the arms of the chair. "We've been out for maybe four hours. It's barely two."

"In the morning?" I squeaked. He answered with a long suffering sigh and I crossed my arms over my chest. "Maybe I'm used to waking up then for work. You don't know."

"The fuck you are. Now get back in the damn bed and go to sleep."

"Stop bossing me around."

"No."

I pursed my lips and we stared at each other, or at least I did my best in the dim lighting. "Listen, Law," I began but he was up and pushing himself out of the chair. "What are you doing?" I broke off at his sudden movement.

"Putting you back to bed, little girl."

The sound I made in the back of my throat at little girl was...unseemly under the best of circumstances. In these it was horny. We both stopped, Law not coming a step closer and I froze where I was with my legs dangling over the bed, hands on either side of me. We didn't speak, our breath sounding loud in the bedroom, and then Law was talking.

"I want to touch you," he said, and then when I only made another low sound in my throat, "Can I touch you?" He asked.

"Yes, please," I whispered, already sliding my hands back behind me so that I could lean my weight on them as Law came forward. "I need you to touch me so bad."

"I know, princess. I know." He came closer, one measured step at a time and then I felt the ghost of his fingers against my thighs. "Can I take your robe off?"

I gave a quick bob of my head and then cursed silently at myself, because what the hell was I doing? Even if we weren't in the dark, I needed to be using my words, not going along with this blindly. "Yes," I told him and swallowed hard. "But only if you get in bed with me."

"Honey…" There was a warning tone to his voice,

but I didn't care. I knew what I wanted, and what I wanted was Law in bed with me.

"I'm not drunk, so stop it with that. I wasn't to begin with, even if you said so," I muttered, already undoing the tie at the waist of the robe I wore. "If you want to touch me, you are going to get into this bed."

I could feel him hesitate. Even in the darkness, there was a weight to Law's presence that told me exactly what the big man was doing even if I couldn't see him clearly. He was hesitating. Hesitating too much, and I knew I had to bring out the big guns.

"Get in bed with me, please. Please, Daddy."

"Fuck." He said the word like he was in pain, but a second later I felt his hand come down on the mattress beside me. "Fine, but you're telling me your safe word."

"Peaches."

He chuckled and I felt the rough touch of his finger against my jaw. "I can remember that."

"What about you?" I asked, already reaching up to put my hands on his shoulders. He was moving in close, the front of him coming to press against me and I almost moaned when I felt his lips against my shoulder.

He slid my robe to the side and kissed my shoulder. "Albuquerque."

I smiled. That fit. I didn't know why, but it worked with who Law was turning out to be around me, which was unexpected. "Got it. Now get in bed."

"Now who's bossy?" He asked, and I heard his shoes hit the floor before he was moving onto the bed, the mattress dipping beneath his weight.

"I'm a brat. It's what I do," I returned and was rewarded with him hooking an arm around my waist and pulling me to him. He went onto his back and cupped my face, his other arm still wrapped around my waist, holding me close.

"This isn't a scene," he said quietly. He was right, it wasn't and that was...different. I didn't come to the Cairn to get into bed with men I had no intention of playing with. I got the sense Law didn't either, but here I was, here we were, doing just that. This was intimacy but of a different kind than the exchange through the boundaries and trust explored through shared kink. This was raw and stripped down to the foundation.

There were no roles or negotiated scenes to navigate. There was only me and Law.

Just us in the dark.

"No, it's not," I replied, my hands coming to rest on his broad chest. I ducked my head and pressed my nose to the material of his dress shirt. It wasn't a scene but it felt just as important, maybe even more. I didn't have a thought in my head as to why Law was getting into bed with me other than I wanted him there. I wanted him close to me, his body pushed to mine while I explored his. I wanted the time to figure out what the hell was going on between us.

But most of all, I wanted him.

"Where were you going?" He asked me.

"To my suite," I said, turning my face into his hand. He had nice hands, softer than I thought they would be, but I could feel the calluses on his fingertips. The warmth of his palm was reassuring, drawing me closer in the cool of the dark room and I ate it up eagerly.

"What the fuck for?" He was annoyed. I could tell by the gruffness of his question, but I wasn't going to let it deter me. Not when I'd gotten him into bed with me. I had more than a few cards in my hand and I was going to play them to the best of my ability.

I rolled my eyes and bit his thumb. "I didn't want an awkward morning," I said, lips still against his thumb.

"What the hell would have been awkward about it?" He moved closer, the arm around my waist tightening, his hand flexing against the curve of my hip.

I shrugged, knowing he could feel the gesture. "I'm sorry you had to babysit me," I said finally and flushed with embarrassment. It was true. I hated that

I'd been a burden to him. I didn't want that. Never that. "You came here to play and instead…" My voice trailed off, and I ducked my head, lowering my forehead to his chest.

"There's no instead," Law gruffed out, hand sliding in my hair.

I lifted my head. "But–"

"Are you pretending we didn't have the talk we did before bed?" His fingers flexed and he twisted his hand in my hair, tugging on the strands to tilt my head back. We couldn't see each other, but I knew he was looking at me. That if the lights were on, we'd be eye-to-eye. I swallowed hard and blinked, grateful for the dark.

"Well, no. But that doesn't mean you were happy tonight."

"Neither were you, princess." I felt a flutter of warmth in my belly at the pet name and Law's hand moved, fingers beginning to rub a circle against my hip. "You should know what I want from you after our talk."

I did know. Or at least, I hoped I knew, but I wanted to hear the man say it. "What do you want?" I asked and he chuckled, the hand at my hip moving to pull the robe up, bunching the soft fabric of it into his fist.

"You want to hear me say it, don't you princess?" If a man could purr then was the sound Law would be making. He would be purring like a satisfied lion at getting what he wanted. He was enjoying this as much as I was. My urge to hear him answer my question matched by his own desire to hear me return the favor.

I smiled, biting my lip. "Yes," I told him, pressing my thighs together. The friction of it a blessing and nowhere close enough to what I needed. Only Law's mouth, his hands, his dick could give me that. I shivered, held my breath, and waited for him to speak again.

"I want you to be my little girl."

I sucked in a breath, and not just because he'd said the words I'd been desperately wishing to hear since he'd called me 'his girl', or when he'd threatened to spank me in Sik Gaek. Words I'd wanted to hear since he'd eaten me out on my table and left me wanting more. My breath was caught short, stolen by the deft play of Law's fingers against my skin as they slipped beneath the robe I wore. He slid them along my hip, slowly moving down the slope of my side until his hand was pressed flat against me, fingers just inches away from my now aching clit.

My fingers flexed and I began to undo the buttons of his dress shirt. I stopped when I had his shirt half undone, my fingers hovering just above his skin. I could feel the warmth of it against my palm but I didn't go any closer. I was waiting for him to say something, to tell me he wanted me to touch him, but most of all I was waiting because he was too.

He hadn't moved his hand since slipping it inside of my robe. His fingers were warm and gentle against my skin, touch so light that if I wasn't concentrating on where his hand was I might think I had imagined it. I moved, flexing my hips forward, trying to get closer to his hand, but still I didn't touch him.

"What's wrong?" He asked, and he moved, but just a finger, the pad of it dipping lower on my body until it was now pressing against my hood. He began to slowly draw a circle against the tender flesh and when I didn't answer him, his hand in my hair flexed in warning. "Honey, answer me."

Right. I needed to talk. It was hard to remember what the fuck I was supposed to be doing when he was touching me. Not when I knew he could and would give me exactly what I needed. What my body craved and wanted from a partner. It would be good with Law. I knew that. The problem I had was keeping my ass focused and not drifting off into the euphoria that I knew could pull me under being with a man like Law.

"You didn't let me touch you in my apartment," I told him. "Do you not like being touched?"

"Fuck no."

"Then why did you not let me move? And my hands? You had them tied, told me to keep them off you." It had been hot. Sexy in the best of ways with each and every move Law had made that night. Ticked every one of my boxes.

He began to move again, the hand between my thighs dipping lower so that he could trail a finger along my slit. I moaned and he let go of my hair. He caught my hand that was still hovering above his chest and pressed it down. My hand flattened against his muscled chest and I went still. The firm muscle under my fingers was warm and I could feel a dusting of chest hair prickling against my palm.

I had welcomed the dark earlier in my vulnerability, but now? God, I wanted to see him in the light.

"If I had let you touch me then it would have been all over." He pressed his hand down over mine, palm warm, his fingers sliding between mine. "If I had let you touch me, I wouldn't have let you go, Honey. Didn't matter if I knew you wanted what I wanted. That you wanted this." He squeezed my hand gently. "I would have taken you."

"I wanted to be taken."

"I know. Keeping your hands off me was the only way to stop that."

"But you're letting me touch you now," I pointed out.

"I am."

My heart began to pound at his answer. *I am.* Did this mean he meant to...to... "Does that mean you're taking me?" I asked, voice breathy, his finger now stroking against my clit in feather light touches. He moved, pressing a finger into me as he began to speed up. I shuddered, my feet pressing against the bed, raising my hips up to meet his strokes.

Law hummed in answer. "I am. God, you're going to be mine, Honey. Do you want that?" The fingers playing over my clit moved to dip into my folds and I moaned at the first thrust of his fingers into me. He wet his fingers, my slickness allowing his fingers to glide over my flesh, and he was circling my clit again. Faster and faster, each and every touch driving my body closer to the edge and I cried out, a sob escaping me from the pleasure Law was giving me.

It had been good with a lot of partners. Some of them vanilla and some of them Doms, not all of them Daddies, but there was just...god, there was something extraordinary about being under the practiced hands of a Daddy, even if we were not playing yet. We were exploring, our bodies, hands and mouths still new to each other, and I moved forward trying to kiss him. I missed, my mouth glancing off his chin, and then again off his upper lip before I was able to hit my target.

We kissed, our mouths slanting together hungrily and I took as much as I could give. My tongue slid against his and I moaned into his mouth when he dropped my hand in favor of my breasts. He curled a hand over one, his fingers moving to twist my nipple. He rolled the sensitive flesh between his fingers, the sharpness of it lighting my body up in a new way.

"Do you want that?" He husked out against my mouth. The obscene sound of his fingers slick with my arousal sliding through my folds, dipping in and out of me filled my ears. It sounded so fucking good.

"Yes," I sobbed, wrapping an arm around his shoulders and yanking his mouth back to mine, but Law was having none of it. He moved, dropping his head lower to replace the fingers that had played with my nipple with his mouth, and god, if that wasn't magnificent.

"Law," I whispered, hips stuttering, trying to keep pace with his hand that mercifully continued to stroke me. "Law!" This time it wasn't a whisper, it was a shout of pleasure. The edge he had been driving me closer and closer to was finally there, and I plunged over the side of it gleefully. The orgasm he'd given me on my kitchen table had been wonderful. The release of that had washed over me in ways that satisfied my body's needs, but this? This was fucking magnificent. It was pleasure and need released in its most pure form and the ecstasy of it left me breathless and weak, my body shaking against him, hot under his hands. He kept circling my nipple with his tongue, lapping at my tender flesh while I sobbed against him, fingers twisting in the loose fabric of his half undone shirt.

"Law."

"Honey."

I lifted my head and aimed a kiss at where I thought his lips were. I hit pay dirt when our mouths connected and I sighed against his. "I like it when you say my name like that."

He didn't answer, just kissed me, fingers still easing me down through my orgasm. When he withdrew his hand from my pussy, I made a sound of annoyance. If I could, I would keep it there forever. His hand pressed to my pussy, thumb to my clit and my cream smeared over his fingertips. He gathered me up against him and that was when I felt his dick against my thigh. I dropped my hand, automatically reaching for it, but only managed to brush my palm against the head of it before he pulled me away.

"But I want you to feel good too," I said.

"Not yet."

"But, Law, I began again when he moved off the bed and pulled me with him, hauling me up into his arms and making me shriek in surprise. I wrapped an arm around his neck and grabbed onto his shoulder to stay upright, but he paid me zero attention and kept walking through the dark room. "Law!! What are you doing? Put me down!"

"No." He shifted me in his arms, hiking me higher. I was about to demand he tell me what the hell he meant by *no*, when he spoke again. "We're getting in the shower," he said, already striding towards it.

My mouth snapped shut. I could live with *no* if we got in the shower. Getting in the shower meant a naked Law and a naked Law meant I was going to get my hands and my mouth on his dick.

CHAPTER NINETEEN

LAW

Getting Honey in the shower was easy because she was sweet again. She'd been quiet, her hands clasped in front of her while I switched on the taps, hit the button for the shower and tested the water making sure it was warm enough. She'd stepped into the shower without a word when I nodded at her to do so.

"You're coming in, right?" She asked when she was standing inside the glass enclosed shower. She was standing in the middle, the spray of the shower head missing her, sliding down only half of her body. Stray water droplets sprayed up and against the glass between us and she moved forward, placing a hand on the glass not making a move to hide her nakedness from me. I liked that she was confident. I liked littles, ones that played in shyness, blushing cheeks and demure looks, but when it came to a submissive's body I did not indulge the same behavior. A submissive had no need for shame with their Dom. Any partner I played with had the body I wanted. There were times when a submissive's confidence was lacking, uncertainty and twisted body image making their presence known, but as their Dominant it was my job to actively take apart those threads until they had no bearing on my submissive. Their love of their own body put back together in the form of what Honey was now giving me.

Pure want. A joy found in sharing her body with me. She liked that I was looking at her, wanted me to do it. I could tell by the way she raised the hand not pressed to the glass and braced her elbow against the rapidly steaming glass. We stared at each other in the low light of the bathroom and I let my eyes wander slowly over her body. She was a beautiful woman, her dark hair down and curling, the ends of it sticking to her body from the water. She had full hips, and a soft belly, tits that were soft and full, the brown of her nipples prettily contrasting against her tan skin. My fingers twitched, the memory of what her nipples felt like had my dick hardening.

"Yes, I'm getting in," I told her, shrugging out of my dress shirt and tossing it to the side on the small table that sat there. Shit like magazines, lotion and candles lined its surface, all meant for a comfortable stay. I tossed my shirt onto the table, covering the items but not before wondering if Honey like candles or what kind of lotion she would want rubbed into her skin.

"Hurry up," Honey said, tapping a finger against the glass.

Those two words had my dick jumping. I gave her a disapproving look, though I enjoyed her behavior. She was a brat through and through. Even if we were just being together in the most basic sense of the word it was enjoyable to have her acting this way. She was comfortable. She was happy. She was bratting as she pleased, even without a scene.

These were all good signs. Honey would not be a flash in the pan or one time hookup. This thing between us was going to have legs.

"Now who's bossy?" I asked her, unbuckling my belt and pants. Her muffled giggle sounded through the glass, but it was cut off when I finished undressing, adding my pants and belt to the growing pile of clothing on the table. When I got no answer I looked up from removing the last thing I wore–boxers–and saw Honey's eyes were wide.

"What?"

"Holy shit," she whispered.

"What?" I asked again.

Her eyes moved up and down the length of me, and she pressed her hand flat to the glass.

"You're beautiful," she blurted out. I snorted at her words. I'd been called a lot of things. Beautiful was not one of them. "Like seriously, fucking gorgeous."

I ignored her words, but I liked how much enjoyment she got from looking at me. I had a good body, I knew that. I worked out six days a week maintaining the body I'd earned from keeping order in the streets, but it was a body that wasn't perfect. There were scars from gunshots and knives, and the tattoos that I used to cover most of them, though I'd given up on that years into the game. Half of my chest was a mass of ink work, a falcon with its wings outstretched and soaring, a star above it and below a forest of plane trees, their gnarled branches twisting into one word: Sokolov. The scene was serene, calming, and it had been my solace–a constant reminder not to forget who I was. That I was, above all things Lawson Sokolov. Even when the money had been good, the seat at the table with the mafiosos and cartel kingpins a little too choice, their goodwill flowing like the liquor they poured for me, that I did not lose sight of my goal.

That I remained my own man at all costs. The pleasure and power those men and women offered me was fleeting, it all came at a price. Everything did.

Honey looked like she was going to go on speaking, which was fine. I liked listening to her. I raised the hand that I'd had between her sweet thighs and inhaled deeply. The sweet and musky smell of it had my mouth watering. I hadn't gotten to taste her, not like the night before and slipped my fingers inside of my mouth sucking off what was left of her cum.

Honey made a strangled sound and I raised an eyebrow at her while I licked my fingers clean.

"Get the fuck in here."

"Manners." I made no move forward and instead closed my eyes, taking my time sucking her taste off my skin. If she wanted me to do a damn thing she was going to learn to show some respect.

"Please. Please, Daddy get in the shower with me."

There it was.

I smiled at her. I reached down and closed a hand around my dick, giving it a slow pull. "Keep asking nicely like a good little girl."

Her eyes were wide and locked onto where my hand was slowly working my hardening dick. I groaned, the ache in my balls growing with each stroke. If I wasn't careful I was going to fucking finish before I got my hands on her. Having Honey climax with my fingers inside of her, her body bowing, hips straining against my hand while she sobbed out my name had nearly been enough to make me lose control like some snot nosed kid getting his first taste of pussy. I'd had to get us up and out of the bed to hold on to my control. I wasn't used to feeling like this. There had never been another submissive that could drive me this wild, made me lose all reason and thought, and I hadn't even been inside of Honey yet. I'd tasted her, felt her, but not had her.

Jesus Christ when I finally had her...

"Please, Daddy." Honey's voice pulled me away from thoughts of how fast I would lose control when I had my thick cock inside of her.

I opened the shower, the warm steam rolling out over me. "Do you even know what you're asking for?"

She shook her head, water flying from the tips of her long dark hair. "No, but I want it if it's with you."

"Good answer." I shut the door behind me and stepped in close to her, forcing her back under the shower spray. The warm water hit her back and Honey's eyes drifted closed when I wrapped an arm around her waist, pulling her towards me. I lowered my head, running my lips along her shoulder. The warm water splashed down around us, the heat and steam of the shower wrapping us up in a cocoon that shut out the outside world. There was no Cairn, no shitty fuckwad of an ex, there weren't billions of fucking dollars waiting for me to finalize details.

There was only here and now. Just us.

"I want to taste you," Honey whispered. I froze where I had been kissing a lazy path up her shoulder to her neck and leaned back to look down at her. Water clung to her eyelashes and she was smiling, looking up at me. "Please let me suck your cock, Daddy. Can I?"

How the fuck was I supposed to say no to her when she was looking at me like this? All doe eyes and 'please Daddy,' it was going to be impossible to deny her a damn thing if we made a go at this. I smoothed my hands down her sides and cupped her hips, fingers digging into her skin.

"Yes. Suck my thick Daddy cock, princess."

"Fuck, yes." Honey moaned, her hands moving to grip my arms. She leaned up on her tip toes and kissed me. It was just a quick press of her full lips to mine, but it was good and sweet. Just like her.

"On your knees, princess." She dropped down to her knees without hesitation, her hands already reaching for me on the way down. I slid my hands in her hair, gathering her dark curls in my hand. "You're a greedy little girl aren't you?"

"Yes, Daddy," she panted, and then reached out with a hand and began to pump my cock.

I groaned and stretched out, putting a hand

against the wall to steady myself. "That's it, princess. Just like that." She slid her hand from the tip of my dick to the base, fingers tight on me as she did so. When she hit the base she did it again, her free hand moving to fondle my balls, the pad of her thumb rubbing against my perineum. She moved, using both hands to circle my dick and slid them up and down my throbbing cock, fingers tight on me while she increased speed. My hips began to lazily thrust up into her hands. This felt too good not to move with her and I tightened my grip in her hair, pressing my hand harder against the shower wall. I was surprised the marble didn't shatter and crack beneath the force I was exerting.

I grunted. "Oh princess." Honey's hands on me were good. I knew her mouth would be better.

"Suck me off. Give me your mouth."

"Yes, Daddy." Honey lips brushed against the head of dick, my pre-cum mingling with the water on her lips and she sighed happily before she began to bob her head up and down, taking me further into her mouth with each movement. My hips stuttered when she dragged her tongue from the tip of my dick to the base and then back again.

"Fucking hell."

One of Honey's hands came up to grip my dick, sliding in time with the slide of her mouth and tongue. Honey moaned, the sound of it vibrating in her throat and my dick. I sucked in a breath when she did it again.

"Princess. Yes, yes."

She looked up at me, our eyes meeting, and I could see she was happy. The sparkle I'd seen in her eyes when she was bratting shone through her gaze. Fuck she was beautiful. On her knees with my dick down her throat and her moans bouncing off the marble and glass of the shower. She looked absolutely perfect.

She moved closer to me, a hand going to brace herself against the wall, and that was when I felt the change. She had been taking her time, slowly at first and then faster, taking me as far as she could into her. Honey moaned, low and deep and I felt my balls tighten, pulling close against my body in time with Honey's faster tempo. She stared up at me, her hot little mouth sliding up and down my dick and I knew what she wanted.

"How verbal do you like your Daddy?"

"You want me to cum down your throat don't you? Stuff you so fucking full of it that you can't swallow it all, isn't that right?"

"Very. I like it when he calls me bad names..."

She groaned in pleasure. Of course she liked that.

"You're my little cock slut, aren't you?" I pushed away from the wall and tilted her head back slightly with both hands.

Again Honey groaned, her eyes fluttering and I saw she had dipped a hand between her thighs, working her clit over. She was getting off on getting me off. Perfect.

"That's it, suck your Daddy's dick like a good little cumslut. I'm going to cum right in your perfect mouth." I sucked in a deep breath, my eyes glued to where she was playing with herself. Her fingers were sliding and dipping through her folds and I fucking wished it was my hand. "That's it, touch yourself you dirty slut. But you aren't going to cum before your Daddy does, are you?"

Honey didn't answer, her rhythm had fallen off and her eyes had closed. I knew from how fast her hand was moving that she was close. Her head was bobbing up and down my dick, the hair I held in my hand was twisted and gnarled by the shower water. I gave her head a gentle shake and asked my question again. "Are you going to cum before your Daddy?"

Her eyes flew open and she gave a muffled 'No', her mouth stuffed full of my cock. It was a beautiful fucking sight. "Good girl. Good little slut." A deep moan from Honey and when she fell back into a rhythm, my hips met her. I thrust forward, forcing my dick further into her mouth and down her throat until I bottomed out.

"God. Fuck yes, princess. Suck Daddy off." My hips were erratic, Honey was moving to match it, her hungry mouth sucking me off, tongue sliding like fucking heaven against my cock. I wasn't going to last. I knew it from the way the ache in my balls had deepened. I had maybe a minute left of this, maybe less. I wanted Honey to cum with me.

"That's it, rub yourself. Play with your pussy for Daddy to see. Do it faster, baby. Let me see you cum."

Her hand moved faster, her breathing was labored now, her world was only my dick and the pleasure of her hand. Nothing else fucking mattered.

Nothing.

"Honey, princess, that's it. Cum with me, princess. Cum with Daddy." I tensed, holding off the orgasm that was about to fucking knock me on my ass. "Cum with me, princess. Do it, do it. I want you to cum with Daddy in 5…4…"

Honey's hand was moving faster, the movements were smaller now, her touch focused on her clit.

"3…"

I could do this, I could hold it off to share this with her. I needed to do this with her.

"2…"

"1. Cum with me, princess. *Cum with Daddy.*" My voice was loud to my own ears. The sound of it was reminiscent of the awful ringing that accompanied gunfire at too close of range, but instead of that pop and then disoriented tinny ringing, it was the spray of the shower and our breathing turning into one mix of white noise.

A strangled cry came from Honey, that beautiful fucking sound was the thing that pushed me over the edge. My body tensed and I looked down at her where she had her thighs clamped tight around her hand, her mouth stuffed full of my cock while she climaxed. I had never seen a more perfect thing.

I came so hard I nearly lost my fucking footing on the wet tiles of the shower. "Princess," I growled, emptying my balls down her throat. I was true to my word and there was more than she could swallow, the white of my cum dribbling down the side of her mouth while she sagged forward, body shaking against my leg.

We were both still for a second and then I pulled in a deep breath, and then another. When I was steady enough I reached down and pulled her up into my arms. She was wobbling and glassy-eyed, she was going to need a tender touch after this. I ran my thumb alongside her mouth, scooping away the cum that was there and moved to wash it off in the shower but Honey caught my hand with hers to stop me. She leaned in close and licked the cum off my thumb.

"That's mine," she whispered, lips still against my thumb.

I bit back a moan and kissed her instead. The

taste of me on her lips and tongue kicking my need for her back into high gear. I could feel my dick starting to take interest. It hadn't even been a full five fucking minutes and I could go another round. This time with her cunt wrapped around my dick, not her mouth.

She was going to be the death of me.

I kissed her again. There were worse ways to go.

CHAPTER TWENTY

HONEY

That's it, suck your Daddy's dick like a good little cumslut.

The shower had been...amazing. The grip of Law's hand in my hair, the way his cock had felt on my tongue, his cum in my mouth. Fuck, it had all been...okay, amazing was a bullshit word, but it was the best I could do right now since I was in a daze. My body felt light and happy, every part of it lit up from inside to the point that I could have been floating for all I knew. If my feet touched the ground it was news to me.

But then again, Law was carrying me so I guess my feet hadn't really hit the ground. He'd toweled us both off, me in my dopey haze, and after getting me into my robe again he'd carried me to the bed and dressed himself.

"I'm taking you to your suite," he'd said, reaching for me. This time my arms went around his neck without hesitation. Law scooped me off the bed and left his room. We were in the hallways of the Cairn with Law striding purposefully and utterly at ease as if he carried me around on the daily. I heard a peal of laughter sound from behind us and a door to a room slammed shut, muffling the merriment. There were voices on the heels of it and I knew we now had company in the hallway. When I looked over his shoulder in the direction of the voices, Law spoke.

"It's just after three. Still plenty early in the club."

"Oh, yeah, I guess I forgot," I waved a hand at the hallway and leaned back against his chest, "about all of this while we were…" my voice trailed off and I blushed, "you know," I finished.

He chuckled, his arms tightening slightly around me and holding me closer. "Yes, I know," he said, the rumble of his voice in his chest comforting. It felt familiar and reassuring in a way that it shouldn't have given this was our first night together–if you didn't count the night in my apartment which I wasn't sure I did–but Law talking to me like this, the way he held me, how we fit together…it all felt right.

So fucking right.

I was basking in the beauty and comfort of that rightness when everything in my world went sideways. Just like it usually did. Because of course, it fucking did.

Christian.

He was at the end of the hallway, just turning the corner and ambling towards us. The woman from earlier was still with him, her arms wrapped around his waist tightly as they walked. She was looking up at him and smiling, her face showing how much she clearly adored the man she was with. It was a pity really given that Christian looked utterly fucking bored.

It was a look I recognized well. The one he gave when the attention he was getting just wasn't up to snuff. The one he got before he started getting mean for fun.

I shivered and pulled my robe tighter, turning my face into Law's chest so that I wouldn't see Christian or the woman with her heart in her eyes. God, I hoped someone told her to put her heart somewhere he couldn't see it. It shouldn't be that bare and open to him. If only someone would–

"Which way to your suite?" Law asked. He'd stopped walking now and was looking ahead. I wondered if he saw Christian.

I lifted my head and swallowed hard. "What?"

"Your suite. Which way is it?" he asked again,

nodding at the hallway in front of us. We were in the main corridor but there was an intersection coming up, one that had three halls that went off in different directions. I uttered a silent prayer of thanks when I saw that Christian was definitely not going up the hallway that had my suite. He'd already crossed through the intersection and was heading right for us.

"To the left," I mumbled quickly with a jerk of my head and then went back to where I was, head pressed his chest and my chin dipped down. "It's the fourth door on the left after that."

"What's wrong?" Law asked. I glanced up at him, from under my lashes to see that he was staring ahead, his eyes narrowed and his jaw set. He hadn't started walking again and the sinking feeling I'd had that he'd spotted Christian grew. There was no way the man didn't know why I was hiding as best I could.

"Nothing," I mumbled.

"Honey." The warning tone was back and the rumble was not so lovely or right this time when it vibrated against my shoulders and side.

"It's him. You see him. Don't pretend like you don't," I whispered, pushing back to look at him, a hand on his chest. "We have to go."

"You're with me now," was all Law said, as if that cleared it all up.

"That doesn't matter," I told him and his lips turned down, while an eyebrow shot up. He did not like that one bit. Shit.

"It matters plenty."

"You know what I mean." Was all I could get out before Christian was talking.

"Well, well, well, isn't this a lucky surprise. Running into *old friends again*." He pulled on the last part of his sentence and I cringed inwardly. He was definitely bored and up for being mean. I looked away from Law, but I could tell that he hadn't. From the corner of my eye I could still see him staring right at me as if Christian hadn't just spoken.

"It matters," he said again, ignoring Christian who was now walking forward. The woman had to let go of his waist, but he grabbed her hand, dragging her with him as he approached us. A shiver ran up my spine at the sound of Christian's voice and I gripped Law's shirt tighter, my knuckles turning white from the pressure.

"We have to go," I tried again.

Law showed zero sign that he gave a fuck. "When we get to your suite I'm going to fuck you." My breath caught in my throat.

"What the hell are you both still doing here?" Christian asked, his voice acid.

"And then I'm going to feed you and put you the

fuck to bed, little girl," Law went on ignoring Christian. "Do you understand?"

"I know you're not really together, princess."

"Yes, Daddy." I ignored Christian and answered Law.

"No." Christian made a strangled sound and the next second the woman he'd been dragging behind him was forgotten. Left where she was standing while he stomped up to us, his face twisted in anger. I'd thought he was handsome before, but now? Now that I'd had Law's hands and mouth on me, his cock in my mouth...now that I knew what he looked like underneath the button up suits and dress shirts. His body as beautiful as it was savage, the hard planes of muscle dotted with scars and covered in dark inky lines that spanned his side from chest to abdomen, stretching and spiraling around arms to the backs of his hands.

Now that I knew all of that?

Christian didn't look handsome anymore. He looked like a boy. And right now he looked like a spoiled, angry boy who was throwing a fit. When we were together–all seven months of it–his anger had scared me, made me anxious and had me hurrying to cave to whatever new bullshit reason he'd cited as pushing him over the edge. I lifted my head and looked at Christian, the anger in his face no longer scaring, but confusing me.

Why the fuck did he care what I did or who I did it with?

"You do not call him that. I am your-" Christian began, but Law was moving, down the hallway and towards the hallway my suite was in, and he was doing it in the same slow pace he'd had all along. He shifted, hiking me higher in his arms, my body cradled close to him. His arms were warm, strong, and I knew so long as I was in them I had nothing to be scared of.

Christian's anger went from confusing to downright comical. Why the hell had I ever been scared of him?

"I want you to think about what you want to eat," he told me, voice soft and even. I tore my eyes away from Christian who was staring at us like we had grown three heads. I gave a quick nod but said nothing. "It had better not all be sweets," Law added, and I grinned up at him, my grip on his shirt loosening.

If he could pretend Christian didn't exist then I could too.

"Honey, get the fuck down," Christian snarled with a jerk of his hand pointing down at the floor beside him, "Now."

"But I like sweets. I want cake," I told Law. Dessert was delicious and I hadn't had much lately. Sweets were a thing I enjoyed when I was relaxed and carefree, but between my work schedule and the constant go go go of the city I hadn't really allowed for any of that. A chocolate cake with double cream frosting would hit the spot. Or maybe cheesecake now that I was thinking about it. The allure of sugar and confectionery delicacies were suddenly very appealing now that Law had forbidden them.

"You can have fruit."

I pouted. "You're no fun."

"Fine. A cupcake then."

That appeased me and I nodded, settling back against his chest. I opened my mouth to point out that two cupcakes were far better than one when Law's arm jostled slightly. My eyes slid to the side to see Christian's shoulder against Law's arm, my feet were nearly touching him and Law turned his body pulling me away from Christian.

Christian's eyes were on me. They were narrowed with anger and he flicked a finger at me, making me flinch despite my dedication to following Law's lead. "Honey, did you fucking-"

Quick as a viper, Law leaned in to Christian, the move so fluid and sudden it startled Christian into shutting the fuck up. For a second I thought Law was going to deck him, but he didn't move his arms, just kept right on holding me while he moved close enough to whisper in Christian's ear. The low rumble of Law's voice was too muffled, his head turned, lips almost brushing Christian's ear. The scene might have even passed as tender to anyone that didn't know better.

Law stepped away from Christian and set off at an amble again, footsteps steady and sure as he turned to the left and went down the hallway to my suite without even a second look behind him. I, of course, looked twice, fuck, I looked *three* times just to be sure I saw what I thought I saw. Which was a speechless Christian, mouth open and eyes wide with shock. There was fear there too, the unfamiliar look of it in his eyes was nice. He deserved to know what it was like to be on the other side of things for once. The woman he had come with was staring after us as well, a lost look in her eyes, arms folded around her body. She was leaning against the wall behind her, all the strength in her gone, and I felt a pang of sadness go through me at the broken look to her.

She looked like a discarded doll. Left by its owner and unsure of what to do next.

I'd been like that once too with Christian. I hoped she left him.

I looked at Christian who still hadn't moved, but whose eyes were on us as we slowly drifted away. When our eyes met, I didn't flinch away. I stared back at him until he looked away first.

"What did you say?" I asked once we were in my suite.

"Nothing important," Law replied. His hands were in his pockets and he was looking around the suite with an amused expression on his face. He moved to the side and considered the fireplace I hadn't been able to make use of. "I'll start us a fire."

"What do you mean nothing important? You left him staring after us like--like," I threw out my hands, "like he was terrified. That can't be from something not important."

He crossed the room to the fireplace and considered it for a moment before reaching out and taking the tinderbox in hand. "It's not important because that prick isn't important. We are not speaking of him again tonight."

I bit my lip and then nodded, because the last thing I wanted to do was bring up Christian. "Fine," I conceded, "but later?"

Law glanced at me over his shoulder. He was crouched in front of the fire, his hands busy with the tinderbox, "Later, we can if you still want to."

"Okay. Thank you."

"Of course, princess."

The familiar glow of pleasure I got when he called me that bloomed into being and I shifted nervously from foot to foot. "I like it when you call me that," I said, stating the obvious.

"I know. Now get in bed."

I rolled my eyes at him because he was back to domineering, but I did want to get in bed so I did what I was told. "Don't take too long."

Law hummed, but he didn't say anything as he worked at the fire. I settled back against the plush pillows and comforter of the bed, pulling the blankets high, up to my chin, and enjoyed the sight of Law doing something domestic. It was doing wonders for my libido, and I knew if I saw the damn man wash a single dish I was going to want to rip his clothes off. When he stood and turned towards me, I was turned on. He stalked across the room towards me, hands already undoing the buttons of his shirt. He tossed it over the back of the velvet settee in the center of the room and then continued towards me.

"I normally stay in this room," he told me, taking off his shoes when he was at the foot of the bed.

"Oh?"

"Yes, Connie told me there was a VIP in it this weekend though. I see she was right."

I giggled. "She was up to something from the beginning. She knew you'd end up here."

"Whether she did or she didn't isn't important really, but I am glad that you have this suite. It's comfortable."

"There's cake already in the fridge too," I said

pointing at the door that led to the kitchen. "I forgot earlier when you said I couldn't have sweets."

"I said not *just* sweets," he reminded me and braced a hand on the bed as he looked me over. "Now, do you remember the three things I told you I would do once I had you back here?"

"Yes," I whispered.

"What were they?"

"You said," I licked my lips and paused before I told him, "you said, you would fuck me, feed me and put me to bed."

"You're already in bed, so this order isn't quite what I wanted, but it'll do. There are two more on that list now to be done, princess. I think you know what's on my mind, but what do *you* want?"

That was too easy to answer.

"I want you to fuck me."

Law's eyes darkened and the smile he aimed at me was soft and sweet as anything I'd seen in my life. I think it was easily the softest thing I'd ever seen in the city. New York was a place not prone to soft or kind, but it did have its beauty. And when it offered that beauty it was rare and precious.

Law was the most precious thing I had ever been offered by New York.

"I want you to fuck me, Daddy."

He came forward then, moving close until he was beside me and I breathed in deep, taking in his scent with a barely restrained moan of happiness. He smelled like sage and sandalwood, warm, clean and woodsy. "Remember your safe word, princess," he said, reaching out and tucking a lock of hair behind my ear.

"Yes, sir."

He cupped my face for a second before he moved in and kissed me. The kiss was slow and gentle, the mirror of the smile I'd been so transfixed by, and when I opened my mouth to him he deepened it, taking my mouth with a groan. I reached for him, hands burying in his hair, fingers twisting in the strands as I pulled him closer to me. Law's tongue moved along my bottom lip, tasting me before it met mine. His arms wrapped tight around me and he pulled me up and into his lap, the sides of my robe falling open and baring my breasts to him. Law broke our kiss, leaning back to look at me, his blue eyes moving slowly over my face.

The hand at my face moved, fingers lightly skimming my cheek before gently cupping it. My eyes closed and I leaned into his hand, turning my head when Law bent forward to whisper in my ear. "This is how I'm going to do it, princess."

I licked my bottom lip, eyes still closed, my body sinking further into Law's hold with each and every second he described what he was going to do to me. Each and every word setting my body on fire. The lust Law inspired in me growing and taking root, until all I could think of was touching him.

"I'm going to tie you down," he told me, rough fingers tensing on my jaw. He turned his head and his lips brushed against the shell of my ear. I shivered, breath starting to come quicker with the thrill of excitement moving through me. "Your sweet body open and ready for me to do what I want with it."

I leaned forward and rested my forehead against him, just at the curve where his neck and shoulder met. "Where?" I whispered, breath catching. "Where are you going to tie me down?" I asked, pressing my palms flat against his broad shoulders.

"The bed, to the corners. I want tie you down and touch every fucking part of you before I fuck you." The arm around my waist tightened with his words, the crook of it pressed to the small of my back, arching my back and forcing me closer to him. "I want to worship you. Are you going to let me do that?"

I sucked in a breath at the tantalizing image. I could see it now, my hands tied down, above my head, Law's big body moving over mine, mouth, tongue and hands covering me from head to toe. "I want that."

"I know," he said, voice all sugared confidence that made my clit ache. "And I have a surprise for you."

I opened my eyes and sat up straighter, lifting my head from his shoulder. "A surprise?"

"The flogger, princess."

My fingers tensed on his shoulders, breath leaving my body in a whoosh and the ache in my clit turned into an all out sweet throbbing. "I want that too," I told him.

"I know, princess." His lips turned up in a grin. "It was all over your face in the Great Room. I know you want me to use it on you. You crave the bite of the leather on your skin, don't you?"

I nodded. "Yes, but…" My voice trailed off and I raised my eyes to meet Law's gaze. He was watching me closely, and when I bit my lip instead of answering him he gave my thigh a squeeze. The dig of his fingers into my skin had my attention, so did the underlying growl I heard in his voice when he asked, "But what?"

"I want it from you. It wouldn't be the same if it wasn't you holding the flogger," I told him. Law's hand on my thigh tightened, fingers pressing harder and I bit my lip. I shifted, pushing my hips closer to him, and dropped a hand to lay over the hand at my thigh. "I want your marks on my skin. Your cock in my pussy."

"Princess," Law growled. He leaned in, claiming my mouth with a kiss, and when he pulled back I knew it was time. His back was drawn up, spine tall and muscles coiled and ready like a notched arrow in a bow ready to be let loose. Hi blue eyes showed no hint of the man that laughed for me. Instead, there was an intense focus that told me he was ready to go forward, but he wouldn't. Not before I told him I was ready.

I took in a deep inhalation and let it out, shoulders rising and falling, my breath warm and fanning against his tattooed skin. "I'm ready, Daddy."

The change was instantaneous. Law's hands on my body began to move and he lifted me up again, drawing himself up onto his knees, our bodies pressing together for a moment before he was forcing me back onto the bed.

"I want you on your back. Arms above your head, feet pointed towards the corners of the bed. Now."

I went back but I took my sweet time, the slow exaggerated movements eating up precious seconds while Law moved off the bed. He came to stand beside the bed and cross his arms, watching me slowly shift into place.

"You're taking too long, princess."

I smirked at him, enjoying being at the center of Law's world. When we were like this nothing and no one else existed. Not for either of us. This was our world. The room, the bed, the limit and span of our bodies and the space between us.

This was it.

It was all that we needed.

Law tilted his head to the side, watching me with a slightly pinched look on his face. A look that only got me going, the excitement I was feeling spreading through my body until I felt dizzy from it.

"Only good girls get surprises, and you do want your surprise don't you?" he asked. "Don't make me take it away."

I went onto my back when he threatened that. I did want my surprise, and I did absolutely want to be Law's good girl. Even if I liked pretending that I didn't. "Fine," I muttered with a toss of my head. Law came around the bed then, hands deftly pulling out padded leather cuffs I hadn't known were there. The cuffs were attached to soft leather straps at each corner of the bed and he secured my wrist, buckling them into the cuffs, testing the tension, tightness and pull of the cuffs at each corner as he went.

"Are you comfortable?"

I gave the cuffs a pull and nodded, settling into the bed. "Yes."

Law left the bed then and went to a chest a few feet away. It was against the wall leading into the bathroom and when he bent over it, opening it, I raised my eyes to the ceiling. My heart was pounding from the anticipation of what was to come. Adrenaline flooded my system so forcefully it was nearly painful, and I worked to keep my breath even and steady. By the time Law returned to the bed, I was squirming, eyes trained on the ceiling and doing my best to be patient.

"Hurry up," I begged. "Hurry up."

I was failing at patience.

Law tutted but made no move to speed up his movements. Something that brought me no end of frustration and I communicated this to him with a kick of my restrained foot. I opened my mouth to throw sass but a well timed smack of the leather flogger against the bottom of my foot had me gasping, the sass forgotten.

"Watch your tone. And where are your manners? What did I say about good girls?" He asked, punctuating his question with another smack of the flogger.

My toes curled at the contact. "Hurry up," I said, unable to resist another chance to poke at him. Indulging my bratty side, finding his boundaries and learning where those edges fit with my own was all indulgence. It was, well it was fucking fun. "Please," I added hastily when I saw the flogger in his hand rise again but it was too late, and this time he brought it down on the side of my foot. The sting of it had me blurting out another quick, "Please, please, hurry up, Daddy."

"You're a little too late with the manners, princess. Now you have to pay."

"But I-"

"Now," he swung the flogger, the bite of it hitting above my ankle, "You," again another strike, this one on my calf, "Pay," he said, each word punctuated by another flick of leather against my skin.

I sucked in a breath, lungs seizing at the contact of leather to flushed skin. "Daddy!" His hand sliced forward, this time the flogger hit right above my pussy, the edges of it flirting with my inner thigh and I moaned. "Daddy."

"You look like you're going to be a good girl for me now. Is that right, princess?" He struck again, my sides this time, and I knew I would have welts there. He was bringing the flogger down with more force now. I knew why. No one would see these marks, not with a shirt covering them. These were just for us.

"Yes," I moaned, when the leather tickled the underside of my breast. "Yes!" I cried, leather kissing my nipple, first on one breast and then the other.

"That's my sweet girl." He dragged the flogger slowly between my breasts, the soft leather tip of it trailing over my skin before it gently rounded the side of my breast. "You are my sweet girl, aren't you?" He asked, pausing, the flogger pressed to my skin but not moving.

I took in a shaky breath, my chest rising and falling quickly. "Yes, Daddy. I'm your good girl." Law hummed and quick as lighting the flogger moved again, the stinging strike of it coloring my sensitive skin pink. I gasped, back arching and hands pulling at the cuffs.

"Next time I'm going to blindfold you," he said, conversationally, as if he weren't taking me in hand with the flogger. As if I wasn't bound to the bed and shaking with desire and need for his cock, the welts on my skin already flashing an angry red and making my flesh feel both overstimulated and starved at the same time. I wanted his hands on me. I needed his touch. His weight bearing down and grounding me in this moment. If I didn't get that I would fly apart and into a thousand breakable pieces.

"I need you, I need-"

Law cut me off, the leather of the flogger moving to press against my jaw. He angled my head back to look up at him and I almost came from the sight of him. He was shirtless, just like in my daydream. A slight sheen of sweat glistened on his muscles, the flogger in his hand looking as lethal as any sword. The flowing lines of his tattoos made him beautiful like a fallen angel.

"What did I say about manners?" He asked, forcing my head back further with a flick of his wrist. His flogger dug into my flesh. "Use your words, princess."

"I'm sorry, Daddy," I whispered and tugged on the cuffs. "I'm sorry but, I need you."

"Then ask for me."

I swallowed hard, my throat moving against the hard leather still pressed against me. "I need you, Daddy, please," I began. "I want you inside of me. I need your big daddy cock filling me up. Please fuck me." My words were needy, my voice shaking and breathy and I pulled at my restraints as I spoke, my limbs unable to stay still with Law's gaze on me. The man's eyes were too much, those blues the color of a roiling sea storm about to break land. I hoped Law broke me. I needed him to.

"Fuck me, Daddy," I husked out. *"Please."*

Law stepped closer, the flogger sliding out from under my chin as he did. He dropped it beside the bed, the clatter of it hitting the hardwood deafening and he touched my chest, a light touch that soothed my sensitive skin.

"Since you asked so nicely, princess, Daddy will give you what you want." He pressed his palm flat to my chest, fingers possessively splayed out against my skin. He leaned down and kissed me, his mouth hard against mine and he was gone before I could return it. I mewled in annoyance, but he tsk'd and tweaked my nipple in response. "Patience," he said, undoing his pants and letting them slide down his thighs. My mouth went dry when I saw he hadn't bothered with his briefs. I liked him bare and ready, his fat cock heavy against his thigh, the head of it dripping with pre-cum I wanted to taste.

I licked my lips, eyes on his cock and Law made a sound that was a mix of amusement and arousal. "You're a greedy little slut."

I nodded. "Only for you."

He kissed me again, a hand moving to slide up and down his hardening dick. I moaned into our kiss, tongue sliding hungrily against his while I kept my eyes fixed on where his hand was, still working his dick. Up and down, up and down, his hand slid and my clit throbbed in time with the movements. I nipped his bottom lip when he made no move to get onto the bed.

Law pulled back, breaking our kiss. "Naughty girl."

"I want you. You said I could-"

"I should make you wait now," he grumbled, but he was moving away and towards the bed table as he spoke, "I should make my dirty princess watch her Daddy's dick," he slid his hand up and circled the head of his cock with his fingers, making me groan, "make you watch him get off and cum all over your beautiful body."

"No, please," I begged, though there was no real steel to the plea. If Law wanted to make me watch him please himself, wanted to cover me in cum from my tits to my toes, I'd let him. I would want and love every fucking second of it and beg him for more still.

He pulled a condom on and my heart sang. He wouldn't make me wait.

"I ought to cover your tits in my cum, mark you up after," he went on, rolling the condom on as he spoke, "Daddy shouldn't give you a fucking fat inch until you are crying for it."

"Daddy," I whined, "please don't."

I was breathing faster now, my breasts rising and falling in little hikes that had Law's eyes on them. My nipples beaded and hardened under his attention and I squirmed, my feet pulling at where they were restrained. I needed him so badly I could barely fucking breathe. My cunt was wet and slick, my arousal making the sheets damp beneath me and I knew this bed was going to be fucking ruined after we were done.

Whatever. Zeus could fucking clean it up.

He came back to the bed and stood there, his dick hard, fully erect and proud. I pushed my hips up as best I could, eager for him, but I didn't get very far before he put a hand over my pussy and pushed me down onto the bed.

"Patience, princess," he said, hand warm and heavy against my flesh. He slid a finger through my folds, getting it wet in my slick and I closed my eyes, a sigh of relief escaping my lips.

"Daddy..."

"That's it. That's my good girl." Law slipped his finger inside of me and then another, before he started to pump them in and out. I lifted my hips eagerly, adding a little extra punch to his fingers and he hummed in approval. "That's it. Fuck yourself on my fingers." He pressed his palm to my clit, grinding it down as I sped up my movements and I moaned at the friction, but it wasn't enough. I wanted more.

"Daddy, more, I need more." I arched my back, fingers curling around the leather strap of the cuffs. "Please, please, please," I chanted in time with his fingers fucking into me. If he didn't give me his dick soon I didn't know what I was going to do. I ground my hips onto his hand and moaned again. I opened my eyes when I felt him get onto the bed.

"Yes," I whispered, watching him as he moved his body. He was above me now, hips between mine, one hand supporting himself while he continued to finger fuck me with his other. I looked down, watching him position himself behind his hand and I held my breath, my hips never stopping taking Law's fingers. It was so close but not, god why was he making me wait? But then he was moving, sliding his fingers out of me, which caused me to groan in frustration at the loss of him. But then...then he was giving me his beautiful dick.

He took it in hand and slid the tip of it through my lips, the first contact had me seeing stars and I moaned, eyes drifting closed, head thrown back when he repeated the motion. Up and down he dragged his fat cock through my folds, urging me to move against him.

"What do you say before your Daddy fucks you? For giving you his big fat daddy cock?" Law asked as he lowered himself down to his elbow, placing it beside my head and bending down to speak in my ear. He fed the head of his dick inside of me with exaggerated slowness and I sobbed. "What do you say, princess?"

"Thank you," I cried. "Thank you, Daddy."

He moved his hips, lazily thrusting into me. "For what, you dirty slut?"

"For fucking me. Thank you for your," he thrust again, this time with more force and my words broke off into a strangled sob.

"For my what?"

"Your daddy cock. Thank you for giving me your daddy cock!"

Law thrust again, pumping his dick inside of me and then again, my breasts jiggling from the force of it as my breath was punched right out of my lungs. Law was big and thick in all the fucking right places.

My pussy ached from the stretch of taking him but it was a glorious burn, just like the welts still reddening on my body. The man was easily worth every bit of exquisite pain he brought me. Pleasure on the heels of each and every instance. Law's hand was at my clit working it in time with his thrust and when I opened my eyes I saw that he was looking down at where he was touching me, his hand moving faster, driving me closer and closer to another mind blowing orgasm while he fucked my body, chasing his own. His thighs were pressed to mine, knees on the bed giving him the leverage to fuck me as he pleased. The force of it would have moved me if not for the restraints keeping me exactly where I was. He was fucking me like my body, my cunt, held the answer to life's questions and he was determined to possess the knowledge at all costs. The man was taking from me with each roll of his hips. I loved it, I wanted him to hollow me out, to eat his fill with both fingers and leave me fucking spent and empty, the remnants of me messy and dirty on his fingers and tongue.

"Princess," he growled, lifting his eyes to meet mine.

"Daddy!" I cried, my orgasm slamming into me and pulling me under. My pussy clenched around his dick, the feel of him filling me up adding to the ecstasy he had given me, was still giving me, fucking it through each and every inch of my body so thoroughly I knew I would never shake Lawson Sokolov from me. He was in my bones now. I had a taste for him, one that was going to leave me hungry and wanting for the man, for the Dominant that was now losing himself in my body with a low groan. His movements became less measured, more erratic and he came with a last hard thrust into me.

"Princess, god." Lawson's head dropped to my shoulder, the arm that had been placed by my head curling behind my neck and pulling me tight against him. He slid his other arm under me and held me tight, hips lazily rolling, teasing out the edge of his release. We lay there, chests rising and falling together, bodies moving as one, sweat and cum slicked skin pressed flush. The comfortable press of the leather against my skin grounded me comfortingly and I closed my eyes, leaning my head against his arm with a content sigh.

I could stay like this forever.

"You're mine, Honey."

I smiled. "I know."

CHAPTER TWENTY-ONE

LAW

My sub was happy. She was satisfied and practically purring with pleasure. This meant I was happy. I looked down at where she was sitting on the floor in front of me, a mess of pillows around her for comfort. The fire I'd started earlier was cheerily crackling away in front of us while Honey sipped the tea I'd made her. I focused on the hair I was braiding. Her dark, thick curly hair felt good in my hands, the strands of it curling pleasingly around my fingers while I worked a braid into being. When I was done, I gave it a tug and tipped her head back to look at me.

"Are you happy?" I asked, knowing she was but needing to hear it.

She beamed up at me, her pretty face brightening with a smile. "Yes, Daddy."

I kissed her forehead, settling my hands on her shoulders. "When you're happy, I'm happy, princess."

"I know." She sipped her tea again and then leaned back against the settee we were on with a content sigh. "We have to go soon, though."

"I know." I squeezed her shoulders not liking the thought of leaving the bubble of the Cairn, but she was right. It was mid afternoon on a Sunday. We'd spent the better part of the day sleeping, eating and fucking. I'd touched, licked, and kissed every fucking part of my little girl, and I'd let her do the same. I enjoyed the hungry and demanding way Honey touched me, the way she kissed me, taking as much as she could.

She was mine, but I was unquestionably hers in return.

But that was here, within the walls of the club. We hadn't talked about life in the city. What the everyday would bring for us. My mind was already on the work I had waiting for me, the way my life was void of Honey's warmth and softness. How I had fucking beat it out of my life with surgeon like precision, leaving nothing but work and numbers. That had been safe, better for the people I'd once loved, better for me. It was preferable to know the people you were soft around were safe. That they wouldn't end up with a bullet in their back or a message carved in their side.

I hadn't bothered picking up the threads of my old life when I went legitimate. Being clean didn't really translate to a white picket fence and a dog with a little missus waiting at home for me. That was for a decent man, and I...I hadn't been that for a long time. My life was safe now, stable at least with the biggest risk coming in the form of conference calls and memo forms. But even still, I worked long hours, I was an asshole when I was overworked, Addie said so. I didn't have hobbies anymore, I was--fuck. Who the fuck was I even anymore? The week since I'd met Honey had woken my ass back up to real life.

I'd lifted my head long enough to look around and see that I was well and truly out of step with the rest of humanity. None of that shit had mattered to me before, but after Honey, I'd noticed. I hadn't liked that I noticed or the prickliness it set under my skin, making me feel restless. Frustrated and full of energy at not knowing where to fucking start when it came to stepping back into who I'd once been.

I'd come to the club to blow off some steam. Get that taste of humanity out of my mouth and force myself back into the familiar coldness of my life. My weekend with Honey had blown that plan to shit. How the hell was I going to work a submissive into it? A little girl that was, not just a little in need of a guiding hand from her Daddy, but a complex woman who was bright and determined? Honey was a challenge I had not figured out yet.

"What's wrong?" She asked, reading my face. Fuck, I needed to work on keeping myself more together around her. But it was difficult. Honey had a way of bringing every wall and boundary I had built up down to the ground. She had access to me in ways I had never allowed another person, not just a submissive.

Now that she had noticed my mood I decided not to beat around the bush. No use starting now. She'd read it immediately. And I was the one who had pushed for honesty. No more lies. Those were my fucking words.

"Trying to figure out how we work when we leave here," I told her, and I felt her stiffen beneath my hands.

"I was trying not to think about that." She said, voice quiet. She turned so that her body was to the side, her back against my thigh. She bit her bottom lip, teeth wiggling the plump flesh for a beat before she let it go and blew out a heavy sigh. "I don't expect anything," she said.

"What the fuck?"

Her brown eyes moved to the side, away from me and towards the fire. "I'm just saying that I know—

that, you know this…this…" Her voice trailed off and I crossed my arms, leaning back in my seat.

"This what, Honey?"

Her eyes flew to me. It was the first time I'd used her name that day. It had been nothing but princess, little girl, baby girl, good girl, and a lot more fucked up shit that I wasn't in the mood to think about right then. If I did, I'd get hard and I could tell from the worried look on her face, the way her brows were pinching together, that sex wasn't going to be on the list of activities I felt like indulging in.

"That this is temporary. Just a fun weekend, Law."

Law. Not Daddy. I didn't like it, though I know I deserved it for using her's first. I took in a deep breath. If Honey was going to dig her heels in about this 'fun weekend' bullshit, I was going to give as good as I got. I wanted this woman. I wanted her to be mine and I would rejoin the living to do it. I would show her this was not just a weekend. It couldn't be.

"It's not just a weekend," I gritted out, not giving a shit about holding my cards close to my chest. No lies. Honesty. "Not for me."

"What?" Her eyebrows flew up. I preferred surprise to the upset look she'd been giving me, even though I didn't fucking get why she was surprised.

I scowled. "What what?" *Jesus this was going off the rails.*

She jabbed a finger at me. "Explain."

I reached out, wrapping my hand around her finger and folding it back into her hand. "It's not polite to point."

Her cheeks dusted a light pink and I saw her throat move in time with a hard swallow. "Sorry," she whispered and she lowered her hand, taking mine with her. I could have pulled away, dropped her hand when my point was made. But I wanted the contact with her. My hands wrapped around hers.

"What do you mean this isn't just a fun weekend?"

"Exactly that. I don't want a fucking weekend with you Honey. I want- I broke off, because what the fuck did I want? Hadn't I just thought that I didn't get a missus and a white picket fence? Though the shit we'd done that weekend, what I knew Honey needed from her man...I didn't think she'd want a white picket fence and a quiet life. "I want you," I finally settled on. That sounded *right*.

Her mouth dropped open. "What the hell?"

This time it was me who was frowning at her. "What?"

"I don't get you."

"Right back at you, sweetheart."

She smacked my leg. "I'm serious, Law!"

I leaned forward, wrapping my arms around her and lifted her up, dragging her into my lap. "So am I,

Honey. What the fuck are you going on about now? I just told you I want you. I don't want this to be a 'fun weekend' or whatever the fuck you are talking about, okay? I want you, goddammit." I glared at her, fully committed to not letting go of her until she understood the damn words coming out of my mouth. What the hell was it with women never listening to everything before they started yelling? "Will you listen to me? I want you."

She laughed. "I want you too."

I stared at her. Her words were too easily won. Hadn't she just been smacking me a second ago? "Is this a trick?"

"Oh my god. Shut up and kiss me." She wrapped her arms around me and pulled me close.

"Fine," I grumbled, but I didn't care because Honey was kissing me. She wanted me. I'd kiss her anytime she wanted so long as she wanted me.

CHAPTER TWENTY-TWO

LAW

We left the club that evening. I took Honey to dinner, some fancy place she was worried about going into because of how she was dressed. "Everyone is going to stare if we go in there with me looking like this," she said, hands twisting in front of her. Some fancy french place Addie had told me she'd made reservations at when I'd told her that I needed a table for two.

"For two? But you never eat with anyone." Addie stated. It wasn't a question, not really. She was right and she knew that. I cleared my throat and glanced over at Honey who was packing her bag up, her hair still in the braid I'd put in.

She looked sweet.

When she looked up at me and smiled, I felt my

chest go tight and I cleared my throat, looking away while I answered Addie's question.

"Yes, two. I have company tonight."

"It's a woman. I know it."

"Addie, swear to god…"

"Right, right, right, boss man. Don't worry. I'll handle everything," she chirped excitedly. "Can't wait to hear about her tomorrow!"

"No, Addie—listen," I began, but she was gone, already hanging up to make the reservations for me. Addie was a great executive assistant. She didn't need to do shit for me outside of work hours, definitely not on a Sunday afternoon, but she did it anyway. She would have been pissed if I hadn't asked her. I wasn't looking forward to paying up for it though with a Monday morning grilling from her. Everything had a price though. I could give her enough details about Honey to satisfy Addie's curiosity.

At least I thought so.

"You wanna put your dress back on?" I asked. The club had had it laundered and the emerald dress she wore like a sex goddess was pristine and waiting. If she changed in the car, we could manage it.

Taylor and I could stand guard to make sure she had enough privacy for a quick change. If she put that damn thing on though…I was sure she was going to end up with more attention than if she stuck with what she currently had on. Converse, jeans and a tank top. I liked the way she looked, fresh faced, hair in a braid, body sporting the mark of my flogger beneath her clothing, and most of all freshly fucked by me.

"What? No! I mean, I don't think so…" She bit her lip and looked out the window at the restaurant that was all lit up inside, people sitting at each and every seat and she sighed, shaking her head. "I should have brought something nicer to go home in."

"What for? You're beautiful like this," I told her, and took her hand. "You don't owe any of those fucks a damn thing," I jerked a thumb over my shoulder at the restaurant and I heard Taylor chuckle up front. "You're here to eat dinner. Our money is good as anyone's in that place. You wear whatever you want, and if they say a damn thing they can answer to me."

"But these places have dress codes and-"

"They won't say a damn thing, Honey." I told her, already making up my mind that I would buy the damn place and turn it into a fucking fast food chain if they did. "Trust me. You trust me, don't you?"

That had gotten her up and moving, she'd taken my hand and followed me into the restaurant. Slowly, but she was walking all the same. The second we hit the door, the hostess turned to look our way, and when I saw their lips turn down, I stepped in front of Honey making it apparent she was with me.

Out of nowhere a man hurried up to the hostess and grabbed their arm, whispering in their ear, their eyes on me as they did so. And just like that the sour look on the hostess's face vanished and they nearly tripped over themselves to greet us.

"Mister Sokolov! We are so pleased you chose to dine with us tonight."

We were seen to a private room where I made sure Honey was comfortable. She ordered off the menu with an excited smile telling me she hadn't had food like this 'in a while, I'm so excited!' When she had the first bite of her meal, she moaned, eyes fluttering closed in pleasure. The sound was almost identical to the sound she made when I was going down on her, which I liked. Turning this place into a drive-thru was off the table then, and I made a mental note to bring her back here as often as she wanted.

After dinner, I took her home and when she pointed out the lights with a grin and a soft 'thank you,' I kissed her slow and sweet and right in front of her door where her nosey old neighbor was peeping at us through the cracked door she had opened like we didn't see her. We ignored the woman and went inside Honey's apartment. It was quieter in here than I remembered, but that was easy without a storm raging overhead.

My eyes landed on the kitchen table and Honey grinned at me when she noticed where I was looking. "Are you up for a repeat?" She asked, dropping her bag onto the floor beside the couch and sauntering over to the table with a sway in her hips. "Daddy?" she asked, looking over her shoulder with a pout.

I groaned, eyes on her mouth. I loved her mouth. "Fuck yes," I muttered, already following her. We spent the next hour with me feasting on Honey's pussy, and this time she touched me as much as she liked. I carried her to bed after, tucking her in with a glass of water on her bedside table. And when I left her there was no question in my mind, or hers, that she was my girl.

Being with a woman like Honey was easy. Affection came easily where she was concerned. But what I didn't get was how she brought that out in me. Why she wanted to give it to me. Because if she was my girl that meant I was her man. I'd fucked up a lot in my life, but this?

This was better than perfect. This shit felt good.

This I was going to protect.

THE END

EXCERPT FOR SWEET RULE
CHAPTER ONE

HONEY

BaristApp has 3 new notifications.

I turned my head and looked at my blinking phone. I'd been ignoring the damn thing for the past twenty minutes when the alerts started going off. Normally, I woke up at the first app notification, eager to see what gigs might be available around town, so that I could plan my day. But not this morning. This morning I had been sleeping, enjoying the dream that had wrapped itself around me like a comfy flannel.

The dream had been about Law, more of a memory than anything else. It had been a distorted loop of our last few hours in the confines of the club when he was him and I was me. The sweet trappings of our dynamic were still there gently influencing our interactions. He was brushing my hair, plaiting it in a braid while he talked to me. I had zero clue what Dream Law had been saying, but I liked the way he'd sounded, the deep rumble of his voice filling my ears, his strong hands in my hair, fingers sliding through it until I'd felt content and relaxed.

The dream had been lovely.

So lovely that when my phone began to go off I chose to ignore it until I couldn't anymore. The pinging of its notifications pulled and tore at the edges of my dream until I knew there would be no repairing it and I had to wake up. I sighed and picked up my phone, but even in my irritation I had a smile on my face.

Will you listen to me? I want you.

I shivered, rubbing my legs together beneath my blankets and breathed in the chilly air of my apartment. I'd forgotten to turn on the heater before bed and the last of the spring thaw was making itself known in the early morning.

I want you.

He wanted me. Law Sokolov wanted me. The joy from that was fierce, the warmth of it enough to make me forget about my cold apartment. I wrapped the quilt around my shoulders and sat up, focusing on my phone. I slid my finger along the screen to see what jobs were up for grabs and instantly hit accept when I saw the familiar name of A Different Brew. I definitely wanted that shift, not only because I'd get to see Tiffany and work in a shop I adored, but because of Law.

I would absolutely get to see him if I took it.

The shift started in 45 minutes which meant I had just enough time to get dressed and out the door. I could skip breakfast so long as there was coffee, but I might not even have to do that if I was with Tiffany. There was a bakery nearby that she loved and I knew all I had to do was offer to pick up something and she'd be game.

I hopped out of bed and made a beeline for my closet while firing off a see you soon text to Tiffany. I heard my phone sound with a text message from where I had tossed it on the bed and knew Tiffany must have sent me a reply. I yanked on my clothes, snagged my bag, phone and pulled on my shoes and was out the door in record time. I was hurrying down the stairs when my phone went off with another ping, but I didn't check.

It was probably Tiffany. I could respond on the subway, but making the train needed to happen first. I sped up, power walked the rest of the way to the subway and it was only when I was securely on the train and sitting down that I checked my phone.

'Stop ignoring me'

I frowned, staring down at the phone in my hand. The message made no sense. When I tapped on the message to look at the sender I saw a number I didn't recognize. It was a New York City area code, but that told me nothing, and when I tried searching the number online it came back as a dead end. I bit my lip, eyes on the text message that was sending up warning bells.

"It has to be a wrong number," I whispered, and shoved my phone back into my pocket. The alternative to that wasn't something I wanted to think about. The only person that would send me a message like that was forbidden to do so. Christian's face flashed in front of me and I shook my head. "It's not him. *It's not.*"

Christian was a lot of things, but going against Connie, Zeus, and now Law, was not something I saw the man capable of doing. The memory of Law leaning in close, whispering in his ear, those few quietly said words had been enough to nearly drop Christian where he stood. He'd gone from taunting and aggressive to silent and frozen where he stood. My phone pinged again and I squeezed my eyes shut, the familiar dread of knowing someone was watching me, that Christian was out there keeping tabs on me, was slowly settling over me.

"It's not," I insisted again, fixing my eyes on the advertisements that lined the top of the subway car. I didn't take out my phone to check the message.

The entire trip to A Different Brew passed by in a

blur, my feet carrying me on autopilot. The worry over the text message had been buzzing in my brain the entire way, so had the phone that was burning a hole in my cardigan pocket.

When it had buzzed as a reminder a few minutes after it arrived I'd nearly jumped, but I'd kept my focus and resisted the temptation to check. I ran my hands through my hair and inhaled deeply, trying to settle my nerves before I pushed open the door to A Different Brew. The familiar smell of coffee beans hit my nose and instantly I felt more at ease. This I could do. This I understood. I raised my hands over my head and stretched as I walked towards the counter where I spotted Tiffany's familiar ginger curls. She was bent over, head low as she took the starting temperatures of the fridges.

"Hey!" I greeted her with a fake brightness I didn't feel.

Tiffany's head popped up and she beamed at me. "Honey! I'm so happy it's you. This is going to be such a good day. Did you get the pastries?" she asked.

I blinked in surprise at her question. I'd wanted breakfast but I hadn't really made the jump to getting some or asking her like I'd planned, not with the eerie text message throwing me off. "The what?"

"The pastries," she said, leaning over the counter to see if I had anything in my hands. When she saw that I didn't she pouted. "Boooooo. Did you not get my text?"

"Your what?"

"My text." She tipped her head to the side and gave me a second look. "Are you...okay?"

"Yeah, I mean-" I swallowed hard and then shook my head, reaching for my phone, "I'm sorry, I'm just a little off is all." I thumbed past my lock screen and saw that I had a message waiting from her. I breathed out a sigh of relief, my eyes drinking in the sight of her *'Get pastries from the fancy schmancy bakery for brekkie! Gus already paid. Just pick them up, please!'*

I smiled when I saw the message. It had been Tiffany, not whoever sent the first. "I'm sorry. I was spacing out and didn't check," I said, lifting my phone up and giving it a wiggle. "I can go get them now though."

She clapped her hands excitedly. "Would you? He told me he got all the good stuff because he's trying to convince you to take the job!"

"Tiffany...we talked about that," I laughed.

"Yeah, but that doesn't mean we're going to give up. Plus, we get bougie bakery breakfast, so what's not to love? Let us woo you with your favorite foods, woman."

I dropped my bag behind the counter and grinned at her. "Yeah, okay. I can tolerate that."

"Awesome!" She hugged me tight and then gave me a gentle push towards the door. "It's all taken care of. Just let them know it's for Gus and they will hook you up."

I saluted her on my way to the door. "On it!"

I rolled my shoulders and stepped out onto the sidewalk. The morning air was crisp and fresh. My earlier good mood slowly returning with each step I took towards the bakery. It didn't have to be Christian that sent the first one. Maybe that one wasn't even for me. That happened all the time in a city as big as New York City. Someone had hit the wrong number before they hit send and bam! I had a message not meant for me.

"That has to be it," I told myself. And because I couldn't take any other truth, I accepted that, lifted my head and enjoyed my walk to get breakfast.

Today would be utterly normal. A good fucking, perfectly normal, day.

∽

"How the fuck..." Law's annoyed grumbling pulled my attention away from the movie that I was watching. I was in his apartment, I mean if you could call this place an apartment. It was a penthouse really, the entire floor was his with the elevator taking you right up to his front door from the ground floor.

"This is super fancy," I'd told him when I'd stepped out of the elevator for the first time last week.

"It is," he'd agreed.

"I get why you replaced the lights in my building," I said, looking around the spacious apartment we were entering.

He chuckled, a hand going to the small of my back. "Wanted you to be able to see is all."

"Sure, sure," I replied, coming to a stop when I caught sight of the glimmering New York skyline visible through his floor-to-ceiling windows. Law's home was more comfortable than mine by a mile, everything in it was luxe and top of the line, while I had a drafty walk up with a heater that banged when it kicked on. But if Law ever thought anything less than about where I lived, he never let on. We'd been dating for three weeks and I'd only started coming to his place a week ago with an equal number of nights spent in each of our homes.

I liked that he made the effort to spend time where I lived, even if I was still struggling with doing my best to figure out how to make it home. I'd bought a handful of houseplants and even hung art on the walls, a piece we'd found wandering around in the Village. It was slowly becoming a place I wanted to be in, a place that felt good to take up space in, and I knew that had a lot to do with who I was becoming with Law. I turned to look over the couch I was sitting on and hit pause on the movie, a fairy tale retelling that was just chef's kiss perfection, and laughed when I saw Law, hands on his hips and glaring at the pot in front of him.

He was making me mac and cheese. When I'd told him I had a craving for the comfort dish he'd assured me it was "not a big deal, it comes in a box, how hard can it be?", but from the way he was standing, I could tell it was plenty hard.

I turned completely, rising to my knees and leaning forward, bracing my elbows on the back of the couch. "You okay in there?" I called out to him, leaning my chin in my hands.

"I'm fine, princess."

"You don't look fine."

Law snatched up the box and shook it over his head. "I swear to god, they didn't say," he lowered it to read the instructions again and then sighed heavily, "fuck, they did say."

"What'd they say?"

He tossed the box to the side and picked up the pot he'd been making the macaroni in. "Some cooking shit. I got this. Go back to your movie."

"But do you need help?" I asked, knowing from the determined set I saw in Law's shoulders he wasn't going to be asking me for help, even if he needed it.

He turned, looking at me over his shoulder and winked. "Daddy's got it, princess. Go back to your movie."

The warmth that always bloomed in my chest when Law talked to me like that hit me square in the chest. "Okay, Daddy." I ducked my head and turned, knowing my cheeks had a faint blush on them. It was hard not to blush when Law talked to me like that. One word capable of making me warm skinned and fidgeting. In the few weeks we'd dated he talked to me like that often. A soft voice, a tender word, the affection blatant and I succumbed to it each and every time.

"That's fuckin' soup. Not goddamn mac. I'll show you mac, ya damn box," he muttered, sounding pissed from behind me, and I giggled.

Law hummed as I heard him pause in what he was doing in the kitchen. "Laughing at Daddy, little girl?" He asked, and I sank lower on the couch, pulling the blanket beside me up to my chin.

"No! It was the movie," I shouted, hitting the play button and muffling another laugh behind my hand. I waited, wondering if Law would come see if I was telling the truth and a minute later I saw he had come to investigate.

"You're lying, sweet girl." He moved, putting a

hand on the couch beside me. His other went to my neck, fingers gentle on my skin. "Aren't you?"

"No," I insisted, but I was smiling. I looked up at him and felt the warmth his words had brought to life spread over my body. He was open faced, his eyes had lost the sharp edge they often had in them when we were in the city, "out in the open" as he called it. There was a past to my man, one that was dark if the signs I'd picked up on were telling the truth, and I knew they were. His tattoos and scars were more than enough proof of it, but he hadn't brought it up, and so neither did I. Whatever it was that had Law slipping into high alert when were in too crowded a space, the way he moved when I insisted on a late night walk in Queens, the outright scary aura the man put off that had more than one wannabe goon on the street backing up and giving us space, was not lost on me. I saw it but didn't ask where the sharp edges and steel in my man had come from.

He hadn't given that to me yet. I knew that meant something. There was a reason he hadn't and I was smart enough to know better than to let my curiosity get the better of me. Law was good to me. He treated me right and there was no cruelty in him when it came to others.

I had zero reasons to push for information Law didn't want to give. But when he was like this, tender looks and soft eyes, he wasn't the man with a past I knew was violent. He wasn't even Lawson Sokolov, CEO of Law Acquisitions now, he was just Law. He was mine.

He moved close and kissed me, lips soft against mine and he pulled back to look at me. "You're lucky white lies are okay, little girl."

I rolled my eyes at him. The move earned me a gentle squeeze on the neck and then he was pushing away from the couch. I raised my arms, reaching out for him, but Law dodged my hands. "I've got unfinished business in the kitchen," he said, shaking a finger at me. "Go back to watching your movie."

I pouted, but did as I was told and turned back to face the television. I hit play on the remote and leaned to the side, the blanket I'd wrapped around myself once more settled over my shoulders. The sounds of Law cooking resumed, along with a curse here and there and I grinned. I was happy. This was perfectly...perfect. At least it was for me. I was smiling, not even focused on the movie that was going on in front of me, but enjoying the domestic feel of the moment—the outright hominess of it when Law called out to me.

"Honey, your phone's going off."

"Thanks." I waved a hand and hopped up from the couch. "I bet it's Elaina letting me know if she wants me to water her plants while she's outta town with the twins," I told him, ambling over to the counter where I'd tossed my bag. When I got closer, I heard the familiar ping letting me know I had a text. I reached in the bag and tried not to laugh when I saw Law in front of me. He looked like he was making a study of the mac and cheese box, hands on his waist and eyes on the box in front of him.

"Just let me-" I began, ready to pressure him into letting me help cook when I saw the messages on my phone. I had several. The first of them was blinking up at me.

PICK UP YOUR PHONE!

I stared at it, fingers going tight on my phone for a second before I raised my other hand and slid the lock screen open. I had to see the others. This couldn't be for me. This couldn't be for me. It had to be a wrong number. I knew it.

I opened the texts and saw I had four waiting. The newest was the one I'd just read. The others were just as unsettling, but the first, the first had to be the worst of them all.

'Honey. Stop ignoring me.'

That cleared it up. The messages were for me. When I scrolled to the top I saw the first message I'd ignored from three weeks ago sitting there taunting me.

'Stop ignoring me'

So it had been for me after all. There were also three missed calls from different numbers to my phone, all within the last fifteen minutes. What the hell was I supposed to do with this?

"What's wrong?"

I jumped, eyes flying from the phone screen to Law who was looking at me. The mac and cheese forgotten beside him. "Nothing, nothing," I said quickly, giving him a strained smile.

"Honey…" His voice had dropped and he crossed his arms over his chest. He knew I was lying. Fuckity fuck. Fucking hell. He wasn't going to let this go.

"How's the mac and cheese coming?" I asked, and started to come around the counter to help him, "I really think you should let me help you with that an-" My phone buzzed again and I jumped, flinging the phone away from me with a yelp.

Law's eyes followed the phone and he flicked a finger at it. "What the fuck is on that phone?"

"Nothing."

"Don't lie to me, Honey. You know that shit isn't allowed." He took a step towards me as he spoke, "And this isn't a white lie. I know the difference, and you know it."

We stared at each other, locked in a standoff, and neither of us moved a muscle. He knew I was lying, I knew he knew it which meant I was kind of screwed on buying time to figure out who the hell was sending me messages.

My phone's text reminder went off and we both looked at it where it lay on the counter.

"Answer me, Honey."

"I don't know," I whispered when I finally found the will to speak. I swallowed hard and reached for the phone with a sigh. "I don't know who it is."

"Who it is what?"

I picked it up and held it out to Law with a shaky hand. "Who's sending me these messages."

Law's eyes narrowed and he took the phone from me. He dropped his eyes to the phone and tapped on the screen. I knew he had seen the messages when I saw his mouth go tight, his chest rising with a deep inhale as he read. "I'm going to kill them."

My eyes widened. "What? But you don't even know who is sending them."

"Doesn't matter. They're dead."

"Law, look I know that-" I broke off and considered his words, "Wait are you serious?"

He was silent, but his look told me everything. The past that I didn't know about, the one that I was content to look past, reared its ugly head and I felt my stomach go tight. "Holy shit, you're serious, aren't you?"

He looked away. "I'm going to find them," was all he said.

"What did that one say?" I asked, nodding at the phone he was still holding.

"How long have they been sending these?" he asked, holding the phone out to me.

"A few weeks," I whispered, and I was glad I had whispered because Law's face got scary.

"This has been going on for weeks and you didn't tell me?"

"It was just one, well, until tonight," I informed him. I reached out and took the phone, my curiosity getting the better of me. I needed to see what they'd sent that had Law swearing he was going to find them. And kill them.

'You owe me and I'm going to get everything from you'

I sucked in a breath and stared down at the number in shock. "Fuck this," I whispered, and hit the block button. "I'm done with that. I should have blocked it sooner."

"No, what you should have done was tell me sooner."

"It's not that big of a deal," I lied, and Law glowered.

"The fuck it isn't. Someone's sending you fucked messages and you don't think it's a big deal? What the hell is wrong with you?"

I jerked back as if I had been slapped. "Nothing is wrong with me. This is just not as big of a deal as you're making it out to be."

"You don't think some creep texting you they're going to take everything from you isn't a big deal? You wanna tell me why you're playing this off?"

I bit my lip and looked away. "Because I don't want anything to ruin this."

"Ruin what?"

"This," I said, throwing an arm out between us. "Us. I don't want you to think I'm too much, or my life is just, I don't know shit and you get tired of it and go."

"Honey." Law moved towards me, arms circling my waist and he pulled me close. "Princess, that's not going to happen. You didn't ask for this bullshit. Why would you think I'd leave?"

Because everyone leaves.

I didn't say it, but the words were loud as anything in my brain. I shook my head. "I don't know."

"You have to tell me what's going on. We're together." He moved, hand going into my hair and he tilted my head back to look at him. "I'm yours."

My breath caught at *the yours*. The soft side of Law once more coming out and making me weak kneed. "And I'm yours."

I leaned into his touch, arms going around his waist, face pressed to his chest. The thump of his heart beat comforting and grounding. "I'm sorry, I didn't tell you. I hoped it was a wrong number."

"Now that we know it isn't, I'll figure it out."

"How?" I asked, closing my eyes.

"Lot of things you don't know about me, Honey."

"I know."

He was silent for a second. "I'll figure it out. You're going to be safe. I want you tell me if someone sends another fucking message to you. Got it?"

I nodded. "Okay."

"Good girl." He smoothed a hand over my hair and dropped a kiss to my forehead. "Everything is going to be okay. You know that right?"

I was quiet but then I opened my eyes and looked up at him with a smile, because I did know it was going to be okay if Law promised it. "Yes."

THANK YOU!

Thank you for picking this book up. This book has a special place in my heart and I sincerely hope you continue to read along with me as The Cairn series continues.

I hope you love Lawson and Honey as much as I do. This couple and their journey together has got to be one of the most satisfying things I've written in a very long time.

I write for a reason and that is for you, dear reader, telling all the stories in the world wouldn't mean a thing if you weren't reading them.

Love Y'all.

ABOUT THE AUTHOR

Rebel Carter loves love. So much in fact that she decided to write the love stories she desperately wanted to read. A book by Rebel means diverse characters, sexy banter, a real big helping of steamy scenes, and, of course, a whole lotta heart.

Rebel lives in Colorado, makes a mean espresso, and is hell-bent on filling your bookcase with as many romance stories as humanly possible!

JOIN MY MAILING LIST!

https://bit.ly/2PCKCZl

facebook.com/rebelwrites
twitter.com/rebelwrites_
instagram.com/rebelwrites

ALSO BY REBEL CARTER

The Cairn Series

Come To Daddy

Honey, Honey

Sweet Rule (Coming Soon!)

The Golden Duet

Once Bitten: Reformed Bad Boy + Good Girl Romance (The Golden Duet Book 1)

Oak Fast Fated Mates

Barista and the Bear: PNR Fated Mate Romance

She's a Luna: PNR Fated Mate Romance

Fairy Suited: PNR Fated Mate Romance

Age Is Just A Number Series

New Girl In Town: Older Woman Younger Man Romance

New Girl In The City: Older Woman Younger Man Romance

Gold Sky Historical Series

Heart and Hand: Interracial Mail Order Bride Romance (Gold Sky Series Book 1)

Hearth and Home: Interracial Mail Order From Romance (Gold Sky Series Book 2)

Honor and Desire: Friends To Lovers Romance (Gold Sky Book 3)

Three to Love: Interracial Ménage Romance (Gold Sky Book 4)

Leather and Lace: Sapphic Marriage of Convenience Romance (Gold Sky Book 5)

Pride and Passion: Enemies-To-Lovers Romance (Gold Sky Book 6)

Printed in Great Britain
by Amazon